romance collection

CHANCE OF LOVING YOU

terri
BLACKSTOCK | *candace*
CALVERT | *susan may*
WARREN

Tyndale House Publishers, Inc.
Carol Stream, Illinois

Library of Congress Cataloging-in-Publication Data

Chance of loving you / Terri Blackstock, Candace Calvert, Susan May Warren.

pages cm

Summary: "An anthology by three bestselling romance authors. For Love of Money by Terri Blackstock — trying to launch her own design firm while waitressing on the side, Julie Sheffield was drawn to the kind man she waited on at the restaurant last night . . . until he stiffed her on the tip by leaving her half of a sweepstakes ticket. The Recipe by Candace Calvert — hospital dietary assistant Aimee Curran is determined to win the Vegan Valentine Bake-Off to prove she's finally found her calling. But while caring for one of her patients--the elderly grandmother of a handsome CSI photographer—Aimee begins to question where she belongs. Hook, Line & Sinker by Susan May Warren — grad student Abigail Cushman has agreed to enter the annual Deep Haven fishing contest. She's a quick learner, even if she doesn't know the difference between a bass and a trout. But nothing could prepare her for competing against the handsome charmer she's tried to forget since grief tore them apart. One chance for each woman to change her life. . .but will love be the real prize?" — Provided by publisher.

ISBN 978-1-4964-0537-1 (sc)

1. Man-woman relationships—Fiction. 2. Life change events—Fiction. I. Blackstock, Terri, date. II. Calvert, Candace, date. III. Warren, Susan May, date. IV. Blackstock, Terri, date. For love of money. V. Calvert, Candace, date. Recipe. VI. Warren, Susan May, date. Hook, line & sinker.

PS648.L6C464 2015

813'.0850806—dc23   2014048498

Printed in the United State of America

21	20	19	18	17	16	15
7	6	5	4	3	2	1

Contents

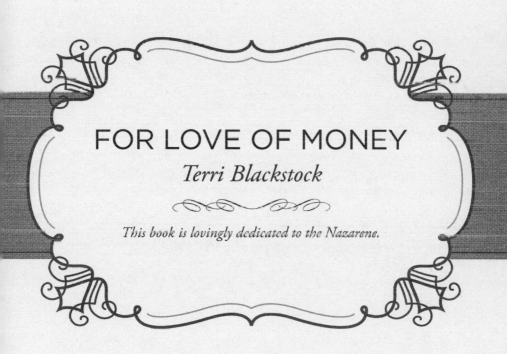

FOR LOVE OF MONEY

Terri Blackstock

This book is lovingly dedicated to the Nazarene.

CHAPTER ONE

Blake Adcock couldn't eat the bowl of hot soup the waitress set before him, any more than he could eat the filet mignon that he'd cut into bite-size pieces so it would look as if he'd tried. He couldn't eat the baked potato that he'd poked at with a decided lack of gusto or the restaurant's famous chef salad that was wilting before his eyes. He'd sat there for three hours, ordering things he didn't want, because there was no place else to go. Home would mock him tonight: the Congratulations banner his employees had hung across his living room; the ribbon tied across his home office doorway waiting to be cut to mark the first milestone of his lucrative new business; the models of his different car designs with Sold signs waiting to be taped on. All the little luxuries his staff had arranged for his "celebration." No, he could not go home and face the consequences of his naive hope . . . not when his dreams had collapsed like the toothpick castle he'd built in third grade.

But that waitress—Julie was her name—didn't mock him. She smiled with full lips the color of raspberries, and her eyes, tired though they were, reflected that smile. "If you aren't hungry for that soup," she said in a soft alto voice with just a trace of amusement, "I could take it back and see if the chef will knock it off your ticket."

He smiled at her and noted the wisp of blonde hair caught in her eyelashes. He had the urge to push it away. "No, it's fine. I'll eat it."

She tipped her head. "Like you ate all this other stuff? You know, where I come from, a meal like this would have fed a family of five for two days, and you haven't touched it. 'Waste not, want not,' my aunt Myrtle always says." She stepped closer and leaned toward him as he shot a guilty look down at the food. "What's really the matter? Is it the rain? You don't want to go out and get wet, so you feel like you have to keep ordering things so we'll let you stay?"

Blake leaned back in his booth and glanced past his reflection on the rain-spattered window. Traffic lights peppered the dark Detroit highway. An interstate leading everywhere . . . and nowhere. His gaze strayed to the reflection of the woman still smiling down at him. *Man, she's pretty,* he thought. He turned back to her and set his chin on his palm. "To tell you the truth," he said, "it's the company that's keeping me here."

"The company?" The thought amused her. "I hate to break this to you, but you're alone."

He laughed softly. "Not when you're standing here, I'm not. I figure the only way I can keep you coming back is to order things."

A blush crept up her cheekbones, and she glanced away, embarrassed.

"It's Valentine's Day, you know," he said. "It's a crime to be alone on Valentine's Day."

She gave him a crooked smile. "Yeah, I've thought that myself." She tipped her head and glanced at his ringless left hand. "What's really the matter? Marital problems?"

He tried to look shocked and insulted. "If I were married, would I be sitting here flirting with you?"

"Stranger things have happened," she told him, that grin tugging at the corner of her lips again.

She knew he wasn't married, he thought. She wasn't looking at him apprehensively. Only warmth shone in her green eyes, filtering through the chill of his failure and pointing him toward hope. Still, it seemed important to clear the notion from her mind. "No, I'm not married or otherwise attached. Matter of fact, I have no ties at all. Not to a woman . . . or a family . . . or a job . . ." His voice trailed off as he realized his levity was giving way to the disappointment with which he'd been wrestling all afternoon.

Julie's eyes instantly widened in understanding. "Oh, so that's it." She studied him for a moment as if gauging his need or desire to talk. Finally she slipped into the seat across from him and leaned toward him with her arms folded on the table. Her eyebrows arched in sympathy. "You lost your job."

This time his laugh held a cynical note. "No, I didn't lose it. Quit it months ago. A pretty good one too."

Her eyes narrowed. "Why?" she asked as if she cared, as if his problems had some impact on her. Was compassion a service of the restaurant, he wondered, or was it just her nature to care about people?

Blake eyed his lukewarm, untouched coffee and brought it to his lips, stalling for time. How did one spill his guts without evoking pity? That was the last thing he wanted from her.

He set down the cup and gave a shrug. "I was a design engineer at GM, but I quit so I could start my own business designing inexpensive vans and cars for handicapped people." He propped his jaw on his hand and looked out the window again. As if to add percussion to his story, the rain began to pound harder. "I had a big contract with a friend of mine who has a business called Access, Inc. He sells specialized equipment like that. He hired me to do twenty vans to start with. Paul said he'd pay me in advance as soon as I finished the prototype, and then I could pay my staff and part of my banknotes and start producing the vans."

His story came to a halt as the injustice of the day returned to him. He was not going to blame this on Paul, he told himself as he stared out into the night. It was not his fault.

"You couldn't finish it?" Julie prodded gently.

He shuffled his plates around a bit. "Oh yeah, I finished

it. And I delivered it today. Only Paul couldn't pay, because he'd made some bad investments that left his business on the verge of bankruptcy. It wasn't a big surprise. He kind of warned me last month, but I was almost finished, and I kept hoping things would turn around." The words were uttered matter-of-factly as if the events were typical.

Julie whistled softly. "That's too bad."

He met her eyes. There was no pity there, and somehow that comforted him. "Yep. So now I'm broke, jobless, and don't have a clue what I'm going to do next."

Julie pulled his untouched soup to her side of the table, picked up his spoon, and took a sip. She tilted her head and looked at him with thoughtful eyes as he watched her. "Doing business with friends doesn't pay. You lose a lot more than you gain. Good friendships are hard to come by. You can find a business partner anywhere."

"Is that another of your aunt Myrtle's nuggets of wisdom?" he asked, smiling.

"No, that one came right from firsthand experience."

"Well," Blake said, "our friendship is still intact. Paul and I go way back. And as far as business partners go, there isn't anyone else who knows this stuff like he does. He's made some major strides in making life easier for disabled people, and he knows what they need because he's confined to a wheelchair himself. He just made some mistakes with his money."

Julie set down the spoon and leveled her gaze on him. "You're pretty forgiving."

He laced his fingers together and lifted his shoulders.

"Forgiveness never even entered my mind. You forgive people for committing wrongs. Paul hasn't done wrong. He just made some mistakes. Besides, what good would it do to be bitter?"

"Well, at least there's a bright side," Julie said.

"A bright side?" He couldn't wait to hear what it was.

"Yes. You still have the prototype. The van. You could market it yourself, couldn't you?"

Blake's shoulders fell a few inches, and he let his focus drift outside the wet window again. "No. I left the van with him. If he could find a way to market it anyway, maybe we could both get our business back on—"

"You gave him the van?" Julie cut in. "Just *gave* it to him? Didn't he pay you anything at all?"

Blake loved her reactions, and he smiled. It was good to have someone to talk to, someone who seemed to care—even if she didn't understand the bonds of childhood friendship. "Yeah, he gave me something. Did the best he could. He gave me a hundred dollars . . . and this." He reached into the briefcase on the seat next to him and withdrew the heart-shaped box of chocolates.

"Valentine candy?" she asked. "You spent—what?— probably tens of thousands of dollars designing that van, and he gave you a hundred bucks and a box of chocolates?"

With a chuckle in his voice, he said, "Actually, there's a little more." He opened the box and withdrew a sweepstakes card. Grinning, he began to read: "'You have won twenty million dollars—'"

"Yeah, right."

"'—if you are chosen the winner. To be announced on February 15 at 8 p.m., drawing held during *Wheel of Fortune*. Sweepstakes sponsored by Sweet Tooth Chocolates and ABC television.'

"See, you scratch off this square to find the number underneath, and if they call it, you win. Guess he figured he was giving me a shot at twenty million dollars."

She ate another spoonful of soup. "And you still consider him a friend?"

He laughed then and met her gaze across the table. "He meant well. I told him that the sweepstakes ticket wasn't worth the cost of the chocolates. But ole Paul, dreamer that he is, said it could be worth twenty million. I took it to make him feel better."

Julie shook her head. "Some people would have thrown it at him. But you're worried about his feelings?"

He brought his napkin to his mouth, even though he didn't need it, then dropped it to the table. "Well, of course my bubble was popped. But so was his. And he had a lot more to lose."

A moment of quiet settled between them, scored only by the piano playing in the corner, the quiet voices of nearby late diners, and the patter of the rain against the window.

"You're a nice man," Julie said.

The words seemed to soften the rhythm of the rain as the tempo in Blake's heart sprinted. This was no bartender type of concern. Julie was sincere, and it showed in her honest, sparkling eyes. His troubles began to seem far away, and the promise of a discovered treasure lifted his heart.

"I'm not so nice," he said. "I'm just doing what's been done for me."

"What's that?" she asked.

He shifted in his seat and leaned forward, locking into her gaze. "There's a story in the Bible about a servant who owed something like a million dollars to his master. No way he could ever pay it back, so when his master called him in to pay up, the servant begged for mercy."

Julie set the spoon down and sat straighter, listening.

Blake went on. "So his master had mercy on him and forgave his debt. But as soon as the guy was outside, he found someone who owed him a hundred bucks, and he demanded payment."

Julie nodded. "And when that person couldn't pay, he refused to have mercy and had him thrown into jail until he could pay his debt."

"You know the story?" Blake asked.

"Yes. Jesus told it," Julie said. He wasn't sure, but her eyes seemed to mist over as she went on. "The other servants went back and told their master what he had done, and the master called him back in. He asked him how he could refuse to forgive such a small debt when he'd been forgiven so great a debt."

"And the master threw *him* into prison," Blake added. "And, see, I'm that guy who owed a huge debt. And Jesus, my master, forgave me. Paid the debt for me. So how could I hold this little thing against my friend Paul?"

She seemed to be struggling with her own emotions. She stared down at the pattern on the tablecloth, then brought her misty eyes up to his. "You couldn't," she whispered. "I couldn't, either. My debt's been paid, too."

She's a believer, he thought. She was like him. His heart leaped, and he blinked back the mist in his own eyes. God had led him here tonight, he thought. Straight into this restaurant . . . to his own special Valentine's gift.

He picked up the heart-shaped box of chocolates, looked down at it for a moment, then handed it to her across the table. "Here," he said in a soft voice. "I want you to have this. No one like you ought to go without chocolates on Valentine's Day."

She took the box as more tears welled in her eyes. "That's so sweet . . . but it's yours. . . ."

"See, I think it was yours all along. God had Paul give it to me so I'd have something to give to you."

She smiled and smeared a tear under her eye. "Thank you," she whispered. "I wish I had something for you."

"Are you kidding?" he asked. "You've given me something, all right. You've taken my mind off my troubles. That's priceless."

She breathed a soft laugh. Opening the box, she took out the sweepstakes card. "Here, at least keep this."

He grinned and left it lying on the table. "Yeah, can't do without my twenty million. I'm holding my breath until *Wheel of Fortune* tomorrow."

She sighed. "Boy, what I would do with that kind of money."

"Tell me," he said, enjoying the dreamy look in her eyes.

"Well, I'd quit this job because I'd be able to finance the fashion show I've been working on to show my designs, and I'd go to New York, to the garment district, and hire designers to work for me, and I could buy all the supplies I need. . . ."

"You're a fashion designer?"

"Yes. I'm working on a line of clothes for women who are tired of the sleazy choices we have in stores today. Modest, pretty dresses for women with integrity and self-respect. But as you can see, I'm just getting started."

As he watched the smile work on her glistening eyes, he wondered if he should ask her what time she got off. Should he take her somewhere? Bask in her warmth a little longer? And what if she said no? The disappointment over his failing business he could take. But rejection from her? He wasn't sure.

"More coffee?" she asked finally.

"No thanks. I've bothered you enough tonight. I hope sitting here won't get you into trouble."

"It won't," she assured him. "My shift ended about thirty minutes ago."

"Thirty minutes? And you've stayed because I—"

A coy smile skittered across her lips. "You needed a friend."

He found himself struggling for some quick comeback that would make him seem less affected by her. "I appreciate it," he said finally.

She stalled for a moment as if waiting for him to make a move.

Should he ask her out for coffee? Oh, that would be smooth, he thought, considering that he had just refused her offer for more coffee. Maybe they could go dancing. It was only eleven, and Valentine's Day, after all. . . .

His thoughts trailed off as he realized he would need every penny he had just to eat for the next week. He could invite her to come watch a movie at his house—but she might find that a little too intimate when she hardly knew him. She didn't strike him as the type who would go home with a virtual stranger.

"Well . . ." She stood reluctantly, reached into the pocket of her uniform for his tab, and laid it on the table. "I hope things work out for you. I know they will."

Her voice alone soothed him. It had a deep honey sweetness, with a directness that lent it a unique credibility. He took the bill, looked down at the amount, and felt his lungs constrict. A hundred and fourteen dollars! How was he going to pay this? The thought of being thrown with the ruthless servant into debtors' prison crossed his mind, and he wished he'd never reminded her of that parable.

While he sat staring at the bill, Julie wandered away toward the kitchen. Blake rubbed his temples. Had he gone insane? Sitting here ordering a meal fit for an Arab prince, all because he was attracted to a waitress who made him feel less alone?

He left a fifteen-dollar tip—fifteen dollars more than he could afford—and took the ticket to the cash register. His forehead beaded in a cold sweat as he pulled out his credit card and handed it to the cashier. He held his breath as she made the phone call to check his credit limit. And when she looked apologetically at him as she set the phone in its cradle, he realized his problems were rapidly multiplying.

"I'm sorry," the young woman said. "But you've already reached your limit on that card. Do you have another one?"

"No," he admitted with a groan. Until a few weeks ago he hadn't needed more than one. On the brink of panic, he pulled out his wallet and found the hundred-dollar bill Paul had given him. "How much did you say it was?"

The cashier checked the bill again. "One fourteen eighty-three."

Blake rubbed his eyes. He had only the hundred-dollar bill and . . . and the tip he'd left for the woman who'd been the only bright spot in his night. If he took it back, the possibility of seeing her again would be ruined, for she'd see him as an ungrateful no-account. But if he didn't . . .

Heaving a sigh, he went back to the table and grabbed the fifteen dollars. The first woman he had related to in months, he fumed, and he had to stiff her! She had probably anticipated a big tip, and she deserved it. He looked in his billfold again, as if by some miracle he'd find a ten or twenty hidden in the folds. But all he had left was the lone hundred dollar bill. Now he almost knew how helpless Paul had felt today.

Well, he'd always been good with IOUs. If he at least left that, it would show her that he wasn't a complete deadbeat. And maybe—when he stopped beating himself up for being an extravagant jerk—it would provide him with an excuse to see her again. He searched his wallet for a piece of paper but found nothing. He looked around on the table and saw the sweepstakes ticket he had left lying there. Hurriedly, he ripped it in half and pulled a pencil out of his pocket. On the back of the ticket, he wrote: *IOU $15. Blake Adcock.*

He set it on the table where she'd be sure to see it and shoved the other half into his pocket. As an afterthought, he added a P.S. *If this is a winning ticket, I'll take you to New York.*

Gulping back his humiliation, he straightened and glanced toward the kitchen, hoping he could leave before Julie saw what he'd done. Jerking the money out of his wallet, he hurried to the cash register and dropped it on the counter. "I'm kind of in a hurry," he said. The cashier gave him a peculiar look that told him one didn't sit for three hours if one was in a hurry.

"Need a receipt?" she asked.

"Why not?" he said, reaching for it. He could at least add it to his loss when he filed his pathetic income-tax return.

He dropped the few cents in change into his pocket. He stuffed the receipt into his wallet and started for the door. But Julie stopped him as she came out of the kitchen. She had put on a fresh pair of jeans and wore a bright-red sweater. Her coat was thrown over her arm. Her eyes looked even more alive against the bright color, and he suddenly wanted to ask if there was an oven available into which he could stick his head.

"If you're up to staying out a little longer," she said, the words tumbling out as if she'd spent all the time in the back summoning her courage and was afraid it would flee, "I know a quiet little café near here where we could go and talk."

With his heart falling to somewhere in the vicinity of his ankles, Blake turned to the glass door and watched the slanted needles of rain cutting down on the pavement. "I-I can't, Julie. I really need to go."

Julie's face reddened, and Blake wanted to do himself bodily harm. With an exaggerated shrug, she said, "Okay, no problem. I should get home, anyway. I've been on my feet for hours, and I have a million things to do."

She turned back toward the table, and he hovered at the door, wishing there were some way to keep her from seeing her tip. "Julie?"

She turned back to him with eyes that hadn't completely given up.

"Thanks for . . . for listening."

Her smile faded, and he saw her swallow. Her eyes lost their luster as she realized that was all he was going to say. "Sure," she said quietly.

He looked down at the floor and called himself every degrading name he'd ever heard, plus a few he invented for the occasion. Then, as she started back to his table, he stepped out into the storm.

The piercing strength of the icy rain as it hit him felt like the only justice he had experienced that day.

❊　❊　❊

Julie Sheffield watched through the window as Blake disappeared into the night, his broad shoulders slumped against the rain and his silky hair absorbing the water. She'd read him all wrong, she decided. She had been sure he was attracted to her, yet . . .

Blowing out a heavy sigh, she told herself that she really did have to get home, anyway. She had a full night of work to do on her dress designs if she was going to stay on schedule. Working with stitches would be good therapy tonight, she thought dismally. It would help her forget the fluttering feeling she'd had when she thought she had finally met someone she might like to spend some time with. Not like the others who came into the restaurant late at night.

"Oh, well," she said, trying to find the bright side. Maybe he'd at least left her a good tip. Heaven knew, she needed every penny she could scrape together these days. Juggling two jobs—or one job and one difficult dream—wasn't easy, and a good tip could pay for the pearl buttons she needed for her latest creation. She looked down at the cluttered table and shifted the plates, looking for the money usually tucked under a saucer or a glass when a customer left. When she saw the IOU propped against a glass, her stomach plummeted.

"You've got to be kidding," she mumbled. She picked up the ripped half of the sweepstakes ticket. The note on the ticket sent her blood pressure up. An IOU for a tip? An *IOU*? And the note about New York was like a punch line in a predictable joke. She glanced around her, humiliated for having spent so much time on a man who probably wouldn't give her another thought. New York, indeed. She hated herself for liking him.

But he wasn't just like all the rest, was he? He had seemed like a genuinely nice guy. Knew the Bible and everything. He seemed to be a real Christian, and that had moved her to tears. She had prayed so many times that God would send her one of his own, someone who shared her beliefs and her values. For a while tonight, she had believed God was answering that prayer. Was her judgment so warped that she hadn't seen Blake for what he really was? He'd paid over a hundred dollars for food he hadn't even touched, and he didn't even bother to leave her a ten percent tip! *Ten* percent? *Five* percent would have been better than nothing.

She looked down at the ticket again, and a ribbon of shame curled through her. What was the matter with her? The guy probably didn't have anything else. Hadn't he confided in her about his misfortune? And he *had* mentioned that all he'd been paid for his work was a hundred dollars and a sweepstakes ticket. Maybe he figured that box of candy was her tip. Maybe he'd given her all he had.

Except his time. He hadn't been willing to give her that, when she'd had to psych herself up to ask if he'd like to go somewhere. She grabbed her purse from behind the counter, her mind weighed down with regrets. *I should leave the candy,* she told herself. Yet she tucked the box under her arm all the same.

As she stood in the rain beneath the dim streetlight waiting for her bus, she looked back down at the ticket. Did the IOU mean she'd see him again?

She honestly didn't know whether to hope for that or not.

✳ ✳ ✳

Julie had overcome her disappointment by the following night and decided that God had intervened to protect her from someone who wasn't what he seemed. She told herself that she hardly remembered the dark-haired Blake Adcock or the blue eyes that had drawn her in from the moment she'd taken his order.

There were more important things preying on her mind. She sat sprawled on her living room floor with an elegant gown draped over her lap as she did the delicate beadwork on it. She had her first show to think of—the show that she had been working on for more than a year. It would be her debut as a solo fashion designer, even if it was in the city's smallest mall with amateur models and was taking every last penny she'd saved.

No, she had hardly thought of him at all, she told herself with congratulations. So what if they'd shared a moment of communion, a moment of reaching out and understanding? So what if he'd given her a box of candy, which she'd tossed into a drawer when she got home? So what if she'd believed his line about enjoying her company? So what if she'd known he was attracted to her, just as she was to him? So what if he'd seemed like a direct answer to prayer?

Maybe the emotion stirring in her because of another lonely Valentine's Day had caused her to imagine things that weren't real. Or maybe they were real, but he had some rule against going out with waitresses or blondes or Christians.

Or maybe she had been too assertive. How was he to know that it had taken every ounce of courage within her to invite him out?

The doorbell rang. Placing her needle between her lips, she stood and laid the gown carefully over her sofa, next to some of her other designs that were almost ready. "Coming!" she mumbled around the needle. Jerking it out of her mouth and jabbing it in the arm of the sofa, she fluffed her shoulder-length hair and brushed back her bangs. It was probably one of the waitresses who'd agreed to model her clothes in the show coming for a fitting, she thought as she rushed to the door. She swung the door open.

"So we meet again," Blake Adcock said in a lazy drawl that belied the dancing delight in his eyes. He thrust a handful of fake poinsettias at her, and she wondered if he'd just plucked them from her next-door neighbor's pots. Despite the cool grin on his face and the suave way his shoulder leaned against the jamb, there was a definite glaze to the same blue eyes her heart had stumbled over the previous night. His breathing was heavy as if he'd run six miles to her door, and one side of his shirttail hung out of his jeans as though he hadn't taken the time to tuck it in completely.

"Well, well," she said, unable to suppress her smile. She cocked her head and crossed her arms as she surveyed the man who had kept her from sleeping last night. "I didn't expect to see you again."

"It took some doing," he admitted. She hadn't noticed the dimples in his cheeks the night before, but the sly smile tugging at his lips enhanced them now. "You *would* choose tonight to take off work. And your boss acted like your address was a matter of national security. I had to bribe the red-haired waitress."

"Bribe her? What did you have to bribe her with, Blake?"

"I'm real good with IOUs," he admitted.

"So I noticed. Did you promise her New York, too?"

Blake laughed and threw a delighted glance toward the eaves over her door. "Oh, boy, are you going to be surprised when I tell you why I'm here."

"I doubt that," Julie said. Somehow the laughter in his eyes was contagious, and she couldn't help matching it. "You're here to give me these stolen flowers and pay off your IOU, right?"

"Wrong," he said, laughter rippling in his voice. "I came because of that half sweepstakes ticket I left you. You know— the one that probably ticked you off because you thought it was worthless?"

Julie narrowed her eyes and bit her lip, trying to hold back her grin. She had to admit he was cute when he was mysterious. "I vaguely remember something like that," she said.

Blake took a deep breath and pulled his half out of his pocket. In a voice vibrating with controlled excitement, he said, "Well, Julie, you might want to go get it. I was just watching *Wheel of Fortune*, and they drew the winning number. If my eyes aren't playing tricks on me, we're about to be rich."

Julie sucked in a breath. "The winning number? How much?"

Blake's grin trembled. "Twenty million dollars," he whispered. "Ten for me and ten for you."

CHAPTER TWO

"TEN MILLION DOLLARS?" Julie threw a hand over her heart and stumbled back from the door. *"Ten million dollars?"*

"You got it," he said with a shaky note of euphoria. He took her hand and started to dance. "We're rich. Millionaires!"

Julie pulled away. "Wait. This can't be. You can't become a millionaire with a little piece of paper."

"I'll prove it to you," he said. "Go get your half. They said we have to head to our nearest ABC affiliate by midnight to claim our money."

Julie's face went slack as she racked her brain. Where had she put the ticket? Her hands fell helplessly to her sides as her eyes darted from place to place around the room.

"Julie, the ticket," he pressed.

She nodded quickly, holding up a hand to quiet him as she tried to think. "Just give me a second," she said. "I need a minute."

Alarm narrowed his eyes. "A minute for what?" he asked slowly.

"To think about . . . where I put the ticket. I don't think I threw it away."

Blake gasped. "You don't think . . ." Carefully, he stepped inside the door. "Are you telling me that you lost a ticket worth twenty million dollars?"

"No," she said quickly. "I didn't lose it. I just can't remember what I did with it."

"Well, think!" he blurted. The cords in his neck began to swell. *"Think!"*

"I'm trying to!" she shouted back. "But you're making me nervous!"

"I'm making *you* nervous?" He closed the door—too hard. "Julie, if you don't come up with your half, my half isn't worth a nickel."

"You think I don't know that?" She darted down the hallway into her bedroom, not caring that Blake was on her heels and that he'd see the cluttered state of her house. "I didn't know it was worth anything! Neither did you. If you had, you wouldn't have left it!" She dug through her dirty clothes hamper for the jeans she'd worn the night before.

"Hey, I left that ticket out of the goodness of my heart."

She found the jeans and yanked them out, then dug into

the pockets, which were distressingly empty. "The goodness of your heart?" she scoffed. "You left that ticket to insult me." She threw down the jeans and dug out her sweater. "To put me in my place."

"What place?" Blake asked as his eyes followed her every movement.

"My place as just another waitress. Because you think I'm beneath you."

Blake snatched the sweater from her hands and frisked the pockets. "Beneath me? You think I'd spend three hours flirting with someone if I thought she was beneath me?"

"Depends on how bad the weather is!" she threw back. She knocked over the clothes hamper and scanned the inside in case the ticket had fallen out of a pocket.

"You thought I sat there because of the rain? Did you really interpret my note and that ticket to mean I was too good for you?"

Julie marched out of her room and grabbed her purse off the couch. "How did you want me to interpret it?" She dumped the contents of the purse onto the coffee table and began sorting through the folded receipts, empty gum wrappers, and loose change with trembling fingers.

Blake joined her. "The same way I interpreted it when Paul gave it to me." He picked up a sticky, unwrapped cough drop and cringed. "Don't you ever clean this purse out?"

"I've been busy!" she snapped.

He unwrapped some folded papers and shook them out. "When Paul gave the ticket to me, I saw it as a gesture of goodwill. He was doing the best he could at the time. I almost left you the whole thing! I didn't have anything else."

Julie glanced up at him, reluctant to admit he could be telling the truth. But it hadn't been his failure to leave a tip that had hurt, she thought. It had been the rejection, the indifferent way he'd shrugged her off and walked out.

"You ought to be thanking me instead of making me feel like pond scum. I had enough of that last night." He opened the last receipt, found nothing, and threw it down. "It's not here, Julie. Where is it?"

She panned the room again. "I don't know," she whispered.

Blake got up and scanned the small house. Her designs were draped over the sofa and hanging from hooks on the wall. Bolts of expensive, elegant material lay on a table with the sewing machine, and notions and accessories were scattered in various stacks without order. "I don't know how you find anything in this place. It looks like a rummage sale." He went to the couch and snatched up one dress after another to look under them. "What *is* all this junk, anyway?"

Julie's cheeks stung as she rushed forward to rescue the dresses from his rough handling. Draping them over her arm, she caressed them as if they were small children who had been abused. "This *junk*," she said through clenched teeth, "is why I'm working as a waitress. They're my designs. I've been working on them for months, and they're good."

"Right now they're in the way," he said. He tossed the cushions off the couch and ran his hands along the edges.

"*They* belong here. *You* don't! Now get your hands off my furniture!"

He reeled around to face her. "Your car! Maybe you left it in your car!"

Julie clutched the dresses to her chest and backed away. His eyes were getting too wild, and she didn't trust him. "I don't have a car. I had to sell it."

Blake's jaw dropped. "What kind of person lives in Detroit without a car?" he asked in a cracked, high-pitched voice.

"The kind who has to spend her money on more important things!" she shouted with indignation. "I'm not above riding the bus!" She started back down the hall to hang up her designs, but he was behind her in an instant.

"Julie, don't you understand? If you find that ticket, you can *buy* the bus! Please! Help me look for it!"

"I *was* helping, until you started mauling my dresses," she said. "I don't like people insulting my work!"

"We're talking about *twenty million dollars*!" he shouted. "Who *cares* about your work!"

"*I* care!" she yelled back.

"Okay, I'm sorry!" he said as if to appease her. "I didn't mean to insult your work. I'm just anxious to find—"

"You called it junk!" she reminded him. "If you had any taste in clothes, you'd know that these are masterpieces. They'll give women options! They can look elegant without looking trashy. Beautiful, without exposing themselves. They're going to be worth a lot of money!"

Blake folded his hands in a dramatic praying gesture and

moaned. "Julie, you'll *have* a lot of money if you'll just find that ticket. Please! Where do you keep your garbage?"

She crossed her arms militantly. "Where do you think?"

"I don't know. Judging by the rest of this place, it could be anywhere!"

Julie marched toward the kitchen and found the garbage can tucked in a corner. "I'll go through it myself! I don't need any glassy-eyed man rifling through my trash!"

"I'm not glassy-eyed," he said as he watched her dump the garbage on her counter.

She pulled out a wet paper towel, a soup can, a potato chip bag. "You could be a murderer for all I know," she muttered as she continued sorting through the trash. "How do I know there is a winning number? How do I even know the sweepstakes entry is authentic? You could have made this whole thing up."

He caught his breath, incredulous. "For what reason? To get close to you? You're beneath me, remember? At least that was your enlightened impression!"

Her hands began working faster, in jerkier motions, as she realized she wasn't going to find what she was looking for. "Last night my enlightened impression was that you were a nice man who needed a friend. I liked you. But you know what they say. You never know a person until you've shared a sweepstakes ticket with him."

His mouth fell open. "Who says that? I've never heard anyone say that."

"I just said it," she snapped.

He snatched the garbage can from her hand and violently shoved the trash back in. "Last night you seemed like a nice woman I might like to know better. I never would have guessed that under all that beauty and compassion was someone who valued an unhemmed dress more than a twenty-million-dollar sweepstakes ticket. Priorities a little mixed up? I think so!"

"I'll be just as well off if I don't find that ticket as I will if I do, because that unhemmed dress is worth a mint if I sell it. I can live without ten million dollars if I have to. Can you?"

"No!" he shouted. "Especially if I lost it all because of you! What kind of airhead loses a twenty-million-dollar ticket?"

"What kind of airhead gives one away in the first place?" she bellowed.

"Then we're both airheads!" he admitted. "We'd make a great pair. We probably deserve each other."

"We probably do!" she volleyed.

He pivoted toward her and brought his angry face intimidatingly close to hers. "Close your eyes!" he said.

"Why?"

"So you can concentrate!"

She closed her eyes reluctantly, furiously.

"Where did you leave the ticket?" he asked.

Her eyes snapped open. "Oh, this is great. Yelling at me is really going to help me concentrate."

"I don't know how else to get through to you!"

"And I don't know how to get through to you! What do you want? Blood?"

"The ticket!" he shouted. "I just want the other half of my ticket!"

"*Your* ticket?" she asked.

"*Our* ticket. The ticket."

"If I find that stupid ticket," she muttered through her teeth, "it isn't going to be *our* ticket. It's going to be *your* ticket. I didn't ask for it, I didn't want it, and I sure don't have to subject myself to this kind of abuse for it!"

"Just *find* it," he ordered, "and we'll talk about what to do with it then."

Julie squeezed her eyes shut and tried to concentrate.

"Think," he said, lowering his voice. "What was the first thing you did when you got home last night?"

"I took off my shoes," she said. "You see, I'd been running myself ragged waiting on one customer who kept ordering—"

"Then what did you do?" he cut in, more calmly now.

"I turned on the stereo. Then I came in here and got something to drink."

"Did you have the ticket then?"

Her eyes opened, and she focused on the wall, seeing the blurry events unfold. "I think so. I remember looking at it and thinking you were just like all the rest."

A slight grin softened his features, but his voice remained sharp. "Then what did you do?"

"I went to—" She stopped suddenly and snapped her fingers in the air. "My sewing basket! I put it in my sewing basket when I got out what I needed!"

Blake threw his hands together and glanced at the ceiling.

"Thank you, Lord," he mumbled aloud, "for giving her a temporary lapse in her insanity."

Julie caught the barb and jutted her chin. Stalking to the sewing basket, she reached into her tray and grabbed the ticket half. She threw it at him. "It's all yours."

Blake caught it and matched it to his half of the ticket. Relief swept visibly over him, and he collapsed onto the couch. "I can't believe it," he said. "You found it. We're rich."

"Not *we*," she said, planting her fists on her hips. "*You*. I don't want anything to do with your money or your insults or your wild greed. Just get out before you start hyperventilating, and take the ticket with you."

"Julie, it's yours, too."

"Go ahead. I won't take it. I may not have money, and I may not have a car, and I may not even have a glamorous think-tank job, but I do have pride. I don't want to have anything to do with a man who calls me an insane airhead. Not even for ten million dollars."

Blake threw back his head and gave a genuine laugh—a laugh that was pulled from deep inside, where tense fear had just been harbored. "That's good. You're almost convincing. But nobody in her right mind would pass up ten million dollars."

"Well, according to you, I'm not in my right mind, am I?"

Blake stood and faced her, undaunted. "Julie, come on. This is no time for making some noble statement."

"I'm not trying to make a statement," she said. "I don't need your ten million dollars, and I don't want it."

"*Everybody* needs it," he said. "*Everybody* wants it."

"Not me."

His smile faded as he realized just how stubborn this lady was. "Julie, we were under a lot of pressure. Both of us. I don't do well under pressure."

"I won't take the ticket," she said again.

"And I won't leave until you do," he told her with an equally obstinate shrug. "The winner has to report to the nearest ABC affiliate by midnight. It's nine thirty right now. I'm not going alone."

"Fine," she said. "Then you'll miss it and lose your fortune."

"Fine," he returned. "So will you."

They stood staring at each other for what seemed an eternity, each certain the other would back down. Finally Blake pulled out his cell phone.

"Calling ABC?" Julie asked.

"Nope," he said. "I'm ordering a pizza. It looks like we're going to be here for a while."

CHAPTER THREE

THE CLOCK SAID 11:18. Julie and Blake sat staring at each other across the single remaining slice of cold pizza, as if it represented the torn sweepstakes ticket that neither would touch. She sat with her lips pursed, trying to ignore the two ticket halves lying on the coffee table like a future fading in and out of grasp. Blake had to admit he admired her. How many women could actually carry a bluff so far?

Anyone else would have taken the money and run. But it was the principle of the thing that motivated him. Besides, he liked her little game. He had always found that the most difficult things in life were the most rewarding.

"So . . . how about those Lions?" he asked to break the silence tingling between them.

"I don't have much time for sports," she admitted. "I wouldn't know." She unfolded her legs, dusted crumbs off her jeans, and started to stretch.

"What *do* you have time for?" he asked. He gave a sweeping glance around the cluttered room. "I mean, besides housework."

Julie shot him an insulted look. "I clean my house," she returned. "Things are just . . . a little out of place right now."

He rubbed his hand over his stubbly jaw and laughed again. "You didn't answer my question, Julie. What does a woman like you do in her spare time?"

"A woman like me doesn't have spare time," she said. "I work too hard."

"If you had money, you could have all the time you wanted."

"Money can't buy time." She stood. "Speaking of time, I don't have any to waste. I hope you don't mind my working while you waste yours." She picked up a container of tiny beads.

Blake gave a soft chuckle and stretched out his arms dramatically before clasping them behind his head. "You know us millionaires. We love wasting time." Offering a lazy yawn, he propped his feet on the coffee table. "You know, if you had money, you could buy a dress like that. You wouldn't have to make it yourself."

Her eyes flashed at him. "I am a fashion designer," she bit

out. "This is an original—*my* original. Why would I want to buy one?"

"Well, it's just so much work. If you had money, you could hire someone to sew those little thingamajiggies on."

"If I sell this dress, I *will* have money, and I'll be able to hire help."

"But you still won't have time."

"I'll have self-respect and a sense of accomplishment," she said. "And you can get your big feet off my table."

He grinned wider, but he didn't budge. "I'll buy you a new table."

"If you don't go claim your money, you won't be able to."

"And you'll be responsible for my poverty for the rest of my life," he returned.

Julie grabbed the needle out of the sofa arm and took aim at him. "If you don't get your feet off my table, I'll be responsible for something much worse than poverty."

Blake dropped his feet and gazed up at her. "You're dangerous," he said, a mischievous lilt to his voice.

Julie gave him a victorious smile and plopped back down in her chair, making a grand ceremony of propping her own feet on the table.

Blake stroked his index finger over his lips and tried to suppress his laughter. This one was a rascal. She'd probably wait until the clock said it was ten minutes to twelve to give in . . . and that was only thirty minutes away. Well, he thought, it only made things more exciting.

He could almost believe she meant to give up the money.

But he knew better. Any minute now she'd start to sweat and fidget. . . .

❋　❋　❋

Any minute now, Julie thought with an inner chuckle. Any minute now he'd start to look at his watch and pounce on that ticket. And he would expect her to pounce on it, too. Apparently he wasn't used to women who had the strength of their convictions. She'd show him how stubborn she could be.

"So what are you going to do with your half?" he asked with his disarming grin.

She glanced up from her work. "Flushing it down the toilet comes to mind," she said. "That is, if you don't intend to take it."

His deep, tumbling laughter made her smile. "I'd dare you," he said, "but I won't."

"You're catching on," she returned with a wink.

He dropped his elbows to his knees and leaned forward. "You know, this may be hard for you to admit, but we're a lot alike."

"Us?" she asked with a laugh. "How?"

"We're both cool," he observed. "We just won ten million dollars each, and we're both pretending we couldn't care less."

"*You're* pretending," she said.

"And we're both pretty confident. You think I'm going to give in, and I know you are."

"Then one of us must be wrong," she pointed out.

"And we're both stubborn."

"One out of three isn't bad," she said.

He looked at his watch, compared it to the clock ticking away on her wall. She glanced at the clock. "What's the matter, Blake?" she asked. "Getting a little nervous?"

"Nope," he said calmly. "We still have twenty-eight minutes. And I'm not going without you."

Julie threw down her dress and raked her hand through her hair. She couldn't concentrate on her work when there was a man staring at her, waiting for her to crack, and when time flew by as though disaster were on its heel. "What difference does it make to you? It was your ticket to start with. Why can't you just take it back?"

"Because I gave it to you. I wanted you to have it. You were nice to me."

"Well, I don't charge for being nice to people. I didn't expect to be paid for it."

"You expected a tip."

"For doing my job, not for being nice to you," she said.

"Well, whatever we expected or got out of it, the fact remains that we both won, and we'll both claim our money. Otherwise—" he rubbed his hands over his face and arched his brows firmly—"we both go on as we have been. Struggling, dreaming, failing, reaching . . ."

Her eyes met his, and for a moment she wondered if he knew more about her than he was telling.

"It would be fun," he said. "I can't think of anyone else I'd rather become a millionaire with."

Julie stood and began to pace slowly. "Let's face it, Blake. You aren't going to believe me until it's too late. And I'm not going to believe you, either. You need that money, and I know you're not going to pass it up."

"You need it too. If you had it, you wouldn't have to keep working as a waitress."

That was true, she thought. But it was his money. His. And he had said such vicious things to her when he thought she'd lost her half of the ticket. She sat back down and pulled her feet onto the chair with her, dropped her head onto her bent knees, and tried to think clearly. He was bluffing, she thought. He'd run out in the next five minutes with both halves of the ticket. He wouldn't really risk losing it all just because she refused to take half.

His patient bullheadedness intrigued her. How many men would care whether or not she wanted it? How many men would have waited the space of a heartbeat once she'd given the ticket back?

She shook her head and looked up at him as he waited for her to change her mind. Despite the things he'd said to her, she couldn't help seeing the gentle vulnerability peeking through his expression at odd times, as if some sense of honor lurked behind his mask of indifference. Last night she had really liked him, but would she have ever seen him again if God hadn't drawn them back together with a torn sweepstakes ticket?

Had God really been behind this? she wondered. Was this how he planned to answer her prayers after she'd cried out in her loneliness? Was he giving her a miracle now, after she'd suffered through heartbreak and injustice? Jack—the man she had been in love with, the fashion designer she had worked for—had put his ego above their relationship. He had fired her when he realized that the customers placed higher value on her designs than on his, even though the designs bore his name, not hers. Crushed but not defeated, she had tried to start over alone. But just as her designs began to get attention, he claimed she had stolen them from him.

Nothing had been easy since then. Not only had she been thrown back to the drawing board professionally, but she'd faced the added problem of rising above Jack's miserable allegations. Plus she had to make a living while she got started. A waitressing job in an upscale restaurant had been the perfect answer. It netted her not only enough to survive but a little something to put into her dresses.

That was why she had related so well to Blake. They'd each had dreams, and each knew failure. Each had clung to a down-but-not-out demeanor through it all, and remained devoid of bitterness or blame. So what would happen when he collected his winnings and went on with his life, fulfilling his dreams? Would he remember the little blonde waitress he'd butted heads with, the one who gave up her winnings for some hazy principle she didn't even fully understand?

Or would she be filed under "history" and never thought of again?

The thought depressed her. But if she accepted the ticket, they would be somehow yoked together. She would owe him, and that couldn't be good.

Her eyes strayed to the clock again. Eleven thirty-eight. It seemed like no time at all since it had been nine thirty. Where had the time gone? And still Blake made no move to leave. He wasn't even showing the typical signs of anxiety, as she was. He seemed relaxed, calm, even a little amused.

"Is it hot in here?" she asked.

He shrugged. "I'm comfortable."

He watched as she lifted the hair off her neck and glanced at the clock again. "Blake, it's 11:38. You'd better go."

"Not unless you come with me."

"Twenty million dollars, Blake! Just go claim it!"

"Uh-uh."

Julie wiped the perspiration from her forehead and watched as the second hand traveled around the numbers. She snatched up the tickets and handed both halves to him. "Blake, please."

He waved her away. "I'm a man of honor," he said seriously and without any particular urgency. "When I give something to someone, I can't take it back. Even if it means I lose in the process. You should have learned that about me last night, when I told you about giving the prototype to Paul. I keep my word."

"But, Blake . . ." Her plea trailed off as she realized it

was futile. Setting the half tickets back on the coffee table, she listened as the clock ticked off agonizing seconds that dragged into minutes.

At eighteen before twelve, their eyes met. *I can't wait to see him grab those tickets and dart out,* she thought.

But that moment never came. Blake's eyes were amused, placating, but never anxious.

Hers, on the other hand, must have been glossy, frustrated, borderline frantic. If he lost twenty million dollars because she refused to take half . . . She clutched the roots of her hair and swallowed hard. Ten million dollars could have gotten her father out from under the debts he had worked at the steel mill to pay off until the day he died. It could have given her mother a new start instead of a grieving end. It could get her church out of debt, feed the poor, support several missionaries. . . . The money would roll over into the next sweepstakes, and they'd never have the chance again. The next winner might gamble it all away. He or she might spend it on drugs or waste every penny.

The clock's ticking sounds punctuated Blake's slow, relaxed breathing. How could he be so calm? If he didn't run out in the next thirty seconds, she'd have to do something. The second hand descended to the two, the three, the four, and still Blake didn't move. But his smile grew more pronounced in his eyes as he noted the changes in her expression.

Twenty million dollars! What kind of person would sit there and let twenty million dollars go down the tubes because of a misplaced sense of honor? What kind of *airhead* would sit calmly on her couch while—? She caught the direction of her thoughts and hauled them back. She was acting the way he had acted earlier. Calling him names when she was just as foolish as he!

Suddenly she sprang to her feet. "My shoes!" she shouted in a rush. "I'll get my shoes and you start the car!"

Blake was out the door in seconds, leaping over the untended shrubs in her yard and fairly skidding on his feet as he reached his car. She grabbed one shoe, hopped around until she could find the other. Finally she got it halfway on and stumbled to the car. In ten seconds flat they were on their way, each clutching half of the propitious ticket as his car threaded through shortcuts and wove its way toward the television station.

"We must be crazy!" she mumbled. "Wasting all that time! We'll never make it!"

Blake only smiled.

A car ahead of them insisted on driving the speed limit, and Julie sat forward in her seat. "What's wrong with these people? Don't they have anything better to do than ruin the lives of innocent people?"

Blake laughed.

He passed the car impeding their progress and made a turn onto a street that would get them to the highway. But half a mile from the on-ramp they heard a loud whistle and a roaring engine. Julie sought the source of the light shining over them. "A train!" she shouted. "Can't you beat it?"

"No," he said. "Just take it easy. It's all right."

"All right?" she bellowed. "How can it be all right? We have eight minutes to get downtown! *Eight minutes!*"

"Sixty-eight minutes," he corrected with a smile. "I turned your clocks ahead when you were paying the pizza man."

The emotional bubble in Julie's chest bobbed between fury and ecstasy, then crashed like a lead ball. "You *what?*"

"Hey," he said with an infuriating shrug, "I may be honorable and all that, but I wasn't about to take the chance of losing twenty million dollars. Not even for you!"

CHAPTER FOUR

"OF ALL THE UNDERHANDED, conniving, manipulative—"

Her reaction seemed not to surprise Blake, though his annoyance was clear in his voice. "So I tricked you into accepting ten million dollars, Julie. Sue me."

Julie set her eyes on the train rumbling by. It was a cool night, and the smell of rain dominated the air, a sign that another storm was not far away. The sound of the heavy train roaring over the tracks seemed to underscore her irritation, though she wasn't sure why his deception had the power to douse her excitement. "I should have known that you wouldn't have that kind of honor," she muttered, "sitting in my living room like you cared whether I took it or not."

Blake's splayed hand raked quickly through his dark hair, then settled back over the steering wheel. "I did care, Julie. I do care. That's why we're sitting here arguing. If I didn't care, I'd have left your house at nine thirty with both halves of the ticket and never looked back!"

"Why didn't you?"

"Because I'm a man of my word. I don't intend to apologize for that."

Silence settled between them as the rusty boxcars rattled past, and Julie focused on a spot on the windshield. He seemed much too close in the tiny sports car, and his expression clearly illustrated his bruised feelings. What was it about this man that his surprises, his unpredictability, constantly left her disappointed?

"Tell me something," she said after a moment. "What if I had been stubborn right up to the last minute? Would you have left me and claimed the money then?"

"No." There was no hesitation in his answer, no doubt in his blue eyes as he regarded her across the darkness. She felt her heart rate speed up, and she wished she hadn't been so lonely for so long.

Blake made a big deal of stretching and lowered his arm across the back of her seat, reminding her of the "smooth" ploys of a sixteen-year-old in his dad's car. He leaned toward her, his lips entirely too close to her ear as he said, "At that point I probably would have picked you up, thrown you over my shoulder, and taken you with me."

A tiny smile broke through Julie's scowl, for his admission

restored a bit of her faith. Yes, that was exactly what he would have done, she thought. Finally she allowed herself to look at him, and her heart halted in midbeat. "Why?" she whispered hoarsely. "Why didn't you just take the money and run?"

"Why did you have to test me?" he parried. "What made you so sure I was a scumbag who wouldn't have given you a thought if you weren't the key to my fortune?"

She gave the idea a moment's thought. "Because men are usually after something. There's almost always a motive."

Blake cleared his throat as if he couldn't accept being cleared completely. "Well, I never said I was completely without a motive." The confession left his eyes smiling. "When I saw you last night, I did sort of hope we could see each other again."

"Last night you didn't even want to have a cup of coffee with me," she reminded him.

Blake dropped his left wrist over the steering wheel and leaned even closer, the arm at her back closing in. The breath of his words whispered against her lips, and this time it was not her imagination. "Last night I wanted very much to spend more time with you," he said. "I wanted to find out everything about you. How many sisters and brothers you have, if you like old movies, where you're from, whether your parents are still living, what you do during the day, what you would like to do, whether or not you're seeing anyone . . ."

"Then why didn't you just ask?" she whispered, paying careful attention to his lips.

"Because I felt like a loser," he said, "and you aren't the type of woman who deserves a loser."

It was too pat, she thought. Too easy. But somehow he seemed sincere. "I'm from a town called Wry Springs," she said. "It's about an hour from here. I'm an only child, and my parents aren't living. Dad worked in the steel mill until the day he died, and we struggled all our lives. I don't have much faith in money or people who have money, because I never had any, and I was happy anyway. My family always found happiness in our relationships with each other. I guess that's why the ticket didn't mean that much to me. I don't need money to be happy. So now all your questions are answered," she said, glancing down the tracks where the end of the train was still not in sight.

"Not all of them," he whispered. "You didn't answer the ones about old movies and boyfriends."

She struggled not to smile. "Yes and no."

He moved even closer. "And which question does the yes answer? Yes, you like old movies, or yes, you're seeing someone?"

Julie felt a hot, sweet heat scalding her cheeks. "You'll have to figure that one out for yourself, Adcock," she whispered.

He smiled. "Would you really trust me to form my own conclusions?"

"I can't trust you with the time of day."

She caught his grin, in spite of her efforts not to. His hand moved to cup her chin. The gentle touch sent a charge through her nerves. "Julie, last night I had a hundred and fifteen dollars and a credit card charged to the limit. My bill was $114.83. I was humiliated that I didn't have a tip, so I got out of there. I spent the rest of the night more frustrated about the woman I would never get to know than the fact that weeks of my work were down the drain and I was broke."

She wet her lips. "You . . . you really thought about me last night?"

He was watching her lips as if giving serious consideration to kissing her. "Did you think about me?"

"Yes," she admitted.

"And what did you think?"

Her words came out in a mesmerized whisper. "I thought you were a cheap creep and that I was better off if I never saw you again."

His eyes danced as if she'd just given him wild praise. "What else?"

"That you were a white-collar snob who wouldn't stoop to dating a waitress."

He blew a low whistle and stroked her cheek with his thumb. "And?"

She struggled not to smile. "That you were a pretty good-looking, cheap, creepy snob."

"Pretty good-looking, huh?" he rumbled. "Now we're getting somewhere."

"I know I'll hate myself for admitting it."

"Then I'll admit something too," he whispered. "I thought you were worth groveling for. I almost went back after I left, knowing I would humiliate myself even more."

"Almost? Is that supposed to comfort me?"

He moistened his lips. "It'll have to do for now. You should know that I sold my coffee table this morning to raise money so I could pay your IOU tonight."

"Your coffee table?"

"Yes. It's a marble-topped antique. Belonged to my grandmother."

"And you sold it to pay my tip?"

"No. I sold it so I'd have a pretense for seeing you again."

Julie swallowed. He swallowed. As they looked into each other's eyes, gone for a moment were thoughts of the sweepstakes, and the money waiting for them, and the time that sneaked by much too quickly.

Gone, also, was the train.

A horn behind them blared, and several more in the line of traffic behind them sounded. Someone rolled down his window and cursed.

"The train's gone," Blake and Julie said together.

Shifting back into drive, Blake jerked the car forward. He reached across the seat and took her hand. And as they drove, Julie thought more about the feel of his hand on hers than she did about the money waiting for them.

But as soon as they reached the downtown area, the excitement seemed to strike them both. "Ten million dollars," Julie whispered in awe. "I'm going to have ten million dollars."

"I'm gonna buy my neighbor, Mrs. Davis, a big flat-screen TV," he said. "She's homebound and half-blind. And I'll buy Paul a Jacuzzi to help with his circulation."

"I'll be able to quit my job and work full-time on my designs," she said in a dreamy voice.

"And I'm getting my mom one of those doorbells that plays some long tune when you ring it. And a new car with Bluetooth."

"I can hire an assistant to help me," she went on.

"I want the latest iPhone for every one of my nieces and nephews."

"I could rent one of those good PA systems for my show," Julie said.

"A yacht," Blake added. "I'll buy a yacht for my church, for Sunday school parties and retreats."

"Ten million dollars," Julie whispered again.

"Ten million dollars," he echoed.

They reached the street on which the ABC affiliate was located, and a coil of panic rose within her. What if it was a mistake? What if the number wasn't the winning number? What if there were two million other winners? What if the ticket was a fake? "Are we going to be brave when they tell us it was all a big mistake, or are we going to break down and cry like babies, then trash the place?"

"I vote for trashing the place," he said, "but since it isn't a mistake, it won't come to that." He took her hand again and squeezed it as he came to a stop in front of the building. "Well, are you ready for this?"

She massaged her stomach. "I think I'm going to be sick. Maybe you'd better go in and make sure it's real. I don't take disappointment very well."

"We'll both go, and we won't be disappointed. Trust me."

"Trust you?" she asked. "The man who turned my clocks ahead?"

"It was for a good cause," he said. "Now come on."

Stark terror changed her breathing rate. "I can't. My legs won't move."

"If your legs don't move, they won't be able to walk in there and claim all that money."

"They'll figure out a way," she muttered. "Just give me a second."

She gazed through the window into the lit offices. No one in there knew the winner was here in Detroit. She wondered if anyone of authority was here. Had they been briefed on what to do if the winner appeared?

"You know, our lives are never going to be the same after tonight," he said.

"Probably not," she agreed. "We'll always look back and remember the night we thought we'd won ten million dollars and were mistaken."

His deep, melodic laughter relaxed her a little. "We're not mistaken. We're rich."

Numbly, Julie forced herself to open the car door. Her feet touched the ground, and she managed to make her legs move. Blake was beside her in a moment, with his arm around her shoulders. But his own trembling told her he needed support nearly as much as she did. "You know," he said with a wry grin as they started up the steps and into the building, "ten million is a lot, but twenty is more. We ought to give some serious consideration to getting married and pooling our winnings."

Julie gaped at him. From the laughing look on his face, it was obvious that the idea had been facetious. But she didn't find it amusing. "Don't press your luck, Adcock. I haven't given them my half of the ticket yet."

"Well, come on, Julie," he teased. "How can you not see that this relationship is blessed?"

Before she could answer, he had swept her into the office and announced their presence.

※　※　※

"The tickets are bogus," Julie said a little while later as they sat in the station manager's office, watching through the glass window as the evening news anchor spoke into the telephone.

"No, they aren't," Blake said. "They're just checking for authenticity. They can't just give twenty million dollars to anybody off the street. And then they've got to set up the satellite feed showing them giving us the money. This whole thing is for promotion, you know. They aren't going to do it in secret."

Julie glanced at him, and her heart fell when she saw the doubt in his face. "Wouldn't it be something if we went through all this and weren't winners, after all?"

"That is not even a possibility, Julie. Just be patient."

He took her hand, laced his fingers through hers. That calloused touch felt like security, optimism, but its slight tremor kept her from completely abandoning her doubts.

"But what if we don't win? I'm just trying to prepare myself."

"If we don't win, we're no worse off than we were before," he said as if he were already beginning to accept the disappointment. "In fact, we're better off because we met each other. Pretty good deal, if you ask me."

She looked up at him and saw that he meant it. He considered that a plus, and that knowledge made the situation seem less urgent to him.

"Not much better off," he added with a grin. "But a little."

Playfully, she swung at him. The door to the outside opened suddenly, and Brett Bodinger, Detroit's award-winning meteorologist, came in followed by perky Susan Stevens, Detroit's award-winning news anchor. A camera crew filed in behind them with tape rolling. Susan Stevens puffed her perfectly coiffed hair and smacked her recently painted lips. "Are you ready?" she asked the cameramen as they flicked on their lights and positioned them over Blake and Julie.

"Anytime you are," one of them said.

The woman turned back to the baffled couple and grinned from ear to ear, making certain that she never put her back to the camera. "Congratulations, Mr. Adcock and Miss Sheffield. You're going to be millionaires!"

It took a moment for the words to sink in.

In that moment, Julie realized she had known all along that the tickets were authentic.

Blake realized that he had never really believed it.

Their stunned eyes met as they both rose to their feet, and finally Julie threw her arms around Blake and squealed with delight. Blake lifted her off the floor and swung her around. She laughed like a little girl on a carnival ride. "We won!" she said over and over. "We're rich!"

The cameras recorded the whole scene without interruption, and then the reporters zeroed in on the way they had gotten the ticket. After the initial feed to New York, the news anchors set them up at their news desk, from which they did satellite interviews with a dozen stations across the country.

"What do you think this win will do to your relationship?" one of the reporters asked.

"Well, I wouldn't say there really is a relationship," Julie said. "I mean, we just met last night."

Blake tried to look wounded. "I'm crushed. We were just talking marriage not twenty minutes ago."

"Blake!" Julie's face blushed to crimson. "*He* was talking marriage," she corrected. "Something about pooling our winnings or some such nonsense. We hardly know each other."

"Do you regret giving her the ticket?" the man continued. "You could have had the whole jackpot for yourself."

"No, I don't regret it," Blake said. "I like having women deeply indebted to me."

Julie caught her breath as the reporters laughed, but the next question left her little time to work her indignation into anger.

"What are you going to do with the money?"

A lyrical note of laughter undulated on Blake's voice.

"It depends on when they plan to give it to us. If we get it tonight, I might go out and buy a restaurant in Greektown or something." The reporters laughed with a shared exuberance that no one in the room could help feeling.

"And you, Miss Sheffield, what do you plan to do with the winnings?"

"I'm a fashion designer," she said, "and I plan to invest most of it in my business."

"But aren't you going to splurge with any of it?" someone asked.

"Sure," she said. "Maybe I'll buy a new pair of shoes."

Toward the wee hours of the morning, Julie felt as if she and Blake were two aliens in a room full of spectators. She was too distracted to find it odd or awkward when he held her around her waist, and her nerves prompted her arm around him as well. And neither had the slightest suspicion just how far those tiny gestures or their flirtatious teasing would be carried when news of their winnings hit the morning media.

* * *

It wasn't yet dawn when the two weary winners were walked back to Blake's car, followed by a throng of cameramen. They filmed as the couple waved victoriously and began to drive away, like a bride and groom off to the honeymoon.

"So what do you think?" Blake asked when they were back on the freeway. "Are you glad you met me?"

"Yes, but you may not be so glad you met me. The reporters were right, you know. It could all be yours."

He chuckled. "I'm glad I met you, Julie. And I'm glad we won together. It wouldn't have been as much fun without you." He suppressed a yawn. "So what do you want to do to celebrate? We could go get breakfast. Any restaurants you'd like to buy?"

"I want to get some sleep," she said. "We have a big day ahead of us."

Blake snapped his fingers as if to acknowledge defeat. His grin was incorrigible, but he let the teasing drop. "How long before we have to be at the television station?"

She checked the digital clock on the radio. "Five hours. That'll give me three hours to sleep and two hours to get ready."

He yawned and stretched. "This'll be fun. Telling everybody how it feels to be stinking rich."

"Should be easy enough."

"Yeah."

He took her hand and held it. It felt more natural than it should have, and no alarms went off in her head. They were quiet, both lost in dreamy smiles and contented memories of the night as they drove to Julie's house. Once there, Blake pulled into her driveway and cut off his headlights. "So you're sure you don't want to spend any of that tonight, huh?"

"Definitely," she whispered. He made no move to get out of the car.

"Well," he whispered, leaning toward her, "I had a really

good time tonight. You're fun to be around. Even when there's no sweepstakes ticket involved."

He moved closer, and she didn't move away. Their lips met in a sweet union that made her heart race. Gratitude welled up inside her, and she wondered if it was really possible for her loneliness to end at the same time as her financial problems. Maybe God really had brought them together. Maybe there was a chance . . .

A light flashed and they jumped apart. Two photographers stood at the window, aiming and flashing, recording their kiss. Just as Blake opened the door to confront them, two cars screeched to a halt at the curb, and more photographers jumped out. "We've got to go inside," he said quickly. "It's about to get crazy. Come on!"

"No!" Julie said, stopping him before he got out of the car. "You can't come in. They'll blow it all out of proportion. Especially after that picture they just took. I have to go in alone."

"But I can't leave you here with a throng of madmen outside your door!"

"I'll be fine," she said. "They want a story, that's all. They're harmless enough."

He surveyed the crowd growing around the car, bulbs flashing. "All right," he said with a sigh. "I have to go home and change sooner or later. Are you sure you'll be all right?"

"I'll be fine," she said, shading her eyes from the blinding flash of the bulbs. "I'll see you at the television station."

"Yeah. And, Julie?"

She turned back to him.

"They're sending a limousine, so don't take the bus, okay?"

She giggled. "A limousine. Thanks, I would have forgotten. Bye."

"Bye."

She climbed out of the car and pushed through the shouting reporters and photographers and ran to her house. It wasn't until she was safely inside that she heard Blake's car starting up.

And she had to admit that he had been right. The best thing so far about winning the sweepstakes was that she'd met Blake Adcock.

CHAPTER FIVE

"Sweepstakes Sweethearts Win $20 Million!"

The headline on the front page of the Detroit newspaper was like cold water flung into a sleepy, groggy face.

"Sweepstakes sweethearts?" Julie cried aloud.

"Pardon?" asked the chauffeur in the front seat.

"Nothing," Julie said absently as her eyes dropped to the picture of Blake and her in an ecstatic clench as he swung her around. "I . . . I was just . . . never mind." Suddenly feeling queasy, she leaned forward in the spacious limo to the stack of morning papers. Her banker had given them to her when he had opened the bank early to take care of the wire transfer from New York. Moving the first offensive one off the stack, she glanced at the second.

"Lovers Split Ticket and $20 Million!" was the next headline. The photo below it was of Blake and her with arms clamped around each other's waist as they laughed together and answered questions.

"Oh no," she said with a moan.

Reluctantly, she looked at the paper beneath it. *"Sweepstakes Winners Talk Marriage."* Beneath the headline was a photo of the two of them in his car, engaged in the kiss that never should have happened.

She brought her hands to her face and covered it as if that could protect her from the wrath of her aunt, who lived across the street from her. "Sweethearts?" Myrtle Mahogan would ask in an accusing, hurt voice. Then she would tell Julie how humiliated she was to see her "little Julie" being mauled by a man Myrtle hadn't even met. It wouldn't matter that Julie had won a fortune. To Myrtle, the imagined shame and disgrace would be much more tangible than the concept of lifelong wealth.

The car that was almost as big as Julie's bedroom pulled in front of the television station, where in moments Julie would be hooked up to an earpiece and broadcast via satellite to a network morning show in New York. The added coverage would force Blake and her into some sort of artificial relationship that would either ruin the delicate feelings they had begun to feel for each other or propel them into something much faster than either of them could handle.

There was only one thing to do, she thought as the chauffeur opened her door for her. She would have to dispel the myth of the "sweepstakes sweethearts" as soon as possible. She decided national television was as good a place to start as any.

* * *

Dressed in a blue suit, Blake sat in the television station, where the employees skittered around him like trained penguins, bringing him coffee, doughnuts, and croissants. Chuckling within, he fought the urge to demand a shoeshine and a snack of grapes, hand-fed to him by some awestruck beauties. He didn't think he had quit smiling since the night before, and the way he figured it, he was probably going to be smiling for the next twenty years—or at least until his money ran out.

He checked the diamond cuff links he hadn't been able to afford when he bought them and, finding they were still shining like the pleasure in his eyes, reached to the makeup table in front of him, to the newspapers that had been brought in while he was being made up for the lights. Glancing at the headlines, he began to laugh. Well, there were worse images a millionaire could have, he thought. If he was going to be labeled "sweetheart" to anyone, he could do far worse than Julie Sheffield.

He grinned as he looked over the pictures, recalling the ecstasy when he'd swung her around and the euphoria as they'd answered questions. But when he came to the picture of them kissing in his car, his smile faded.

Wait a minute, he thought. This was taking things a little far. How would this look for Julie? She would be humiliated and embarrassed. And he didn't blame her.

A commotion arose across the studio as the subject of his thoughts entered and was engulfed in a crowd of well-wishers. Quickly he dropped the papers in the trash can and searched for something to cover them with. A sign beside the mirror that read Keep Smiling was all he found, so he tore it down and stuffed it in the wastebasket to hide the papers, in the remote chance that Julie hadn't seen them yet. Then he stood to wait for her.

Fashion photographers would have killed to get her for their magazine covers if they saw her today, he thought as he watched her smiling and talking with the camera crew. She was attired in a loose-fitting dress, belted at the waist, and it had an original and untrendy style. It was probably one of her own designs, he thought. The purple background of the printed cloth was a nice foil for the blended swirls of yellow, green, red, and black. The silky fringe of her blonde hair teased close to her long eyelashes as she dipped her head shyly and answered questions.

Their eyes met across the room, but hers darted away. Her face flushed the color of young rose petals, and he knew that she had seen the papers. Now she would be uncomfortable just talking to him, he thought with a surge of anger.

His dazed excitement over the money temporarily

assuaged, he ambled toward her, hands in his pockets. Was it just the way she looked that was making his heart do an aerobic workout, he wondered, or was it the lady herself?

The crowd seemed to hush as he approached, as if everyone waited to hear the first exchange between the now-famous "sweethearts."

"Hi," he said.

She swallowed and glanced away. "Hi."

"Did you get any sleep?"

"No," she said. "Too many reporters outside. You?"

"Too excited."

"Yeah," she whispered.

Feeling as clumsy as a nerd with the class beauty, Blake sought out the news director in the crowd. "When will we be on?"

"Not for thirty minutes or more," the man said.

"Then could I have a moment alone with Julie?"

"Certainly," the director obliged, and everyone smiled with approval. "Right this way to the greenroom."

The porcelain tightness that passed over Julie's face told Blake that he'd made a mistake. She didn't want to be alone with him, and she especially didn't appreciate his asking for privacy in front of the entire staff of the television station.

The greenroom wasn't green at all but a bright blue that did nothing to calm the nerves of those waiting to be tele-vised. Soft, overstuffed couches filled the room, and there was a wet bar in the corner and a monitor on the wall so they could watch what was going on in the studio. Julie went in and stood awkwardly in the room. Blake knew that for every step forward he had made with her, the morning papers had pushed him ten steps back.

The news director reached for the door to close it, but Blake stopped him. "Leave it open," he said. "We don't need that much privacy."

"Sure?" the man asked.

"Absolutely."

When the man had left them alone, Blake turned to Julie. "What's the matter?"

"I'm tired," she said. "I'm not used to getting a lot of sleep, but I usually get some."

"Yeah, me too."

There was more on Julie's face than fatigue, Blake thought as he watched her drop her clutch purse on the couch and flop down. She slipped her finger through one of her gold earrings. "Do you know what they're saying about us?"

He lowered to the arm of the couch across from her. "Yeah. Afraid I do."

"Well, it isn't true!"

Blake chuckled. "I know it isn't."

"Well, *they* don't know it." She took a deep breath and rubbed her hand over her forehead. "And my aunt doesn't know it."

"Julie, I'm sorry. I shouldn't have kissed you last night. I should have known—"

Julie nodded as if she agreed with him. "And you shouldn't have teased about marriage, Blake. That was like throwing a bone to a pack of starving dogs, and now they want even more. But I was as much at fault as you for the kiss. I didn't exactly fight you off."

He was silent for a moment as he recalled the kiss that had gotten them into so much trouble. A sly grin crept across his face at the memory, and he turned to a soda machine in the corner as if studying the selection of beverages.

"What's so funny?" she asked.

He gave a shrug. "Nothing."

"No, tell me. I want to know."

He turned back to her and leaned against the machine. "I was just thinking that no matter how much it was blown out of proportion, I think if I had it to do all over—" he rubbed the smile on his face—"I'd still kiss you."

"Blake . . ."

He shrugged helplessly. "Sorry, but you asked."

Julie dipped her face and studied the paisley pattern of the carpet, fighting the flattery that nevertheless seemed to calm her. "Well, we have to fix this. We have to make sure that the reporters have nothing else to go on. In fact, we should proba-bly go out of our way to make it clear that we're not involved."

Blake slid his hands into his pockets and paced to the window, glanced out, then turned back to her. "What if we did the opposite? What if we gave them what they wanted until it was old news and they left us alone?"

"Absolutely not," she said adamantly. "I don't want another failed romance to wind up in the Detroit gossip columns."

"Another?" he asked. "Has this happened before?"

Julie closed her eyes. "Forget I said that. I just meant that I don't like to play games."

"I'm not asking you to. We don't have to do anything. All we have to do is smile at each other now and then—be ourselves—and they'll have a field day with it."

"That's why we have to go as far to the opposite as we can. We can't smile at each other, Blake, and we can't touch each other, and we can't be in the same car together or the same house. We've got to tell these people that we didn't even meet until the night before last and that there is absolutely nothing between us!"

"Julie, it'll just make us more mysterious. They'll hound us until they have something. This is the kind of story people love."

Julie got up. "I don't care! It's my life we're talking about! My reputation!" She took a breath as if trying to calm herself. "Maybe I should invent a boyfriend. Or you could tell them you're engaged."

Blake leaned back against the windowsill, playing along. "You mean lie?"

"Well, you didn't mind lying last night about the clocks. Just a little lie."

"Yeah, that could work. I could bring Lola on TV with me. She's had me pegged as husband material for a while now."

"Lola?" Julie asked, a surprised sparkle of jealousy in her eyes that was not lost on Blake.

"Yes. She's a little brassy, of course, but I like her free

spirit. Maybe you could lend her one of your classy dresses to wear, since most of her wardrobe is only appropriate for the stage."

"The stage? What is she? A singer?"

"No, Lola's a little tone-deaf." He chuckled, then shrugged. "I guess I could get her on the news with me later today. It would certainly dispel the rumor that you and I are involved. That is, if you're sure that's what you want."

Julie stared at him for a moment, but slowly her gaping mouth closed. A soft grin pulled at her lips as she regarded him. "You aren't dating anybody named Lola."

"Sure I am."

"You don't even know anyone named Lola," she challenged. She studied him as if uncertain.

A smile broke across his face. He flung out his arms dramatically. "All right, you caught me. But I'll be glad to go out and find someone for this afternoon's broadcast if it'll make you feel better."

In spite of herself, Julie seemed relieved. "I don't think that will be necessary. As long as we don't flirt, I think we can manage."

Blake closed the distance between them. "But see, that's the hard part," he said in a low voice. "By the way, have I told you what a knockout you are this morning?"

A rosy blush painted her cheeks. "Thanks."

"That one of your designs?"

"Yes."

"Nice," he whispered.

She studied her purse for a moment, tracing the pattern with a finger as she searched for a change of subject. "So, did they wire your money all right?"

"Yeah. Four hundred thousand, to start. The bank opened early for me. Funny how accommodating they can be when you have money. They even gave me a digital camera for making a deposit over two thousand dollars. The way I see it, they owed me about two hundred cameras. What did you get?"

"A deposit slip," she said. "I would have liked a camera."

"I'll give you mine," he said.

She laughed softly. "I couldn't believe it. It felt strange getting a deposit slip for almost four hundred thousand dollars!"

"Cheapskates," Blake teased. "I thought they'd give it to us all at once."

"I'm glad they didn't. Just imagine getting a check for four hundred thousand dollars every year for twenty-five years."

"Yeah, well, the IRS is getting a pretty big check every year for twenty-five years too."

"Render unto Caesar what is Caesar's. You won't hear me complaining."

Blake laughed. "Me, either. I can scrape by on four hundred thou a year, even minus the taxes. If they'd just set me loose so I could spend it."

Julie went to the window and looked out. Her eyes lost their dreaminess and took on a practical glint. "I guess I should postpone my fashion show. If I had more time, I could do it up really nice. I'm going to quit my job today so I have more time to work on it."

"You're going to quit?" he asked.

"Yeah," she said. "I was only working as a waitress to support myself until I could get my designer business off the ground. I don't have to do that now. I just hope the mall will work with me on another date for the show. I had to do some pretty fast tap-dancing to make them agree to it in the first place."

Blake was behind her before she knew it. His hands closed over her shoulders, and he looked over her head, out the window, seeing worlds farther than the brick building in their view. "Julie, sweetheart, do you hear yourself? You put all that cash in the bank this morning and you're worried about whether the mall will let you do your fashion show. You can afford to buy the mall. You can have that show anywhere, anytime you want."

Julie looked over her shoulder at him, and the truth of his words seemed to dawn in her eyes. "You're right."

"Then forget about it and just have fun for a while. You'll never win ten million again."

She turned to face him, her big, innocent eyes meeting his; she smiled in a way that only he, a fellow winner, could understand. It held the suppression and the ecstasy of disbelief . . . and the beginnings of belief.

And it made his heart do drumrolls.

"How am I going to make it through live television if I don't have you to prop me up?" he whispered.

"No touching," she maintained, though the mesmerized look on her face told him she didn't mean it.

"We can't even hold hands?"

"We *especially* can't hold hands."

He brushed the hair out of her eyes. "But what if we really did want to get involved? What if we really wanted to make all those headlines come true?"

"*If* that were the case," she whispered noncommittally, her eyes sparkling like morning sun, "we'd just have to do our hand-holding in secret."

His face brightened. "In secret, huh? I like it."

"I said *if.*"

A grin captured one side of his mouth. "I heard what you said," he whispered.

A knock sounded, and they leaped apart as if they'd been caught doing something more than just smiling at each other.

"We're about to go on," the news director said. "We need to get a sound check."

Blake's hands plunged into his pockets. Julie's wrapped around her purse. Together they walked to the set, staying a few feet apart. But the director had other plans. The tiny bench they were seated on was meant for only one, but he insisted that they sit there together. "So we can get you both on the screen at once," he explained. "Just cozy up together."

So they made the most of it, sitting awkwardly, shoulder to shoulder, until the director insisted that Julie lean more into Blake. She did as she was told, but Blake felt her stiffness and knew that if she hadn't been so nervous, she would have been protesting loudly.

They inserted their earpieces and clipped on their mikes. Near the camera was a monitor, where they could see the host of the show talking with an actor. "We're following *him*?" she whispered.

Blake sensed a note of awe in her voice. "I'll bet *he* never made ten million in one night," he mumbled into her ear.

The actor's interview ended, and a soup commercial followed. "Stand by," the director said. "New York wants to do a sound check. Say something."

Blake took the gauntlet. "That wasn't her in the car with me, Aunt Myrtle. It was Lola. The photographers just superimposed Julie's head over the body."

Julie slapped at his chest, incredulous, though a smile did battle with her glower. "Blake, stop it. If you say anything like that on the air, I promise I'll get up and leave."

Blake grabbed her hand, wrestling her still. "Yes, Aunt Myrtle, they forced us into that kiss. The photographers cut out the terrorists holding guns to our heads."

"Blake, I'll kill you!" Julie hissed.

"Perfect," some laughing, New York voice said in their earpieces. "That's exactly how we want you to play it."

Julie's smile faded. "Play it?" She looked at Blake. "I mean it," she whispered as if to keep them from hearing. "I don't want to feed this fire. Please . . ."

He held his fingers up in a Boy Scout salute. "I promise. I won't embarrass you."

"Stand by," the director said again, this time chuckling.

❇ ❇ ❇

Julie tried to put some stock in Blake's promise. But the memory of his cheating with her clocks and playing into the press's hands with talk of marrying their fortunes reeled back through her mind.

They waited, tense, as the theme music played and the host mentioned that it was half past the hour. And then, before they could catch their breath or wipe their palms, they were on the air.

"Sweepstakes sweethearts" were the first words out of the host's mouth, and Julie thought she was going to be sick. When he'd finished telling the viewing audience the unique reason for their splitting the ticket, he turned to the camera. "Julie, Blake, how do you feel today?"

"Like ten million bucks," Blake said.

Julie threw him a look, wondering if he'd spent his five hours alone that morning figuring out that line.

The man laughed. "Julie?"

"I feel great," she said.

Blake threw her a look that asked if that was really the best she could do.

"Any further thoughts of pooling the winnings and making it legal?"

Julie wondered if her face was searing in living color. "Uh, I think we should clear something up," she cut in before Blake could answer. "This 'sweepstakes sweethearts' business is a little too much hype. The fact is that we only met two nights ago, the night he gave me half of his ticket."

"But there must have been something there if he gave you half of a twenty-million-dollar sweepstakes ticket."

"It was a tip," she explained.

"You must be some waitress!"

"It was the uniform," Blake interjected. "I have a weakness for women in uniform."

Julie gasped and glared at him.

Blake winced, waiting for her to strike him. The crew erupted with raucous laughter.

"Tell me," the host said, thankfully changing the subject, "what do you plan to do with the money, Julie?"

Julie cleared her throat and tried to regroup, telling herself it would all be over soon. "I'm a fashion designer, and I plan to invest in my business, but I haven't had time to think of specifics yet."

"She designed what she's wearing," Blake added. "Isn't that a knockout?"

Julie ground her heel into his foot, out of the camera's view. Blake flinched and set his teeth.

"Fantastic," the man said. "Ten million ought to get you well on your way. What about you, Blake?"

"I don't know," he said in a strained voice. Julie lifted her heel, and he breathed with relief and glanced at her with an expression that one would wear in the presence of a lunatic. Then, bringing his eyes back to the camera, he added,

"Maybe I'll buy a castle or something. A couple of pinball machines. Who knows?"

"Who knows, indeed," the host said as if those three words held the wisdom of a whole council of wise men. "Are you planning any grand celebration together? Besides the one we've already read about?"

"I promised to take her to New York," Blake blurted, and Julie's eyes flashed again. Fearing another dig into his foot, he quickly covered himself. "Really, Julie meant what she said. We aren't involved. We actually just met night before last, and we know very little about each other. As a matter of fact, I've been seeing someone else."

"And he's not my type at all," Julie threw in.

"And I don't generally like blondes," he added.

On that ridiculous note the host thanked them and broke for the weather, and Julie and Blake remained motionless on their seat.

"If I had a gun," she mumbled through compressed lips, "I'd shoot you right here on national television."

"Julie, I'm sorry. Those things just slipped out."

Julie stood, jerking the earpiece and mike off, and raged down at him. "Just slipped out? The bit about New York? How could you?"

"I just told the truth. I get all stammery when I lie. You didn't want me to get all stammery on national television, did you?"

Julie groaned viciously and started off the set, and Blake

limped after her. "And why'd you have to crush my foot that way? I probably have a fracture in the shape of your heel."

"That isn't my heel print, Blake. It's teeth marks from ramming your foot into your mouth every time you opened it!"

"Julie, it's no big deal," he said, hobbling faster. "I'll do better next time."

"Yeah." She swung back to face him. "I just bet you will. You'll just stiffen your spine and stand up for my honor and reputation, won't you, even though you don't generally like blondes!"

Blake nodded innocently. "I'll make Aunt Myrtle proud of you. And just for the record, I made up the bit about not liking blondes."

Biting her lip, Julie crashed her heel into his other foot. He yelped and grabbed it, hopping as she stalked away. "Are you crazy?" he shouted after her.

She turned at the door and wagged a finger at him. "Yes! The next time you decide to let some innuendo about me 'slip,'" she said, "remember that I have other shoes at home. Sharper ones!"

She was thankful Blake had the good sense to stay quiet as she hurried out the door.

CHAPTER SIX

Julie slept hard that night and most of the next day. It was dark when she finally emerged from her bedroom. She peeked out the window and saw that some reporters still lurked out in front of her yard. She had turned off her cell phone so it wouldn't wake her; now she turned it back on so she could call her aunt Myrtle. The phone began ringing instantly. Too tired to talk to another reporter, she silenced it. One after another, her voice mail alerts popped up on the screen.

She listened through ten messages; then a familiar voice startled her. It was Jack, the designer she'd once been in love with, the one who had betrayed her. He had heard of her win and wanted to congratulate her. He thought they might have dinner, if she would call him back.

Julie sighed and stared at the phone. She supposed she was more attractive to him now that she was rich. The thought brought back sad memories of rejection and pain. He had shaken her life after their last meeting a year ago, when he'd fired her from his design studio. No, she wouldn't call him now. His business had suffered when she'd left and taken her talent with her, even after he'd spread word that every design Julie had created since had been stolen from him. When she heard of his lag in profits, Julie determined that God had taken vengeance. But the scars on her heart hadn't healed, and she was not about to expose them to Jack again.

Wrenching her thoughts away, she went to the kitchen, looked in the refrigerator, and sighed when she saw how empty it was. *I'm a multimillionaire,* she thought, *and I don't even own a carton of milk.* Right now she would have given a whole year's payment for a pint of yogurt. She was afraid to go to the grocery store for fear she'd never get out alive when the press and well-wishers surrounded her. But she'd bet it wasn't that way for Blake. He was probably ordering everything in.

She laughed lightly. They were so different, yet she couldn't stop thinking about him. She would have to stop, though, because the last thing in the world she needed now was to fall head over heels in love with him, only to find later that it couldn't work. Then the whole world would know about the split. It would be worse than last time, when everyone had watched and waited for her reaction to Jack's callous behavior and his contention that she was washed up as a designer. But *everyone* in the fashion circles had been only fractional compared to *everyone* who was following her alleged affair with Blake through the media.

The doorbell rang. Julie cringed and refused to answer it. A hard knock followed.

Was Blake having these problems, too? she wondered. Or was he enjoying all the attention?

If only the press would get tired and leave, she could concentrate on her work. She wondered if she'd see Blake again, now that they had nothing throwing them together. The thought of not seeing him again disturbed her, and she leaned back in her old, lopsided recliner and closed her eyes. She felt herself relax as she realized the worst part was over. There were no more interviews, at least for a while.

A purposeful knock sounded at the side window of her living room, and she sprang up and sucked in a breath. *A photographer,* she thought. He had found a way to get past her fence!

The knock sounded again, louder this time, and she rushed out of her recliner and looked around the room for a weapon. Her eyes fell on a seam ripper on the coffee table, and she grabbed it. It was the first time a photographer had actually knocked on her window. He must be pretty desperate—and a little crazed—if he was willing to do that.

Holding her seam ripper out in front of her as if it were the weapon that could save her, she slowly stepped toward the window. This was it, she thought. It had gone too far, and she was going to put a stop to it!

Gritting her teeth, she stepped beside the window and took a few deep breaths for courage. She didn't care what the papers said about her after this. She'd had enough, and she was going to make sure that this reporter didn't get away without a few of his seams ripped!

Slowly she reached her hand under the curtain and threw back the lock. Then, as quickly as she could manage, she flung open the window and closed her eyes as she thrust forward the measly weapon.

"Julie, no!" came a strangled voice. A hand reached out to grab her arm as a body came through the window and thudded to the floor.

Wrestling free as she realized her seam ripper wouldn't do the trick, she reached for a lamp and swung it high in the air.

"Don't kill me. I give!" the man said in a high-pitched whisper. "It's me, Julie!"

Julie stepped back from the window and flicked on the lamp she clutched in her hand. The face of Blake Adcock winced up at her.

CHAPTER SEVEN

"Blake, what are you doing here?"

Blake gave her a haggard look, but that familiar grin broke through his scowl. "I can't talk right now," he said with a groan. "I'm wounded. Are you going to help me up, or do you plan to take a few more stabs?"

Julie set the lamp down and kicked a pile of laundry out of the way. "Did I hurt you?"

"Almost." He stood and checked the contents of a loaded pillowcase he carried. "Luckily those clothes on your floor broke my fall. And the ice pick—or whatever it is—only caused a minor flesh wound."

"It's a seam ripper," Julie informed him.

"A seam ripper," Blake repeated. "Terrific." He showed her the scratch on his hand. She hadn't even broken the skin.

Julie grabbed a sock off the floor and used it to pat the scratch.

Blake jerked back. "Julie, I don't mean to insult you, but I'd rather not have my wounds attended to with a dirty sock."

"It isn't dirty," she said. "That pile is clean laundry. I haven't had time to fold it yet. Now give me your hand." Reluctantly Blake extended it. "So how did you get over my new fence without getting hurt?"

Blake glanced down at his torn jeans and the scratch on his leg. "I didn't. Take it from me, that fence is effective."

Julie assessed the damage and gave him an exasperated look. "Are you crazy?"

"Hey, I had a security fence put in today. I thought I had it figured out after I climbed over mine. No one even saw me leave. I walked away and called a cab, and he dropped me off on the street behind here."

"Why did you do all that?"

"Because I wanted to see you."

He looked at her through the dim, flickering circle of light cast by the lamp. She felt suddenly self-conscious about her hair inching out of its binding. His voice dropped in pitch. "You said that we'd have to do our hand-holding in secret. If we hadn't won gazillions together, we'd be on a dinner date with my coffee table money. Right out in the open. You know it's true."

"I don't know any such thing."

"Face it. You're a snob. If I weren't a zillionaire, you'd go out with me."

"No, never," she whispered. His lips were much too close, and he smelled of wintergreen.

He grinned, not believing a word. "Sure?" he asked. "You liked me that first night. I know you did."

"I was trying to get a tip."

"Yeah, that's you. Miss Mercenary. But even if you were after a tip, I liked you. I would have had you head over heels for me by now if it weren't for the money."

He was too close, and her heart was pounding too hard. She couldn't help the grin tugging at her lips. He made her laugh when she didn't want to. She feared she had already fallen for him.

"So what do we do now?" she asked.

He cocked his brows. "I brought food," he said. "From the looks of your refrigerator the other night, I gathered you don't have food in the house, and I figured you wouldn't go out to shop. So I decided to feed you. I brought a picnic."

He reached into the pillowcase and pulled out a tablecloth and spread it on the living room floor. She fell to her knees, giggling. "You brought everything?"

He shrugged. "I would have brought it in something more romantic than a pillowcase, but I didn't think I could sneak in effectively with a basket." He reached in and pulled out an elaborate brass candleholder. *"Voilà!"* He pulled out a candle and set it in the holder. "And now, to set the mood . . ." He reached into his pocket and withdrew a match, then lit the candle. "Ah," he said when the flame caught and lit her face with a faint golden hue. "I knew you'd be beautiful in candlelight."

She swallowed. "Blake . . ."

He set the candle on the tablecloth and pulled out the food, grinning at the unsettled look on her face. "Peanut butter and jelly," he said. "It was all I had."

"It's my favorite," she said, sitting down. She took half a sandwich and bit into it. "Crunchy," she said with a smile.

He sat also and regarded her for a moment. "You're very easy to please," he said. "You know, my mother said I should snap you up before some fortune hunter does."

Her eyes laced with amusement. "Your mother said that? I never thought of you as having a mother."

"Did you think I was born in a test tube?"

"Guess I just never considered it."

"Maybe you thought such a *manly* man didn't need a mom."

"No, everybody needs a mom. I miss mine. She died five years ago."

"I'm sorry." Blake's eyes took on a sudden grief as if he'd known her mother.

Julie looked at her bare feet. "No, it's okay. She was suffering. Cancer. But I have a lot of peace because Mom found Christ just before she died. She was in a Christian hospice, and the sweet woman who ran it won her to Christ, so she had a happy ending. I owe a lot to the Spring Street Hospice Center. I'm looking forward to giving them a fat donation."

"Maybe I will too," he said. Julie watched as he pulled a can of Sprite and two plastic cups out of the pillowcase. He divided the soda into both cups and handed her one. "To our money," he whispered. "May it bring great happiness."

She watched him drink. "How is the money going to bring you happiness?" she asked.

He ran his finger around the rim of his cup. "It's going to get my business going, for one thing."

Their knees touched as they sat cross-legged, and they leaned toward each other as if some magnetic force drew them together. "How? I thought your business depended on your friend Paul. If his business is floundering, how will your money help?"

"I'm going to help him," he said. "I'm going to give him the money he needs to get back on his feet."

"Bad idea," Julie said. "He didn't manage his own money well. How do you know he can manage yours?"

"He will," Blake said.

"I know you mean well," she said, "but it might just ruin your friendship. Believe me. I've been in business with someone I cared about before."

"The designer you mentioned? The one in the gossip columns?"

"Yeah."

Blake reached out and his hand tightened over hers. "What happened?"

Julie ran the fingers of her free hand through her ponytail. "He got jealous of my designs, fired me and humiliated me,

FOR LOVE OF MONEY

slandered me publicly, then hired a new young designer with less talent. It was a much safer relationship for him."

"Oh." Blake studied her hand with a scowl. "I'm sorry."

"It's okay," she whispered. She took a deep breath and reached for her sandwich, trying to seem unaffected. "He's suddenly interested again, now that I have money. Thinks I'm a fool. Anyway, my point is that when it comes to business, you should stay as far away from people you care about as you can. I learned that the hard way."

Blake's face was solemn, and his eyes glistened. "Then you and I won't do business together. We'll keep it strictly personal."

Once again, she fought the grin on her face. "But we have to think. Why are we attracted to each other? Because of the money? Because we treat each other like human beings when everyone else treats us like we cured cancer?"

"We liked each other before all that, Julie. God brought us together. Let's just remember that." He kissed her hand, making her heart jolt. "But I don't intend to get to know you by scaling your fence every night. I've decided it's time for me to keep my promise to you."

"What promise?"

"To take you to New York."

Julie caught her breath. "No, Blake. That's a bad idea."

"Couldn't be," he said, combing his fingers through her hair. "I'm just suggesting we go for the day. Manhattan is a great place to spend time together and find out what we really feel for each other—without the media to draw conclusions for us. I mean, think about it. With all the celebrities and hotshots there, we're two of the littlest fish in the sea. Nobody will even notice us."

"I'm not going to New York with you," she argued. "I can't."

"Yes, you can."

"What will people say?"

"They'll say, 'Where'd they go?' We'll leave secretly."

She sat paralyzed for a moment, considering it. No phones, no photographers, no interviews. If they could, indeed, get away without anyone knowing, she might have some peace. And some time with Blake.

"When would we leave?" she asked.

"In just a few hours—before dawn. If we leave that early, the press won't see us," he said, his eyes sparkling as if she'd already consented.

"But what about airline tickets?"

"Leave that to me. You just start digging for your walking shoes, and I'll line everything up."

Julie didn't move just yet. "*If* I go, I'd pay my own way. And we have to behave appropriately. I don't want to give Christ a black eye by making it look like I'm some high-rolling 'sweepstakes sweetheart' who's too intimate too fast with some guy I met in a restaurant just two nights ago."

"Too intimate too fast?" he asked, amused. "How do you figure that?"

"We kissed on page 1, okay?" she reminded him.

"But I didn't mean to kiss you on page 1. I thought I was kissing you on page 3."

She tried to bite back her laughter and shoved him. "I'm serious!"

"So am I! I'll be a perfect gentleman, Julie," he promised. "I want to honor Christ, too. And I always keep my word."

Reluctantly Julie agreed to go.

✳   ✳   ✳

It was well after midnight when Blake called Paul and reminded him of every favor he'd ever done for him.

"I think mine tops all of yours, Adcock," his friend said in a groggy voice. "I gave you the twenty-million-dollar ticket, remember?"

"Oh yeah, there's that," Blake agreed. "But I need one more little bitty favor, buddy."

"What little bitty favor would that be?" Paul asked.

"I want you to pull some of those strings of yours and hire a luxurious private plane to take Julie and me to New York."

"Now? Do you know what time it is?"

"Yes, but the lady wants to go before dawn. You wouldn't let a little thing like sleep stand in the way of a favor for a pal, would you?"

"A private plane," Paul said with resignation. "And someone to fly it, I presume?"

"Yeah, that would be nice," Blake said. "But I want it to be so discreet that even the pilot doesn't know about it."

"The pilot has to know about it," Paul said. "Unless you intend to fly the plane."

"Oh yeah. Well, just tell him to keep quiet. I have a little lady here whose reputation is already in dire straits. We seem to be a volatile combination, at least in the papers, and I don't want any more explosions."

"Got it," Paul said. "I know just the plane. But it'll cost you. Think you can come up with the bread?"

"I think I can manage to find a few extra bills lying around," Blake said. "How long will it take you?"

"Two hours," Paul said. "Meet me at the charter terminal at the airport, and we'll have you on your way."

"We'll be there," Blake said.

"So I finally get to meet her, huh?"

"Yeah. But don't get your hopes up. The lady only dates new money these days."

"As opposed to borrowed money?" Paul laughed.

"Hey, I am not giving you a loan," Blake said. "It's a gift. As you just pointed out, you gave me the ticket."

"I'd rather consider it an investment," Paul corrected. "One that you won't regret. And if God had intended for me to keep that ticket, I would have. So pack your bags and meet me in two hours. If I see any reporters lurking around—"

"Create a diversion," Blake finished. "Take an employee hostage or something."

"You got it, buddy."

It didn't take long for Julie to change into a versatile dress that would work for the nicest of places as well as the most relaxed. When it was time, they called a cab to meet them two blocks away and made their way quietly out her back gate. Julie didn't remember when she had ever had more fun as they stole through the night to the waiting cab.

Paul was waiting for them at the express gate at the small private airport. Julie observed the blond hunk whose disability was only apparent by the wheelchair in which he sat. The man reached for Julie's hand when Blake introduced them and pressed a kiss on it that told her his charm more than compensated for his problems. "You look even lovelier in person than you do on television," he said.

She gave him a skeptical grin. At this late hour, she knew she probably had dark circles under her eyes. She turned to Blake. "Your friend just lost all his credibility. I'll never believe another word he says."

"I'm wounded," Paul said, a hand over his heart. "She doesn't believe me."

"Take it from me," Blake said, "her verbal wounds are much better than the ones she inflicts with her seam ripper and the heels of her shoes. So where's the plane?"

"Over there," Paul said, pointing out the large window to a plane warming its engines on the dark runway. "That jet over there."

Blake's grin was instant. "Perfect."

"Perfect?" Julie asked, astounded. "That's just for us? It'll cost a fortune!"

"We *have* a fortune. Two of them."

"Not for long if we spend it this recklessly." She turned back to Paul, who watched her with laughing eyes. "Couldn't we take a Cessna or something?"

He shrugged. "I could've gotten a crop duster, but the man said he wanted luxury."

"But . . . a jet? I don't know."

"I'm paying for this part," Blake said, taking her by the arm and leading her to the door. "And it's already arranged, so please try to grin and bear it." He turned back to Paul, who rolled behind them. "Poor thing. She just has to endure so much."

"Be kind to her, Adcock. Every now and then dress her in a burlap sack and feed her cold cereal so she'll feel a little more secure."

"You two are impossible," she said. "I'm not a cheapskate. It's just that I don't like to spend money."

"I see the difference," Blake said. "Don't you, Paul?"

Paul nodded adamantly. "It's very clear to me."

"Oh, let's just go. I'll try to enjoy it without thinking about how many bolts of silk I could buy with this money."

"I'll buy you all the silk you want when we get back," Blake said as he pulled her out onto the tarmac. He bit his lip like a little boy trying to suppress his delight. "Oh, this is gonna be great!"

CHAPTER EIGHT

"THIS ISN'T AN AIRPLANE; it's a hotel with wings!" Julie exclaimed when they had boarded the luxurious jet.

"Oh, don't exaggerate, Julie," Blake said. "It doesn't even have a swimming pool."

Julie gaped at him as he stepped inside as if he'd been raised there, dropped his duffel bag on the floor, and plopped down on a couch. "Blake, what has gotten into you? This isn't necessary. We could have taken a plane a tenth this size and it would have been fine."

With a flourish, he propped his feet on the coffee table and clasped his hands behind his head. "But I wanted to impress you."

Julie laughed and laid her big purse on the floor, kicked off her shoes, and stepped over them. "Impress *me*? I was impressed a few days ago when you couldn't even afford a tip!"

The exclamation struck Blake as funny. As if he couldn't contain the silly giddiness that was so apparent on his face, he began to laugh.

"What's so funny?" she asked, trying not to catch the laughter herself.

"I was just thinking," he chortled, "about how I couldn't even afford to put gas in my car a few days ago. . . ."

"And now you've rented *Air Force One*."

"Yeah. And if it flies well, I might even buy it."

Julie's face flushed, and she peered out the window to remind herself that they were still on the ground. "And if it doesn't fly well?"

Blake lifted a rugged brow. "You can swim, can't you?"

The plane began to roll down the runway, and Julie tumbled to the sofa as her hand slapped over her stomach. "I just hope the designer put as much attention into this thing's engine as he did into its carpeting."

"I don't know," Blake teased, examining the deep pile. "This is pretty nice carpeting."

It wasn't until they were in the air that Julie managed to loosen up. If the engine wasn't strong enough to support a bar and enough couches to fill a hotel lobby, they would have crashed by now, she reasoned. Besides, there was something to be said for the boyish enthusiasm Blake exuded.

"Why don't you go to sleep?" Blake asked when her spirits mellowed enough to make her pull up her feet onto the sofa.

"Can't," Julie said. "It isn't every day I fly off to New York on a jet with a man I hardly know." She watched, smiling, as Blake sifted through a stack of brochures about New York. "I like Paul," she said. "Tell me about him. How did he become a paraplegic? Was he born that way?"

"Nope. In college he was our first-string tight end." He glanced up from the brochure. "I, of course, was the quarterback."

"Of course."

"Paul and I used to get into some real messes." Blake chuckled as if the old days were spelled out on the pages of the flyer he was holding.

"So what happened to him?"

Blake's face sobered. "We were driving home for spring break our senior year, and an 18-wheeler ran us off the road." His voice dropped to an almost-inaudible level as the memories flashed through his mind. "The car rolled a couple times. To make a long story short, Paul had a lot of injuries. I walked away, but he never walked again."

Julie straightened. "Oh, Blake. I'm so sorry."

He nodded and met her sympathetic eyes. "I felt guilty for years. I'd been driving, and I kept thinking that if he'd been driving, maybe his reflexes would have been sharper, or maybe I would have been hurt instead of him. But Paul is a Christian, and he trusts God's sovereignty. He really believes that it would have happened the same way no matter who had been driving. He never blamed me for a minute."

"No wonder he's been so good at helping disabled people."

"Yeah. He turned his handicap into an advantage and built his business out of his own frustrations. How many people do you know who could take something like that and make it into something positive?"

"So you wanted to be a part of it?" she observed softly.

"Sure. There are people who need those cars and vans I've designed and Paul wants to sell. It wouldn't be fair if he had to let it all go."

"And that's why you loaned him money."

"Just a little," Blake said defensively. "Just enough to get him going again. I can afford it."

Those four words were becoming all too familiar. Julie stood and felt the plane jerk as it hit an air pocket. She quickly dropped back down and hooked her seat belt. "Blake, I know you mean well when you say that, but even ten million dollars has to run out sooner or later. If you aren't careful, you're going to I-can-afford-it right back to where you started. We're only getting four hundred thousand a year, before taxes."

"Julie, you haven't got any idea how much money that is, do you?"

"Well, it isn't like I've had experience. I know it's more than my father ever saw in his entire lifetime. I know that if it's spent right, it can make life easier, more secure."

"It can make life fun!" he exclaimed. "And I'm going to show you as soon as we reach New York."

"Spending money has never been fun for me," she said.

"That's because you never had any before. You just wait. This'll be a ball."

"If I shop," she argued, "it will be for my business. For cloth and accessories and retailing ideas . . ."

"You need to resolve to spend it only on things you don't need."

Julie breathed out a heavy sigh. "I could never do that." She set her hand on the window as if she could reach through and grab a handful of cloud. "You know, my family was lucky to have food on the table. I always did all my shopping at Goodwill when I was growing up. But I tried to put things together with style, and pretty soon I started to like finding old clothes and setting trends with them. By the time I was in high school, I lost my image of the poor mill worker's daughter and became the dare-to-be-different queen. Just as one of my ideas would catch on, I'd try something else. I realized then that I could set trends, and I didn't need a fortune to do it. I can make women look good without looking cheap. They can be stylish and trendy and still dress modestly. Even when Jack stole my designs, he didn't get the concept. He didn't understand about glorifying God with what you wear. All he knew was that the designs sold well."

"Did they keep selling well for him?"

"Not after he made his own changes to them. They bombed."

"Then God fought that battle for you. He's honoring what you do. Even the sweepstakes money may be God's way of telling you that he wants you to succeed."

"You think so?" she asked. "Because sometimes I wonder if it's not just a test. And if it is, I wonder if I'll pass."

"Test or reward," Blake said, "whatever it is, I intend to have fun with it."

✳ ✳ ✳

The cab driver who took them to Times Square chattered on the phone incessantly in a language they couldn't understand, but when he pulled to the curb and let them out, Blake tipped him a hundred-dollar bill.

Julie gasped. "Blake! You accidentally gave that man a hundred dollars!"

"It wasn't an accident," he said against her ear, keeping his voice discreetly low.

"You can't go around tipping hundred-dollar bills!" she whispered.

"Want to bet?" he asked with a grin. He ushered her into a restaurant with white tablecloths and a maître d' who looked as if he didn't approve of them. Blake gave him a hundred-dollar bill for a table.

"Why did you do that?" she asked. "It's not very crowded here!"

Blake grinned. "I just wanted to. It's fun."

Julie moaned and scanned the menu on the wall as the maître d' checked for a table. "Look at these prices! And this is breakfast?" she whispered. "I can't eat here!"

"Why not?"

"Because I don't want to pay for this!"

"Then I'll pay for it."

"*You'll* be out of money by the time he gives us a bill!" she said.

"Julie, don't be ridiculous. We deserve a little—"

"You want to know what I deserve?" she asked, raising her voice. "I deserve an Egg McMuffin. That's all I need."

"Julie, you're acting like a pauper. You said you were going to loosen up and try to spend a little."

"Blake, I have very specific plans for my money. I don't need you making plans for me, thank you. I agreed to this trip because I needed to relax. How can I do that eating fifty-dollar eggs? You can stay here if you want," she said, "but I'm going to find a more practical place to have breakfast."

Like a teenage boy who had been dragged away from a wild day at the fair, Blake woefully followed her back to the busy sidewalk. "So much for that tip."

"Well, maybe next time you won't be so quick to do that. We could have eaten two really nice meals on that hundred dollars."

They reached a diner just across from the jumbotron at the center of Times Square, and she threw her hands up. "See now? This is more like it."

"This is a mom-and-pop diner. Don't you want to try something more fun?"

"No, I don't. I'd just like to eat a normal-priced breakfast in peace, if you don't mind."

He followed her in and surreptitiously tipped the hostess a hundred dollars before she led them to a table by the window.

"That's much better," Julie said when they had been seated. "Now isn't this nice?"

"I should probably thank you," Blake said with a resigned sigh as he perused his menu. "Without you I'd probably be spending like there was no tomorrow."

"Would you be tipping thousand-dollar bills instead of hundreds? Come on, Blake. You're already spending like crazy, with or without me."

"I'm just having fun. And besides, it gives pleasure to others. What's wrong with that?" he said.

She drew in a deep breath and let it out in a rush. "I'm sorry," she said. "I'm just very tired. All this excitement and not enough sleep."

"Maybe coffee will perk you up."

As the waiter poured her coffee, Julie felt the energy seeping back into her already.

✳ ✳ ✳

Blake couldn't get enough of observing Julie's face as she finished her breakfast and watched the rush-hour activity on the sidewalk. Her eyes were huge as she seemed to take it all in. People flew past with purpose and direction in their strides, but their faces were strained and tense. Still, she took great joy in the famous area she had seen so often on television.

He sat watching her, remembering her sweet smile the night he'd met her in the restaurant. She only got more beautiful the longer he knew her. And that was unusual. Before, it had always seemed that women lost their appeal when the mystique wore off. There was always some fatal flaw in them.

It wasn't that Blake was a perfectionist when it came to women. He wasn't, really. It was just that he liked spontaneity, and it seemed his whole relationship with Julie had been based on just that. So far, she had none of the major flaws that had made him flee other women. There was no pretense with Julie. If anyone could keep his millionaire's feet on the ground from here on out, Julie could.

✳ ✳ ✳

"So what are our plans for the day?" Julie asked after Blake had tipped the waiter a hundred dollars. She had started to protest again but then realized that the waiter probably needed the tip. A hundred-dollar tipper in her restaurant would have made her week.

He grinned. "I was just thinking of a cruise around Manhattan. It's only a few hours, and then we can come back and we can go to the garment district."

"A cruise!" she said. "That sounds wonderful." She waited

at the table as he made a phone call. As he led her out, she felt that thrilling twitter of anticipation. A cruise around Manhattan Island with Blake Adcock was about the most romantic thing she could think of.

That twitter of anticipation, however, turned to a jolt of disbelief an hour later when Blake led her to the dock where the boat awaited them. The staff were lined up as if they were greeting royalty, and Julie was baffled to see that they were the only passengers. "I thought this was a regularly scheduled cruise boat," she said.

"It is," Blake said.

"Then why are we alone?"

"Because I rented the whole thing just for us."

As the boat's engine began to roll, Julie realized she should have known.

CHAPTER NINE

As they cruised around the bay, Julie drank in the sights of Manhattan and the Statue of Liberty and the droves of people lined up to tour the statue. Blake drank in the sight of Julie taking in the sight of Manhattan. Watching her enjoy it was already one of the highlights of his day.

"It's a beautiful day," Julie acknowledged as they returned to the dock. "I'll never forget it."

Blake pulled her head against his shoulder and stroked her hair, watching the way it glided through his fingers. "Beautiful," he agreed.

"Thank you," she whispered.

He dropped a kiss on her temple. "My pleasure. Let's go find a nice place to eat lunch," he said.

She wondered what *nice* meant to him. Another class-conscious maître d', or was he going to buy out an entire restaurant?

"I'm not that hungry," she said. "I think I'd just like to get a salad somewhere."

"Julie, I know you're hungry. You just don't want to spend any money. But loosen up," he urged gently. "This is fun. It's as bad to hoard money as it is to blow it."

"Blake, watching money go down the tube is not fun for me. It upsets me terribly. That 'fun' could support the Spring Street Hospice Center for years."

"The money isn't going down the tubes. Think of it as a contribution to the New York economy."

"New York will live without our contribution."

He tugged her into another restaurant with white table-cloths and a snobbish maître d', tipped him as he had the others, and got them a table. She had that look on her face when they sat down.

"Okay, if it makes you feel better, from now on I'll be as frugal as a monk."

"Sure you will," she said skeptically. His charm seemed to be working, sapping the irritation right out of her. "Are you telling me you've abandoned your wish for a Jacuzzi for Paul and an iPhone for every niece and nephew?"

He chuckled lightly. "Not really," he rumbled.

"And the fancy doorbell for your mother?"

"I was thinking of getting one that plays Handel's *Messiah*."

"The whole thing?"

"Well, no. Maybe just the 'Hallelujah Chorus.'"

"And the yacht?"

"My church doesn't want one," he said. "I'll get them a bus instead."

"Oh, Blake . . ."

"'Oh, Blake . . . ,'" he mimicked. "You know, this whole thing is just unreal. Who in the world would have guessed that I could spend almost a million dollars in just two days?"

"A million dollars!" Julie shrieked. "Are you serious? You only *had* a little less than four hundred thousand!"

"Funny how being rich gets you deeper into debt!"

Julie looked queasy. "Tell me you're kidding," she whispered. "Tell me you haven't really spent every penny you had."

"Don't worry; I still have a fortune. I still owe a fortune. It's not what you have but what you owe. Right?"

Julie's face turned pale.

"I'll be good from now on," he said. "I promise not to throw any more money away. But if I run out of money, I'll always—"

"Have mine to fall back on?" Julie muttered.

"Well, yeah. I was thinking this morning, and I have this great idea about our teaming up. We pool our money and open a building with Sheffield Fashions on one side and Adcock, Inc., on the other. We borrow the whole ten million of mine against our future payments, so we can have it now, and then we aggressively invest yours. We live off earnings from our companies and our stock dividends. So I've spent a little much. . . . But with yours added to mine, it could work. The money would grow along with our businesses, and we'd have even more coming in each year."

She gaped at him, her disappointment clear. "You've given this a lot of thought, haven't you?"

"Well, yeah. I mean, doesn't it sound like a wise idea? We make a good team, Julie."

"I thought you said we wouldn't do business together. That we'd keep this strictly personal."

"Well, we would. I wouldn't interfere with your business, and you wouldn't interfere with mine. We'd just pool the money. What do you think?"

She stared at the lantern on their table as if the light had suddenly illuminated something she didn't want to see. "If you'd wanted my half, Blake, you shouldn't have given me the ticket."

"I don't want your half, Julie. I'm not regretting that. I'm just saying—"

"That you've already blown yours and now you want mine."

He closed his eyes and sighed heavily, then leaned in and took her hand. Locking onto her gaze, he said, "Julie, you've got me all wrong. I'm not after your money. It was a bad idea, okay? Stupid. Don't let this ruin our time together."

"All right," she said. "I'll try."

But he could see that it would require great effort because his idea had already been planted in her mind.

CHAPTER TEN

JULIE COULDN'T SHAKE the feeling that the money was the driving force in her burgeoning relationship with Blake. It changed how she looked at every effort he made for the rest of the day, and it made her spirits lag like a four-day-old helium balloon.

That afternoon Blake wanted to shop, but Julie couldn't stand the thought of watching him throw more of his money away. She suggested that they split up and do their shopping separately, then meet back at the Russian Tea Room at six. Blake seemed surprisingly happy to oblige.

For the first time since she had won her ten million dollars, Julie learned just how much freedom it gave her. She strolled in and out of retail dress and accessory shops from

West Forty-Second Street to West Thirty-Fourth; she felt anticipation and excitement growing inside her at the new career opportunities her money afforded her. She would open a retail shop, she decided at some point during the afternoon, an outlet in which to display and sell her designs, a place to offer women the opportunity to have dresses custom-designed for them. She could hire specialists in silk and cashmere, and junior designers to execute her creations.

It was midafternoon when she began to miss Blake. She wondered what he was buying. She wondered how many hundred-dollar bills he'd doled out today. She had to admit—though never to him—that it *was* fun watching his face as he passed out those bills. The thought made her wish she'd stayed with him today, just to see his brilliant eyes and the looks on the faces of those with whom he shared his wealth. He was right after all, she decided. It was fun to have money. She didn't intend to be without it again.

Strolling down Broadway with a wrapped bolt of silk under one arm and a bolt of hand-printed fabric under the other, she saw a man's watch displayed in the window of a store. It reminded her of something Blake would wear, for it was both down-to-earth and elegant. It was practical enough to work in, but with its white-and-gold contrasts, it was suitable for the swankiest dinner club patronized by the world's most eligible bachelors.

Eligible bachelor, she thought, her heart tumbling on the words. They would go home soon. In a few days, the press would grow tired of them, and they would become caught up in their own endeavors. Blake Adcock would have the coveted reputation of the town's most eligible bachelor, and women would line up for him. Men would line up for her, too, but it would be for no other reason than the money. How would she handle that? How would he?

The thought that she would have to carefully guard against those after her money depressed her. But the thought that Blake would, too, depressed her even more. What if they both wound up in relationships with barracudas and gold diggers? What if they lived lives of misery because of the people this money would attract?

She went into the store and checked the price, gasped at the cost, then decided that she wouldn't spend it on him. She thought of putting the money into the bank instead, drawing interest on that amount, and watching it grow.

But then she wouldn't see Blake's surprise and joy that she had spent some of her money on him.

She considered the watch again and thought that buying it would mean playing into his hands. Hadn't he already devised ways of getting her money for himself? Wasn't he really one of those gold diggers circling her as his prey?

Of course not, she told herself. Not Blake. Not the man who had no bitterness when his business failed. Not the man who put his best friend's feelings over his own disappointment. Not the man who had shared Christ with her in their first meeting.

But was he still the man she'd met in the restaurant that night? Was she the same woman?

Ashamed that spending money on Blake was such a battle, she decided to step off the cliff and buy the watch. When it was wrapped and ready, she hurried to the Russian Tea Room, anxious to see Blake's face when he opened it.

❋   ❋   ❋

Julie felt her heart leap with joy when she saw Blake waiting for her with several big bags under his arm.

"Hi," she said, biting her lip as if she held every secret in the world just under the surface of her smile.

"Hi," he said as if he too had a secret. He got the maître d's attention, and the man led them to their table. They took their seats, the corner of the table between them.

"Did you clean out the city?" she asked as they leaned close together.

"Just about. You?"

"I bought some cloth," she said, still grinning. She set down her bolts on one of the empty chairs but held the watch behind her back.

"Cloth?" he asked, his eyebrows arching in frustration. "Julie, didn't you buy anything for yourself?"

"The cloth is for me," she said on a thread of laughter.

"I mean, something irrational. Ridiculous. Even just that new pair of shoes you told the press you would buy."

"I decided I could live with what I had," she teased.

"Julie . . ." The look on his face was despairing, as if he

had tried and failed to show her good sense. "You're a millionaire. You need to act like one."

"Okay, okay," she said, giggling. "If it'll make you feel better, I did buy something kind of ridiculous. In fact, it is so ridiculous, I'm embarrassed to show you."

Blake's expression relaxed. "Good," he said. "I was beginning to wonder about you. What did you get? Don't tell me—let me guess. That crystal pineapple in the window of Tiffany's."

"No," she said, still holding the box behind her back.

"What, then? Show me."

That familiar heat crept up Julie's cheeks as she held out the small wrapped box. "You open it," she said. "It's for you."

"For me?" The curious, amused look in his eyes faded to poignant surprise. "You bought something for me and nothing for yourself?"

"I told you," she said softly, "I bought the cloth."

Stricken, he held her gaze for a moment as if her gesture meant worlds to him. "Thank you," he whispered.

The gratitude in his voice made her laugh, more from nerves than amusement. "Blake, you haven't even opened it!"

"It doesn't matter," he said. "It's the fact that you thought of me that counts. It means a lot to me."

"Oh, boy." Julie covered her face. "Am I glad I didn't buy you that roll of toilet paper made of fake hundred-dollar bills. I almost did, you know."

"It wouldn't matter if it was a gag gift," he said. "It's just so important that you—"

"Blake, just open it, for heaven's sake! I'm breaking out in a cold sweat!"

"Okay," he said. "I'll open it."

His hands trembled as he tore into the wrapping. If he was really that moved that she had bought him something, she thought, she'd have to make a habit of it.

He looked up at her as he pulled the top off the box. And when his misty blue eyes fell to the watch, he tipped his head and lifted his brows as if he'd never been so moved in his life. Then he pulled it from the box the way one would handle the crown jewels.

"I'll never take it off," he said softly.

"Well, you'd better. It isn't waterproof."

He swallowed and held his hand out to her. "Come here."

Obediently, Julie leaned into him, and he slid his arms around her. He buried his face in her hair and held her desperately tight. "I missed you today. So much."

"Me too," she whispered. Then, pulling back, she tried to lighten the intensity of the moment. "Well, aren't you going to show me your toys?"

He let her go, and his hands went into his pockets. "Sure," he said. "Only, I didn't exactly shop for myself, either."

"What?" She looked at the boxes he'd dropped into the chair next to him. "Nothing for yourself?"

He shook his head slowly.

"Not even cloth?"

A grin tore at his lips.

"Not even a pool table or a pinball machine?"

Breathing a heavy sigh as if the moment of truth were approaching, he reached for one of the small boxes and handed it to her. "Open it," he said softly.

She knew her eyes were shining as she took the box. Biting her lip, she tore open the paper.

It was a diamond bracelet, shimmering white, and probably worth more than she'd made last year. She jerked her hands back. She saw people at other tables looking, and she wanted to hide under the table. "Oh, Blake! I can't accept this. It cost a fortune!"

"You're worth a fortune," he said, smiling as he pulled the bracelet from the box and draped it on her wrist. "And I insist."

"But I'm not the diamond type. Blake, please. I can't wear a bracelet that cost more than a year's mortgage!"

"Yes, you can," he insisted. "I want you to. You wouldn't deprive me of the pleasure of seeing you in this, would you?" He clasped it, then held her hand to admire it.

"Oh, Blake," she murmured. "You shouldn't have."

"But I did," he said. His kiss pushed through all her barriers and all her reservations, but somehow the fear was still there.

The feeling that he would not—could not—be hers, the feeling that tomorrow would come and she would find herself alone and aching and humiliated just as she had a year ago with Jack, kept rushing her heart. Instead of seeing the gift as his offering to her, she saw it as her own money draining right before her eyes. He'd probably already borrowed on his. Spent next year's and the next year's . . . now he would want hers.

But she wondered if it was a trade-off—her money for his love. Maybe it was worth it.

He tipped her face up to his and gazed into her eyes. "I think I fell in love with you while you were eating my soup that first night," he whispered. "I had prayed for help that night, and God led me right to that restaurant. I had never been there before. And there you were, Julie. It was the worst time in the world to fall in love, but I had no control over it."

A lone tear rolled from Julie's eye, and she reached up to frame Blake's face with shaking hands. He kissed her again and she felt she'd been released, but she wasn't sure to where. Was it a paradise? Or another heartbreak? It seemed impossible that she—a woman who had been hurt more than her share, a woman who couldn't imagine anyone loving her without motive—could really love a man like Blake without getting her heart broken.

Blake didn't demand a reply from her. Instead, he wiped the tear under her eye. "I didn't get the chance to give you your most important gift," he said, his voice growing hoarse.

"Blake, the bracelet is too much already. You shouldn't have—"

"Just open it," he said quietly, handing her another small velvet box.

Holding her breath, Julie gazed at him for a moment, then looked down at the box. Carefully she opened the top. The three-karat diamond ring startled her, and she caught her breath.

"I love you, Julie," he whispered, tipping her face back up

to his. "And I think we make a good team. Forget my idea for joining forces in business. What I really want is for you to be my wife."

In the seconds it took for Julie's heart to begin beating again, a million thoughts raged through her mind. He had suggested marriage the night they'd won the money and told her more than once that if he ran out, they would always have hers to fall back on. Was that what all this was about? Was it all a ploy so he could correct the mistake he'd made by forcing her to keep her half of the ticket? Had he so enjoyed having money that he couldn't stop thinking what twice as much would do for him?

Could greed really drive someone into feigning love and asking for a lifetime commitment? How would she ever know if it was real?

Tears sprang to her eyes. "I . . . I can't take this," she said. "I'm sorry." She thrust the ring into his hands, trying to keep her tears at bay.

"Julie, why?"

"Because."

"But I love you," he said. "Maybe it's too soon. Maybe I jumped the gun. But I missed you this afternoon, and I realized that I don't want to go home and resume our separate lives. I want you with me—"

"Don't! Don't push it," Julie bit out. "Please."

She could hear the surprise in his voice. "Why? You owe me an explanation, Julie," Blake said. "Tell me why!"

Her face burned, and suddenly it all seemed clear to her.

All the tenderness and romance, all the attention . . . "Why do I owe you, Blake? Because of the ticket? Because of the money?"

"What?" Blake asked. He seemed completely baffled. "What has the ticket got to do with—?"

"I have to go," Julie choked, cutting him off. "I'm sorry, Blake. I'm not going to marry you. You gave me the ticket and made me keep the money, even though I would have been fine to just give it to you. But now I'm in this too deep, and I have plans and hopes and dreams. And it's not fair for you to spend all of your money and come after mine. I can see through all this, Blake. The bracelet and the ring, the trip and everything . . . they're all investments. You're hoping for a huge return, and you can get it by marrying me."

Blake's face drained of color as he sat frozen before her. "That's what you think?" he whispered as if she'd knocked the wind out of him. "You think I wanted to marry you because my money is running out? Is that the kind of man you really think I am? Greedy and selfish and conniving?"

"Money changes people!" she shouted. "Maybe you were that way all along—I don't know. But you're not the man I hoped you'd be."

"You got part of that right, anyway," he said sadly. "Money does change people. It changed you. You couldn't have cared less about money the night we won. Now you're hoarding it, scared to death somebody's going to take some from you. Well, I don't want your money, Julie! And forget the proposal, because you're not the woman I hoped you would be."

Swiping at her raging tears, Julie unclasped the bracelet and thrust it at him, grabbed her bolts of fabric, and ran out of the restaurant.

※　※　※

Blake threw down enough money to cover the bill, grabbed his things, and raced out behind her. He caught her standing on the street trying to hail a cab.

"Where are you going?"

"Home," she said. "I'll take the next commercial flight out." When a cab passed her, she put both bolts under one arm, then roughly dug into her purse with her other hand. "Here. My half of dinner tonight." She threw some bills at him. "I guess I owe you that much."

"You don't owe me anything," he muttered, trying to give the money back.

She tried to stop another cab, but it sped past. She couldn't stop her tears. "I didn't want it to end like this."

His eyes flashed to hers. "Then what did you want, Julie?"

She stopped and stared down at the sidewalk, trying desperately to hold herself together until she was away from him.

"Answer me, Julie," he said more firmly. "What is it you want?"

"Nothing!" The word seemed to rob her of every ounce of strength she possessed.

"Exactly!" he returned with equal desperation. "You

don't want anything because you feel so unworthy. You can't let yourself love me because you can't believe that I could actually love you for yourself. There has to be some reason, doesn't there? Some motive?"

"Yes!" she cried. "Yes, there has to be a reason. There always is. You want what I have."

"But I have what you have, Julie! I don't need your money!"

"You'll owe everything you won in six months, Blake!" She touched her forehead with her fingertips. "It's not that I don't want to share. I just don't want to be wanted for the money."

"Is it so hard to believe that I love you because of you?"

"Yes!" she shouted. "Yes, it is. We hardly know each other. We met four days ago! The money complicates everything!" A cab stopped, and the driver got out and loaded her bolts of fabric into the trunk. She wiped her eyes and turned back to Blake. "I have a plane to catch. I have to go."

"Then go! Run away and see where it gets you!"

And she did. Julie got into the cab. When she arrived at the airport, she ran to the ticket counter. Fortunately she was able to purchase a ticket for a plane leaving within the hour. She made her way through security, then ran to her terminal. They were already boarding, so she went down the jet bridge and into the coach class of the commercial jet. When she was seated, waiting for it to take her back to Detroit, she realized she was still running.

When she finally made it home, Julie crawled into her bed

and lay in a ball for ten minutes, allowing herself only that amount of time to cry out her heart. Misery was inevitable for her, she thought, for she always fell for the wrong men. Great sobs racked her body, and she wished with all her heart that Blake had been different. She could have convinced herself of that if she'd tried, she thought. But she would always know, in the deepest corridors of her soul, that he did not love her for herself any more than Jack had.

There was only one thing to do. She would launch headfirst into her business, hire a staff, finish her designs. Maybe that full-speed-ahead work would make her forget Blake Adcock. And maybe it would soothe the wish gnawing in her heart that he would come storming through that door at any moment and shake her fears and accusations right out of her.

Weeks passed as Julie worked ceaselessly, drawing out the new ideas she had had since returning from New York. Her new formal creations were sadder, with flowing, romantic lines and softer fabrics. They each reminded her of her days with Blake—of the wind rustling through his hair on the cruise around Manhattan, the sunlight bathing their faces, the laughter in his eyes—but she didn't want to be reminded, so she worked harder.

She found a building in which to sell her line, with studios upstairs where several junior designers worked executing her designs, and several expert seamstresses put them together.

Already she was taking orders from people who had seen her on television in her own design, and so her custom business was getting under way. She capitalized on the dramatic, everyday styles that her customers seemed most interested in. Her fashion show was back in the planning stages, and her waitress friends had been assured that they could still model her clothes.

To anyone looking in from the outside, it would have seemed that Julie Sheffield was on top of the world. No one would have guessed that every night Julie cried herself to sleep because no amount of work could smother the regret still smoldering in her heart.

It was raining one night when she got home. As she rummaged in her drawer for a sweater to change into, she ran across the box of chocolates Blake had given her that first night, the chocolates that had once held the sweepstakes ticket. She remembered how moved she had been when he'd given her the candy. She had almost cried.

It had been raining that night, too.

She looked out the window that Blake had climbed through. The steady drizzle left her tiny house feeling even smaller and lonelier. She gazed out through the rivulets of water tracing designs on the panes, recalling the night he had brought her a picnic. Peanut butter and jelly sandwiches and candlelight in a pillowcase.

He had talked her into running off with him in the night.

What was it her mother used to say when Julie was in high school? *"There's no point in starting something you can't finish. You can't learn from it or lay it to rest until you've seen it through."*

Her mother had been referring to the dozens of dresses Julie had started with bits and pieces of secondhand dresses, then abandoned from frustration and fear of failure. Now, in the loneliest days of her life, she wondered if her mother might have used the same advice about love. Julie had left things hanging with Blake, had run away as fast as her plane would carry her, and she couldn't put him behind her until their relationship was laid to rest once and for all.

New tears rolled down her face, and she leaned her forehead against the windowpane, remembering his words that had seemed so true. *"I had prayed for help that night, and God led me right to that restaurant. I had never been there before. And there you were, Julie. It was the worst time in the world to fall in love, but I had no control over it."*

Was it all a lie, or had she ruined the truth in it?

She got her phone and pressed a fist to her mouth. If only he had called her when he'd gotten back to Detroit, maybe he could have convinced her that she was wrong about him. More than anything else in her life, she wanted to be wrong.

But he hadn't called. And he hadn't come over.

Had any of it actually been real?

A persistent, gnawing need to know took hold of her. If it was real, she had to hear him say it. And if it wasn't, well, perhaps she could go on with her life without thinking of him three hundred times a day.

Controlled by an irrational need to hear his voice, she

bit her lip as tears rolled faster down her cheeks. With a trembling hand she picked up the phone and dialed Blake's number. He answered on the second ring.

"Hello?" It was quiet behind him, and his voice seemed much too close to her ear. Much too familiar. Much too sweet against the bitter silence she'd suffered since she'd seen him last.

"Blake?" she choked out. "It's Julie."

He caught his breath, then said softly, "Julie." His tone teetered between relief and apprehension.

Julie grabbed a tissue out of the box on her bed table and wadded it over her eyes. "I . . . I just wanted to ask you one thing, Blake," she said.

"What?" he whispered.

She swallowed, steadied her voice, and went on. "What we had in New York. That morning on the boat . . . and in the restaurant, when you said you loved me. Was it real? I have to know the truth."

She held her breath and waited an eternity before Blake's broken voice reached across the line. "It was real, Julie. It was real."

Closing her eyes, she ended the call and lay back on the bed, staring at the ceiling. *Why? Why didn't he say it was an illusion?* she asked herself miserably. *Why couldn't he just have taken that opportunity to lay it to rest once and for all?*

The phone rang almost immediately, but Julie only looked at the caller ID. It was Blake, of course. But she was too confused to talk to him, and she needed time to think.

So she lay staring at the ceiling as the phone rang incessantly, her painful tears soaking into her pillow.

*　*　*

"Answer, Julie," Blake whispered. "I know you're there." He held the phone to his ear as he paced across the bedroom. Finally it had come, the call he'd been praying for, the sign that said she still cared. He had been too hurt and too proud and too stubborn to make a move before, after the things she had accused him of, but her whispered question had changed everything. Now it was time to get her back.

But the phone continued to ring. An anxious, broken mist welled in his eyes. "Answer!" he cried aloud. Was she just lying there beside it, listening and refusing to pick it up? Was she that determined to lay their feelings to rest?

He counted out three more rings and told himself that he would get dressed, hightail it to her house, and break in again if he had to, if she didn't answer in the next thirty seconds. . . .

Suddenly the ringing stopped, and he heard her presence on the other end, though she didn't speak.

"Julie," he said, bending over suddenly as if she would hang up if he stood erect. "Julie, don't hang up. Please."

She didn't hang up, but she said nothing, and he found himself groping for the right words. It was several moments before he came up with anything. Rubbing his moist eyes, he sat on the edge of his bed and closed them. "Julie, I wish

I'd never seen that sweepstakes ticket. I wish I could just turn back time to the night in the restaurant when you ate my soup and brightened my night. The best thing about winning that money was that I got to know you in the bargain. And now that's the only important thing."

The sound of her muffled sob broke his heart, and he tried to steady his voice. "Julie, you've got to trust me. You've got to trust yourself."

"But I can't do that," she rasped, "because my judgment always stinks."

Blake opened his mouth to speak, but before the argument could leave his tight throat, Julie had hung up again.

Defeated, he threw down the phone and slumped over it, shoving a splayed hand through his wet hair. There must be something he could do, he thought miserably. There must be some way to prove his love for her.

Tell me what to do, Lord. Show me how to fix this.

But nothing came to mind. He paced his house—back and forth, back and forth—running scenarios through his mind, alternately begging God for help, then concocting schemes of his own. But he couldn't see any good outcome from any of them.

✳   ✳   ✳

I need closure, Julie thought as she held the box of chocolates in her lap and navigated her way to his house. She needed to undo the tender memories that seemed to hold her captive.

She reached his house in the secondhand car she had recently bought and pulled quietly up to the curb. She got out in the rain, clutching the box to her heart, and opened the gate on his fence. Then she stole up to his front porch and laid the box of chocolates down in front of the door.

She straightened up and looked at the door, knowing he was in there, just on the other side. All she had to do was knock, and this misery could end. But she would never know if it was her or the money. She would always wonder.

She turned and hurried down the steps and back across his wet lawn. As she got into her car to drive away, she wished she'd never won the sweepstakes. How different might things be if they'd had a losing number? Would he have sold that coffee table, come to pay off his IOU, and started a relationship without the complications of millions of dollars?

With all her heart, she suddenly began to hate the millions of dollars she had won. None of it was worth the loss of a relationship that could have been so good. The money had become a master over her, even though she would have vowed she was above that.

"No one can serve two masters."

She began to weep as she drove home, realizing that in hoarding her money and protecting it from Blake, she had forgotten about her relationship with God. The money had even ruined that.

"Forgive me, Lord," she said aloud. "Please forgive me, and show me what I need to do."

✳   ✳   ✳

After an hour or so of pacing and thinking, Blake knew there was only one thing to do. He had to go to Julie's house, see her face-to-face again, declare his love for her, and not leave until she believed him.

He grabbed his keys and rushed to the front door, threw it open . . . and almost stepped on the box of chocolates. Frowning, he stooped down and picked it up. He looked around for some sign of Julie, but she was gone.

Was this really the end? Was it her way of saying that she wished she'd never met him?

Suddenly sapped of his energy, he went back in and sat at his table. He opened the box, remembering the sweepstakes card that had been inside it. The card that had changed his life.

Things had been so simple just before that. He had given her the box, and she had gotten tears in her eyes. He had realized that God was in this. He hadn't gone there by chance, hadn't stumbled on this special woman by accident.

And if God had led him to her, wouldn't God help him find a way to get past the money and win her back?

An idea came to mind, perking him up instantly. He tore through his drawer for a business card he'd kept, then dialed the number of the public relations director at ABC in New York. He asked for her extension, then waited for her to answer.

"Jeanine Stegall."

"Mrs. Stegall," he said in a rush, "this is Blake Adcock. The one who won ten million dollars a few weeks ago?"

"Yes, Mr. Adcock. How are you?"

"Well, not so good," he said, heart pounding as if the end of his dark tunnel was in sight . . . but still just out of reach. "But I think you can help me. You see, I'd like to give the money back. At least, the part I haven't already been paid. Is there some way I can just cancel the rest of those payments and throw my money back into the jackpot for next year's Valentine's drawing?"

Mrs. Stegall was apparently stunned. "Mr. Adcock, have you been drinking?"

"No. I'm stone-cold sober. Scout's honor."

Mrs. Stegall cleared her throat. "Well, this is highly irregular."

"But can it be done?"

"Absolutely not. We gave you that money. The amount of paperwork was astronomical. The IRS is involved, and several banks and governmental agencies. We can't undo it!"

"But I don't want it!" He messed up his hair, trying to find the words to explain it to her. "See, it's kind of a God thing. I mean, I don't think I'm the guy God meant to have all this. Maybe he just gave it to me to hold for a while, maybe to teach me something. I've learned, okay? I can't deal with this money."

"Then I suggest you give it to a charity of some sort, Mr. Adcock."

"I'd do that, Mrs. Stegall, except how do you know which

ones are legitimate? I mean, maybe God actually had me holding it for somebody else, you know? Like, somebody who really needs it, somebody who can do something with it that would help Christ's Kingdom and meet people at the point of their need. . . ." Even as he spoke, it became clearer to him.

"I wouldn't know about that, Mr. Adcock."

"Well, I just mean that there's got to be a person or group or foundation or something that could do a lot more with this money than I could. If I could figure out who that is . . ."

"That's your responsibility, Mr. Adcock. I just dispense the winnings. I can't tell you how to spend them."

He groaned with frustration. "Well, thank you very much for your help! You're all friendly and gushing when you're giving me money, but the minute I try to give it back, it's all business!"

"Mr. Adcock, do you hear yourself? This really isn't making a lot of sense."

"Oh, just forget it." He clicked the phone off and threw it across the room. It hit the back of the couch, then bounced to the floor. He stood there a moment staring at it, then snatched it back up. It still worked, so he hit Paul on speed-dial.

"Hello?"

"Paul?" Blake's voice cracked as turmoil wobbled in his voice. "I need somebody to talk to, buddy. Can you spare a couple of hours?"

"Sure, Blake," his friend said. "I'll be right over."

JULIE NEVER WENT to sleep that night, so when she rose the next morning, she looked in the mirror and moaned at what stared back at her. She looked like a phantom, was nauseated from crying, and her head ached as if she'd been banging it into a wall. For a while, she blamed Blake. But it wasn't his fault, she realized finally. It was the money.

The stupid money that she'd never even wanted in the first place. The money that had brought the two of them together and had ultimately torn them apart.

Two masters.

"I don't want to serve money," she told the Lord. "I want to serve you. I trust your will so much more than my own.

If I didn't have to keep wondering if the money was the motive . . ."

If she could just get rid of this money, things would be clearer. It wasn't making her happy. Maybe it could make someone else happy, instead.

The Spring Street Hospice Center.

Not so long ago, she'd told Blake that she was going to donate a big chunk of money to them. They needed it. Their work was crucial. They could share the Good News of Christ and give peace and even joy to terminal patients. If she gave them the money, they'd never have to raise funds again, never have to wonder if they'd still exist from month to month.

Joy like Julie hadn't felt in weeks sprang up inside her, and she knew this was God's idea, not hers. Hope grew within her as the day rolled on, and she called her lawyer to draw up the necessary documents to have her money donated to the hospice. All she kept for herself was the seed money she needed to keep her business going.

And as the finality of what she was doing became clear to her, she felt as if the weight of ten million dollars had just been lifted from her shoulders.

✳ ✳ ✳

Paul did everything in his power to talk Blake out of what he was about to do. "Aw, don't do it, buddy," he pleaded as they found the building with the sign that said *Spring Street Hospice Center*.

"Give me one good reason why I shouldn't," Blake said with more verve in his voice than he'd had in weeks.

"Give me one good reason why you should," Paul returned.

"Because," Blake said, "you wouldn't take it all."

"I let you give me only what I needed, but I think this is crazy. Give me another reason."

"Okay. Because they need it. They led Julie's mom to Christ before she died. Think of all the people they could help. They meet people's physical needs so people will trust them with their spiritual ones. Isn't that what we've always said we'd be about in our own work?"

"Blake, for heaven's sake, there are other ways to help them."

"For heaven's sake is precisely why I'm doing this."

They parked the car, then sat and let it idle for a moment.

"You're doing this for Julie," Paul accused. "But what if you make this grand, sacrificial gesture and you still don't get her back?"

Blake set his teeth and swallowed at the blunt question. He'd given that a lot of thought. "Paul, I'm doing this because the money has made me lose the only things that matter to me. Julie was right. I don't know how to handle it, any more than I knew how to handle her. It caused me too much pain."

Paul set his elbow on the window and rubbed his face with his hand. "But, Blake, if you give it away, you won't ever be able to get it back."

"I don't ever want it back," Blake said. "All this money

has taken away my pioneer spirit. That grit that made me shuck my job and try designing those cars. When I had the money, all I wanted to do was sit back and let somebody else do the thinking for me. And that's not the way I want my life to be. Struggling is part of the challenge. It's also part of the reward."

Paul moaned and looked fully at his best friend. "Are you sure, man?"

"I'm sure," Blake said. "Are you with me or not? You can wait in the car, you know."

Paul opened the door and wrestled his chair out of the backseat. "How often does a guy get to watch his best friend give away a fortune?"

Blake only laughed as he got out of the car to set his life back on the right track.

❋ ❋ ❋

Julie wore her biggest smile since she'd won the sweepstakes as she signed the last of the documents that turned over her winnings to the Spring Street Hospice Center. It had taken a full day to take care of the tedious business. She drove back to her house, and as she pulled into the driveway, she saw a familiar car waiting. She looked up to her porch, and there was Blake sitting on her steps.

Her heart began to hammer. What would he think when he learned what she had done? Would she regret doing it if he reacted badly?

She got out of her car and slowly walked toward him. When he got to his feet, she saw that he held the box of chocolates in his hands.

They faltered for a moment, absorbing the sight of each other with remorseful eyes.

"Blake, what are you doing here?"

"I have to talk to you," he said carefully. "Can we go inside?"

She nodded and unlocked her door, and he followed her in.

Just get it over with, Julie thought. Either he wanted her, or he didn't. "I need to talk to you too," she said.

Blake's defense barriers sprang up at her cool voice, and that vulnerability in his eyes seemed to vanish. Instead, he looked guarded. She sat down and gestured for him to follow, but he remained standing. One hand slid into his pocket, and the other clutched the heart-shaped box.

"You first," he said.

Julie gulped back her tension. "You were right," she said, her raspy words tumbling out too quickly. "About my changing because of the money. So I figured there was only one thing to do."

He waited, his body tense as a bowstring, as she struggled for the words.

"I can't help wondering if you want me for my money. So I got rid of it. I'm a little better off than broke right now, but I have no hope of getting my ten million back. It's gone. Take me or leave me." Tears filled her eyes as she mumbled the words, for the astonished look on Blake's face told her that he would leave her.

But instead of watching him walk away, she watched the guarded expression fall from his eyes as a smile slowly stole across his face. Before Julie knew what was happening, he had covered his face with both hands and was laughing hysterically.

"What's so funny?" she bit out.

Blake stopped laughing and reached for her hand. He pulled her up and stepped close to her, still laughing. "I'm sorry . . . I didn't mean . . . It's just that . . . so funny."

Julie jerked her arm free. "It is not funny!"

"Yes, it is. Don't you see?"

Julie planted her fists on her hips. "No, I don't see! Why don't you tell me?"

"You gave up the money so you could have a fighting chance with me!"

Fury pumped through her veins. "I did not. I gave it up because I couldn't serve two masters. Because the Lord showed me that I had changed. That the money was making me miserable. Other people needed it more than I did. . . ."

"That's priceless!" Blake shouted, doubling over again. He banged his fist on the table as he shouted with laughter. "I can't stand it!"

Julie took a deep breath and wondered if she should call someone, if the pressure of the money had finally made him snap.

He wiped his moist eyes and tried to speak. "See . . . mine's gone too."

"Of course it is, Blake. That's why I thought you wanted *my* money."

"No!" His gales of laughter almost blew her over. "You don't understand. I didn't spend it all. I invested some in Paul's business and some in mine." He sniffed and leaned back against the table as if the laughter had taken too much from him. "And the rest . . ."

A deep frown wrinkled her forehead. "You spent the rest, didn't you? Even what they haven't paid out yet."

"It's not where you think." He took both of her hands in his and brought one to his lips. He kissed it, then touched her face, so gently that it brought tears to her eyes.

She gulped back her emotion. "Then we're both broke."

"Right," he said and started laughing again. "And if you thought I'd turn and run because I couldn't get yours, you're wrong. I've never been so happy to hear anything in my life. Now I can prove to you that I wasn't after your fortune. Now I have a chance . . . "

Her face changed. "Then you still want me? You still . . ."

"I still love you," he whispered, the mirth still dancing in his eyes. "But you may not want me."

"Of course I want you! I've always wanted you. I've been miserable thinking about all the trouble you were getting into with all that money."

Blake began to laugh again. "Well, you were right. See, I gave mine away too. Even what I haven't gotten yet."

"What?" She pictured him handing thousand-dollar bills to everyone he saw, until there were no more left. "Blake! Who on earth did you give it to?"

"The Spring Street Hospice Center," he said. "Your story about your mother coming to Christ there kept harping on my mind. I thought it was the best use of my money."

Julie stepped back, awestruck. "The hospice center? You gave it to the hospice center?"

"Have you seen their building lately?" he asked. "They desperately need a bigger place, and they need all kinds of equipment. They need more staff members, more beds—"

Julie flung her arms around Blake's neck, and he stopped midsentence and lifted her from the floor, holding her as if he couldn't bear to let her go again. "Oh, Blake," she whispered against his ear. "You *are* the man I hoped you would be. I love you. I think I loved you from the beginning, that first night when you talked about Christ with me, and I knew that you were the kind of man I'd prayed for, but the money muddied the water and I was so afraid . . ."

He breathed out a long sigh of relief, and she felt a tear run between their faces. She wasn't sure if it was his or hers.

He set her carefully down, then wiped her face and gazed at her with wet eyes of his own. Then he handed her the heart-shaped box, the one that had started all this trouble. "I wanted you to have this," he said. "Open it."

She pulled the top off, as she had done just weeks ago, and saw all the uneaten pieces of chocolate in their little brown cups. But pressed down into the center one was something that hadn't been there before. It was the sweepstakes ticket that he had left her that first night, the one the television station had laminated and allowed them to keep as a souvenir, with the fifteen-dollar IOU and the note that had made her so angry.

"I was going to tell you that I was dead broke, that I wouldn't have given all my money away if I was so greedy that I'd connive to get yours. I was hoping you'd see that I didn't care about the money and let us just start over, from that first night. Give me one more chance."

"I'm the one who needs another chance."

He took fifteen dollars out of his wallet and handed it to her. She took it. "We've already been to New York," he whispered, "so now that I've paid my IOU, we can start fresh. How about just a dinner date here in town? Or . . . a lot of dinner dates . . . that might lead to . . . something even more important?"

She smiled. "Starting slow is good. I like that. And yes, I'd love to have dinner with you."

"No doubts? No fears?"

"Just about your using your credit card to pay for it." He laughed, and a smile glowed in her green eyes. "It won't matter that we aren't rich anymore, Blake. Because we *are* rich, whether we have money or not. Being broke might be our greatest asset."

He crushed her against him, then began to laugh in a deep rumble against her ear. "Well, you know when I said I was broke? I didn't mean *totally* broke."

She stepped back and looked at him. "What do you mean?"

He shrugged with that boyish charm that had never failed to enchant her. "I still have a little something."

"Like what?"

"Like . . . when I said I invested some in my own business . . . I made sure I'd have a tiny bit to pay back some debts and get my business off the ground . . . and a tiny bit to live on while I struggle."

"Blake!" she said, grinning. "How much, exactly?"

"Just a million," he said. "Split over twenty years. That's not so much. I've prayed a lot about what a healthy balance is. I think it's having enough to live on, enough to spend a little on people I love, enough to give away some. And I wanted a little nest egg just to get a family started . . . if and when it leads to that, and I mean absolutely no pressure by saying that. . . ."

She smiled at the thought.

"You think we'll ever regret it?" she asked as they walked out to his car. "Giving up all that money?"

"No," he said. "Because that ticket won us a lot more than money, and we won't ever have to give that away." He leaned down to kiss her, and as he did, her heart sent a prayer of gratitude to heaven.

"Besides," he said against her lips, "there's always next year's sweepstakes."

DOUBLE CHOCOLATE CINNAMON COOKIES

Preheat oven to 350 degrees. Line a cookie sheet with parchment paper.

Ingredients:

- ½ cup coconut oil (in solid form)
- ½ cup packed brown sugar
- ¼ cup white sugar
- 1 tsp vanilla extract
- 1 egg (or egg substitute)
- ½ cup whole wheat pastry flour
- ¾ cup unbleached all-purpose flour
- ⅓ cup unsweetened cocoa powder
- 1 tsp ground cinnamon
- ½ tsp baking soda
- ¼ tsp salt
- ½ cup dark chocolate chips

In a large bowl, mix oil, vanilla, and sugars until creamy. Add egg, blend until smooth.

In a medium bowl sift together the two flours, cocoa powder, cinnamon, baking soda, and salt. Add flour mixture to coconut oil mixture, stir until just combined. Stir in the chocolate chips.

Use cookie scoop or form rounded tablespoons of dough and drop onto prepared baking sheet.

Bake at 350 degrees for approximately ten minutes, until edges are set and the middles are still somewhat soft. Transfer to a wire rack for cooling.

Yields approximately eighteen cookies.

ABOUT THE AUTHOR

TERRI BLACKSTOCK is a *New York Times* bestseller, with over seven million books sold worldwide. She is the winner of three Carol Awards, a Christian Retailers Choice Award, and a Romantic Times Book Reviews Career Achievement Award, among others. She has had over twenty-five years of success as a novelist. Terri spent the first twelve years of her life traveling in an Air Force family. She lived in nine states and attended the first four years of school in the Netherlands. Because she was a perpetual "new kid," her imagination became her closest friend. That, she believes, was the biggest factor in her becoming a novelist. She sold her first novel at the age of twenty-five and has had a successful career ever since.

Recent books include her acclaimed Intervention series (*Intervention, Vicious Cycle,* and *Downfall*), stand-alones *Shadow in Serenity, Predator,* and *Double Minds,* and series, including the Moonlighters series, the Restoration series, Newpointe 911, Cape Refuge, and the SunCoast Chronicles.

In 1994 Terri was writing romance novels under two pseudonyms for publishers such as HarperCollins, Harlequin, Dell, and Silhouette, when a spiritual awakening prompted her to switch gears. At the time, she was reading more suspense than romance, and felt drawn to write thrillers about ordinary people in grave danger. Her newly awakened faith wove its way into the tapestry of her suspense novels, offering hope instead of despair. Her goal is to entertain with page-turning plots, while challenging her readers to think and grow. She hopes to remind them that they're not alone, and that their trials have a purpose.

Terri has appeared on national television programs such as *The 700 Club* and *Home Life*, and has been a guest on numerous radio programs across the country. The story of her personal journey appears in books such as *Touched By the Savior* by Mike Yorkey, *True Stories of Answered Prayer* by Mike Nappa, *Faces of Faith* by John Hanna, and *I Saw Him in Your Eyes* by Ace Collins.

ALSO BY TERRI BLACKSTOCK

Moonlighters series

Truth-Stained Lies
Distortion
Twisted Innocence

Intervention series

Intervention
Vicious Cycle
Downfall

Restoration series

Last Light
Night Light
True Light
Dawn's Light

Cape Refuge series

Cape Refuge
Southern Storm
River's Edge
Breaker's Reef

Newpointe 911 series

Private Justice
Shadow of Doubt
Word of Honor
Trial by Fire
Line of Duty

Sun Coast Chronicles series

Evidence of Mercy
Justifiable Means
Ulterior Motives
Presumption of Guilt
The Sun Coast Chronicles (an anthology)

Seasons series with Beverly LaHaye

Seasons Under Heaven
Showers in Season
Times and Seasons
Season of Blessing

Second Chances series

Never Again Good-Bye
When Dreams Cross
Blind Trust
Broken Wings

Stand-Alone Novels

Shadow in Serenity
Predator
Double Minds
Emerald Windows
Seaside
Covenant Child
Miracles (*The Listener* and *The Gifted*)
The Listener (formerly *The Heart Reader*)
The Gifted
The Heart Reader of Franklin High
The Gifted Sophomores

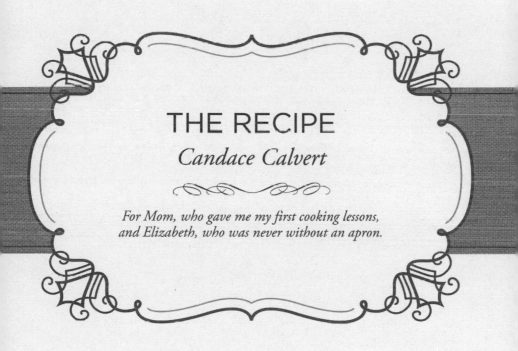

THE RECIPE

Candace Calvert

*For Mom, who gave me my first cooking lessons,
and Elizabeth, who was never without an apron.*

CHAPTER ONE

LUCAS MARCHAL FULLY EXPECTED his grandmother to show no interest in her hospital dinner tray; her appetite had dwindled to almost nothing. But in his wildest dreams he wouldn't have imagined that her dour, no-nonsense nurse's aide would lift the dish cover, scream, then stumble backward and fall to the floor.

He bolted toward her to help, vaguely aware of other San Diego Hope rehab staff filing through the door.

His grandmother's roommate, chubby and childlike despite middle age, pitched forward in her bed to utter a lisping litany of concern. "Oh . . . my . . . goodnethh. Oh, my!"

"Here." Lucas offered a hand to the downed nurse's aide. "Let me help you up, Mrs.——"

"No need," she sputtered, waving him and one of the other aides away. "I'm all right. Weak ankle. Lost my balance, that's all. After I saw that . . . *horrid* thing." Revulsion flickered across her age-lined face. "On your grandmother's plate."

What?

Lucas's gaze darted to the remaining staff now gathering around his grandmother's tray table. They stared like curious looky-loos at a crime scene. Lucas was all too familiar with that phenomenon, though as an evidence technician, he operated on the other side of the yellow police tape. He turned back to the nurse's aide—Wanda Clay, according to her name badge—who'd managed to stand and retrieve the dish cover she'd dropped in her panic. "What's wrong with my grandmother's dinner plate?"

"It was on the rice," Wanda explained, gingerly testing her ankle. It was hard to tell if her grimace was from an injury or from what she was struggling to explain. "Sitting there on the food, bold as brass." She crossed her arms, tried to still a shudder. "Black, huge, with those awful legs. I haven't seen one of those vile bugs since I left Florida."

A *cockroach*? On his grandmother's food? It could snuff what little was left of her appetite—and his hope that she'd finally regain her strength.

"It's probably scurried away by now." The nurse's aide rubbed an elbow. "That's what they do in the light. But I saw it, plain as can be. And you can bet I'll be reporting it to—"

"You mean *this*?" A young, bearded tech in blue scrubs

pointed at the plate. Then made no attempt to hide his smirk. "Is this what freaked you out, Wanda?"

"I wasn't scared," the woman denied, paling as she stared at the tray. "Startled maybe. Because no one expects to see—"

"A black olive?" the tech crowed, pointing again. "Ooooh. Horrifying."

Someone else tittered. "Yep, that's an olive—was an olive. Sort of cut up in pieces and stuck on the rice. A decoration, maybe?"

"Oh, goody." The roommate clapped her hands, her expression morphing from concern to delight. "Can I see? Is it pretty? Can I have a party decoration too?"

"Hey, Wanda," the tech teased, "what form do we use to report an olive to—?"

"I think that's enough," Lucas advised, raising his hands. "No harm, no foul. Okay?" He reminded himself that law enforcement saw its own share of clowning. But . . . "We have two ladies who need to eat."

"Yes, sir." The technician nodded, his expression sheepish. "Just kidding around. I'll get your grandma some fresh water."

"Thank you." Lucas glanced toward Wanda. "You're not hurt?"

"Only a bump." She rubbed her elbow again, lips pinching tight. "Some decoration."

"Yeah."

Lucas watched for a moment as Wanda helped the chattering roommate with her tray; then he glanced toward the window beyond—the hospital's peaceful ocean view—before returning to his grandmother's bedside. He slid his chair close, his heart heavy at the sight of her now. Asleep on her pillow and far too thin, with her stroke-damaged right arm lying useless across her chest. For the first time ever, Rosalynn Marchal actually appeared her age of seventy-six. So different from the strong, vibrant woman who'd essentially been his mother. A woman whose unbridled laughter turned heads in more than a few fancy restaurants, who shouldered a skeet rifle like she intended to stop a charging rhino. A still-lovely senior equally at home in a gown and diamonds for a charity event or wearing faded jeans and a sun hat to dig in her wildly beautiful garden high above the Pacific Ocean. She was an acclaimed painter, a deeply devoted believer. And a new widow. That inconsolable heartbreak had brought her to this point . . . *of no return?*

No.

Lucas watched her doze, torn between the mercy of letting her dream of far better times and the absolute fact that if she didn't eat, drink, move, breathe, she'd succeed in what she'd recently told her pastor and her grandson: *"I'm okay with leaving this earthly world."* Lucas couldn't let that happen even if his grandmother's advance medical directive, her legal living will, required he honor her wishes regarding life support. She'd beaten the pneumonia that brought her to the hospital this time, and the therapists said she still had enough physical strength to regain some mobility, as long as she mustered the will to take nourishment.

"Here's that water," the technician said, setting a pitcher beside the food tray. He cleared his throat. "I'm sorry about that kidding around earlier. It wasn't professional."

"No harm done . . . Edward," Lucas told him after glancing at his ID badge. "I appreciate the help all of you give my grandmother."

"Pretty special lady, huh?"

"The most."

"If you need to get going, I can help feed her tonight," Edward offered. "I know she's on Wanda's list, but I don't mind. I have the time." He shrugged. "And after all that joking around, I'm probably on her list too. Wanda Clay's ever-growing—" The young man's gaze came to rest on the Bible on the bedside table, and he appeared to swallow his intended word. "Her hit list."

Lucas smiled. His grandmother's powerful influence for good. Even in sleep. "Thanks, but I can stay tonight. Things look pretty decent out on the streets."

"You're a cop, right?"

"Evidence tech—CSI," Lucas added, using the TV term everyone recognized.

"Cool."

"Sometimes. Mostly it's like being a Molly Maid. With gloves, tweezers, and a camera. Not as exciting as on TV."

"Still sounds cool to me." The tech moved the dinner tray closer. He pointed to the tepid mound of boiled rice. "I guess I can see how someone might think that thing was a bug."

Lucas inspected the offensive olive. "You think it's supposed to be a garnish?"

"Yeah." Edward snickered. "Some bored dietary assistant getting her cutesy on."

✳ ✳ ✳

"It's not like I'm sous-chef at Avant or Puesto," Aimee Curran told her cousin, citing top-ten local restaurants. She tucked a tendril of auburn hair behind an ear and sighed. "Or that I even get much of a chance to be food-creative here. But . . ." She raised her voice over the mix of staff and visitor chatter in the San Diego Hope hospital cafeteria so that Taylor Cabot could hear. "At least working in a dietary department will look good on my application to the culinary institute."

"You're serious about it. I can see it in your eyes," Taylor observed, mercifully offering no reference to Aimee's failed and costly past career paths. Nursing, right up to the moment she panicked, then passed out and hit the floor during a surgery rotation, followed by early childhood education that . . . just didn't fit. "Aunt Miranda would love it, of course." Taylor slid an extra package of saltines into the pocket of her ER scrub top. "She was such an awesome cook."

"She was." Aimee's mother had been a school nurse, but her kitchen was her beating heart. "Apron time" with her only daughter had meant the world to her. And to Aimee.

"If I win the Vegan Valentine Bake-Off, it means admission to the culinary institute with fully paid tuition," Aimee explained. "I can't qualify for more student loans. So this is it."

"I didn't know you'd gone vegan."

"I haven't. Not even close, though Mom taught me to respect organic and local foods. It's just that there won't be so many entries in a vegan contest. It's a calculated risk. And I need to win, Taylor." Aimee's pulse quickened. "It's my last chance to honor my mother with a choice I'm making for my life—my *whole* life. I've got to do that. I can't bear it if I don't."

"I think . . ." Taylor's voice was gentle. "I think that your mother would be proud of you, regardless."

"But it just seems that everyone else has found their calling, you know? You've got your career in the ER. My brother's starting medical school up in Portland, and Dad's found Nancy." Aimee smiled, so very happy for him. "Now they've adopted those two little rascals from Haiti . . ." Her eyes met Taylor's. "The contest is being held on Valentine's Day."

"Your birthday. And also . . ."

"Ten years from the day Mom passed away." Aimee sighed. "I'm going to be twenty-six, Taylor. It's high time I got myself together and moved on."

"I understand that."

"I know you do." Taylor's husband, a Sacramento firefighter, had been killed in an accident almost three years ago. Taking a job in San Diego was part of Taylor's plan to move on.

"So what are you going to wow those bake-off judges with?" Taylor asked after carefully tapping the meal's calorie count into her cell phone. The old familiar spark of fun warmed her eyes. "Some sort of soybean cheesecake?"

"Not a tofu fan," Aimee admitted, her nose wrinkling. "I thought I'd go through Mom's old recipe tin and adapt something—you know, ban the chickens and cows, but keep the sugar."

"And all the love. Aunt Miranda was all about 'stirring in the love.' I think I asked my mom once if you could buy that at Walmart in a five-pound sack like flour."

Aimee smiled. "The first phase is tomorrow. I've got to pass that. The bake-off finals will be televised. Professional kitchen, top-grade tools . . . ticking time clock." She grimaced. "Nothing like pressure. But at least the hospital dietary kitchen gives me a chance to handle more equipment than I have at my apartment and practice my chopping and slicing techniques." She shook her head. "Mostly when nobody's looking, since the biggest part of my job is tray delivery. But I've been known to add a few artistic, signature Aimee touches and—"

"Hey, Curran!"

Aimee turned and saw a familiar young man in scrubs cruising toward them. Beard, husky build. That rehab tech, Edward.

"Hey there," he said, plunking a hand on the edge of their table. He grinned at Aimee, raised a brow. "Was it you?"

"Was *what* me?"

"That cutesy olive on Mrs. Marchal's rice."

"I don't know what you mean," Aimee told him, afraid she did. Why was he making a big deal out of—?

"A black olive, cut up like some kind of decoration? I think someone got pictures of it."

"Really?" She hesitated. Was he flattering her? Or . . .

"Wanda thought it was a cockroach. She screamed like a banshee and fell down on her—"

"What?" Aimee's heart stalled. *No.* This had to be a bad joke.

"Anyway," he said, waving at a passing student nurse, "Wanda's probably gunning for your department. Grumbling about 'malicious mischief' and things like that. Thought you should know." Edward winked, smacked his hand on the table. "But thank 'em for me, would ya? Highlight of my day."

Aimee closed her eyes as he sauntered away. *Please . . .*

"Aimee?" Taylor leaned over the table, touched her hand. "You okay?"

"I . . ." She met her cousin's gaze and groaned.

"Oh, dear." Taylor winced. "A 'signature Aimee touch'?"

"It was a *daisy*. I snipped all those little black petals really carefully. I didn't even know whose tray it was. But I thought it was sort of cheery. And now, when I'm still on probation, I might be accused of doing something malicious . . ." Another thought made her breath catch. "Wanda's pretty old. Do you think she got hurt? Broke a hip or—?"

"I doubt it," Taylor interrupted, her expression reassuring.

"Wanda is sturdier than she looks. But I do think you should go over there and explain. Apologize to her. And to the patient, too, if she was upset by it."

"Oh, great. I just thought of something else." Aimee squeezed her eyes shut again. "I think Mrs. Marchal's grandson works for the police department. Can this get any worse?"

CHAPTER TWO

Aimee Curran, Dietary Department.

Lucas read her name badge, noticing how very pretty this young woman was. He'd be lying if he said he hadn't thought that same thing each time she delivered the cart of trays to this department. She had a sort of creamy-fair complexion, an intriguing tangle of reddish hair . . . amazing eyes and full lips, along with a small but nicely curvy figure—despite that shapeless hospital uniform. Definitely attractive. Though today Aimee Curran looked every inch a guilty perp.

She'd pulled the olive caper. It didn't take gloves, tweezers, or a fingerprint kit to prove it. Lucas could tell by the look in her eyes—beautiful blue-green and completely guilty, though she hadn't admitted anything yet. She must have heard about the olive cockroach incident. He tried not to enjoy her squirming, but . . .

"Do you know when Wanda's expected back?" Aimee asked, tugging at a wavy tendril of her shoulder-length hair. "She didn't go home sick, did she?"

"No. And not that I know of," Lucas told her, answering both questions. He decided not to add that he'd seen the nurse's aide holding an ice pack to her elbow. And probably weighing the wisdom in reporting the incident. Considering the embarrassment factor, he doubted he would if he were in her shoes. "She said something about taking her break once the food trays were gathered up."

"Oh." Aimee attempted a covert glance at his sleeping grandmother's basically untouched dinner tray. Then squared her shoulders and pasted on a smile. "How did your grandmother enjoy her meal?"

You're gutsy; I'll give you that.

"I'm afraid she hardly touched it," Lucas reported, that reality diluting his current amusement. "She hasn't been doing well with food. I think maybe the medications are making her drowsy. I was going to ask Wanda if we could try some of that liquid supplement. Strawberry or—"

"I could do that," Aimee offered in a hurry. "Any flavor she wants. Iced, warmed, or room temperature. Any way she likes it."

"She hates it."

"Oh. Then maybe I could find her something else, Mr. . . ."

"Marchal. But Lucas is fine. And look . . ." He decided there was enough misery in this room; no need to let her stand there with that worried look on her face. "Someone scraped it off the rice. My grandmother didn't even notice your olive thing."

Her teeth caught her lower lip, and her shoulders sagged a bit. "You saw it?"

"I photographed it." Seeing the worry come back into her eyes, he added, "I mean I had my phone out, and . . . Here, wait." He lifted his Droid from where it lay beside the Bible, tapped the screen, and scrolled to the trio of shots he'd taken. He spread the sharpest image larger.

Aimee glanced toward the door, then stepped closer to look.

"See? I got a nice shot of the body and all the little legs."

"Those are petals—it's a flower!"

"Maybe that was your intent, but look at it. Check the other two shots. It looks like big black bug."

"Hardly." She stepped back, hands on her hips. The blue-green eyes narrowed. "Maybe if you knew how to take a decent picture . . ."

"I'd better know how. I'm a photographer." He decided that, pretty pout or not, he didn't have time or energy for a verbal joust. And he didn't exactly like her attitude. It was the last thing he needed today. "Crime scene photographer. Which, considering everything, just might fit here."

Aimee's mouth sagged open for an instant; then her lips compressed in a tight line. "I'm going to go find Wanda."

"Good idea. And I'd be gentle if I were you. She's been traumatized by a cockroach."

＊　＊　＊

Aimee stepped outside the doors of the rehab and extended care wing, met instantly by a merciful sea-scented breeze. February, sixty-four degrees, and sunny. Perfect—wasn't that what everyone always said about San Diego?

She leaned back against the sun-warmed pink stucco and sighed. That exchange with Lucas Marchal had been any-thing but perfect and did nothing to help her current situation. Maybe even made it worse. She shouldn't have taken the bait, gotten so defensive. But he'd seemed nice at first, helpful. And good-looking, of course; she hadn't been blind to that these past weeks. Tall, confident, with those crystal-blue eyes, curly dark hair, and incredible smile. And irritating smugness. Aimee frowned, recalling his jab: *"Crime scene pho-tographer. Which, considering everything, just might fit here."* She hadn't committed any crime. She just . . . needed to find that nurse's aide, Wanda. Make it all right again.

Aimee scanned the employee parking lot. One of the other aides said Wanda liked to take her breaks out here, and—ah, there, sitting on the tailgate of an old SUV, eating her dinner from a Tupperware container.

"Wanda, hi," Aimee offered tentatively as she approached. If the woman had walked out here and climbed up on that tailgate, she probably didn't have a broken hip. Lucas Marchal couldn't add that to the crime sheet. "Such a blessing to work where we can get a little ocean air during our breaks."

Wanda shifted on the tailgate and stared at her.

"Aimee Curran," Aimee chirped, fanning her name badge like a game show hostess showing off a prize. "From the dietary department."

"Ah," Wanda uttered. The look in her steely gray eyes offered a translation: *"Aha. I'm not surprised."*

Oh no. Was Wanda rubbing her elbow?

"I came to see if you're all right," Aimee explained. "After . . . I mean, I heard that you were startled by my food garnish. So—"

"What on earth were you thinking?"

Aimee's stomach sank. "That it would look cheery?"

"I can't imagine anyone being cheered by an olive." Wanda's lips twitched downward as she swept a wiry wisp of gray hair away from her forehead. Her expression said *cheery* was a foreign concept altogether. "Did Rosalynn Marchal look like she could be cheered?"

"I'm not sure." What was Aimee supposed to do? Admit that she'd never even bothered to check whose tray it was? That the whole purpose of the garnish was practice for the contest?

"I hoped it might make Mrs. Marchal smile, maybe," she hedged.

Wanda Clay was definitely rubbing her elbow.

"She barely eats. Hardly talks," the aide reported. "If you ask me, the poor woman's trying to die. Not that I blame her.

Life isn't one lick fair. Sometimes you get tired of the battle." She pinned Aimee with a look. "Maybe someone like you, young and all perky-happy, can't understand that."

"I'm sorry," Aimee breathed. "I shouldn't have added the garnish. I'm sorry if you were injured because of that, Wanda." She winced as the woman raised her arm, displaying an ugly purple bruise below her elbow. "Oh, dear. Are you going to file a complaint against the dietary department? It really wasn't them. It was me. Only me. And I feel so bad about this. Really." *Please don't get me fired . . .*

"I've been icing it. Seems to move okay. So far. I haven't called my charge nurse or gotten all those comp forms yet, but—" Wanda stopped midsentence as a chunky little dog appeared from somewhere behind her in the car. "Hey there, little man. Finished napping?"

Aimee was astounded by the woman's adoring smile; it completely transformed her face.

"He's so cute," Aimee said, taking in the dog's squat stature, fox-like nose, snowy chest, and huge upright ears. "And friendly," she added as the little dog scuttled forward, tail wagging, to greet her. "Is he a corgi?"

"Same as Her Majesty's favorite dogs," Wanda confirmed, still smiling at him. "Only this fellow's just plain and simple Potter."

"Like Harry?"

"Like Colonel Potter. From *M*A*S*H*." Wanda's expression morphed into the unhappy twitch from before. "It was an old TV show. You're probably too young to know it."

"But I do. My mother loved that show. She even had a *M*A*S*H* T-shirt." Aimee stroked the dog's chin, wishing Wanda's smile would return. She had a feeling this wasn't going well at all.

The woman checked her watch and put the lid on her Tupperware dish.

"I really am sorry, Wanda. If there's anything I can do to help . . ."

"You really mean that?" The aide met Aimee's gaze like a drone strike.

"Of course."

"Your shift ends at five thirty, right? After the dinner tray delivery?"

"That's right. I just finished up." Aimee had no clue where this was heading. "Why?"

"Potter's under a vet's care. I have to give him meds—an injection, too—for another two weeks. Three times a day. That's why I have him here with me. I've been trying to do it all on my breaks: walk him, do the meds, and feed him, give him a little love, but it's hard to get it all done in such a short time. Especially since he's skittish with injections. If you could help me . . ."

Aimee grimaced. "I'm not good with needles."

"Not that." Wanda looked at Aimee as if she were certifiably crazy. "I wouldn't trust you with my dog. I meant if you could stay for an hour at dinnertime and volunteer to help feed my list of patients. Only for two weeks."

"I've asked for the day off tomorrow . . ." Aimee decided

against mentioning a contest to prove her expert culinary skills. "But I could check my schedule, maybe. Give you a call?"

"Do that. Sooner rather than later." Wanda rubbed her elbow again. "I think this arrangement will help everyone."

Amy forced herself to smile, said good-bye, and then headed across the parking lot to her own car. She tried to focus on the positive: phase one of the Vegan Valentine Bake-Off would happen tomorrow. It was the first step in her new future. And despite today's regrettable olive glitch, it seemed that she'd managed to save her hospital job. Even if she was being blackmailed by the grumpy Wanda Clay, forced to spend unpaid hours feeding the woman's assigned patients. Which included the grandmother of . . . Aimee groaned aloud.

Lucas Marchal.

CHAPTER THREE

"Yoo-hoo. Miz Marchal, helloooo . . . Good morning! You're awake!" The roommate, Margie, waved from across the room, every inch of her round face scrunched with delight. She pointed at her tray. "Yay, muffins!"

"Meaning she'd be happy to have yours, too." Lucas chuckled, thinking he'd buy the eager cheerleader a dozen muffins if she could keep that fleeting smile on his grandmother's face. It was encouraging to see her propped up on her pillows, face washed, and long snowy hair resting in a single braid over her shoulder, courtesy of some high school volunteers who'd helped this morning. "It *is* good to see you awake," he agreed. "You've been missing all the excitement around here."

"You're referring to . . ." His grandmother's voice was halting and thin, an effect of the stroke, but her eyes were still skeet-shoot sharp. "The unfortunate acrobatics inspired by my dinner tray?"

"You saw that?"

"Certainly." His grandmother's brows rose. "And most of your equally unfortunate handling of things afterward. I've never known you to be so immune to the charms of a pretty girl."

Aimee Curran? Pretty, absolutely. Charming? He couldn't see it. Clearly the only reason she'd been here was to save her skin and—

"Did it really?" his grandmother asked.

"Did what really what?" Lucas calculated the sips of water he'd managed to get his grandmother to take. Not nearly enough. "What do you mean?"

The rare smile teased her lips again. "Did the garnish look like a bug?"

"Enough to call the Orkin Man." He smiled in spite of himself, remembering Aimee's hands on her hips, the narrowing of those amazing eyes. "She said it was a flower. An olive flower. I thought I was going to fall over myself. Laughing."

"Don't be so quick to judge. After all, art . . ." His grandmother glanced down at the fingers that had accomplished so many bold brushstrokes. Too weak now to even hold his hand. "Art is very individual. A gift. We use what we are given."

✳ ✳ ✳

Why in heaven's name did she choose black beans as an ingredient? It was a huge mistake; Aimee felt it in her bones, which were at risk of melting in the stifling heat of the Vegan Valentine test kitchen. She fanned herself with a checkered dish towel, sneaking a glimpse across the other seven competitors' cluttered workstations. Slab after slab of tofu—silken, soft, regular, firm. All boring, common, safe . . . and smart. Black bean brownies? Seriously? But it was too late now . . .

"French silk cheesecake," a voice shouted overhead, "be ready for your oven in four minutes. Lotus flan, you're on deck. Chocolate heaven torte, confirm your baking time, please. Ten minutes for your assigned oven, black bean brownies."

Oh, please . . .

Aimee thought she heard snickers from somewhere behind her. It was almost impossible to tell for sure among the incredible barrage of kitchen sounds: the whir of industrial-size metal mixers and half a dozen food processors, the clatter of measuring spoons and *chunk-thwack* of steel knives against cutting boards, the constant dinging of timers. And the concussive sound of her own heart slamming against her ribs. The air was a potpourri of melted chocolate, scalding almond milk, grated vanilla beans . . . and nervous sweat. Why am I here? Why did I think I could—?

"Black beans," a contest official noted, pausing beside her. His accent sounded European, German maybe. His apron, unlike Aimee's, was still pristine white. "Eight contestants, eight unique desserts. A mystery basket of three must-include main ingredients. A trip to the pantry for basics, plus a challenge item chosen from the wild-card shelf. And you, Miss Curran, are the only one who elected to use the beans." His eyes met Aimee's long enough to make her stomach do a dangerous nosedive, but gave no clue as to whether or not he approved. "Interesting choice."

"Yes." Aimee glanced down at the mixture she'd managed to blend into a smooth batter: Dutch cocoa, oats, maple syrup, coconut oil, vegan chocolate chips . . . and the wild-card beans. She fought a cockroach-garnish flashback. "I was just thinking of changing the name to 'kamikaze brownies.'"

The official laughed, then tapped a finger on her table. "Interesting can be good. Be ready for that oven, okay?"

"Yes, sir."

In the next forty-five minutes, she'd patted the thick brown batter into the prepared baking pan and checked the oven temperature a minimum of three times, each tick of the timer ricocheting through her head. Aimee had prayed—her first time ever to do that in oven mitts—then finally slid the hot brownies from the oven, hoping they tasted as good as they smelled. They did smell good—wonderful, even. But it still took all of her courage not to run from the room after she set the plated and chocolate-drizzled desserts in front of the assembled judges. And then waited and waited . . .

It happened all at once, in a dizzying rush. Whoops of

excitement around the room as one by one the Vegan Valentine Bake-Off finalists were called, by the contestant's full name in addition to the recipe name, until—

"Aimee Curran, black bean brownies."

Wait . . . me? Me?

She was sure she heard it wrong, was afraid she'd slip off her kitchen stool or—

A microphone was thrust into her face, then a TV camera, with a blonde reporter somewhere behind it all.

"We're here at the Vegan Valentine Bake-Off kitchen, with finalist and rising culinary star Aimee Curran, whose very creative offering of black bean brownies wowed today's judges. Yes, I did say black beans, folks, and these surprising brownies are wonderful! Miss Curran, can you tell us how you're feeling right now?"

"Um . . ." Aimee stared, dazed, into the camera. "I . . ."

"Someone told us that Valentine's Day is also your birthday," the reporter prompted. "You'll be competing with three other finalists to win top honors and full tuition at a local culinary school. I'd call that a very auspicious day all around. Any hint of what dish you'll be making?"

"I'm not sure yet." Aimee's heart cramped. "I'll be adapting one of my mother's recipes. She was an amazing cook."

"I'm sure of that." The reporter pressed the microphone close again. "We also hear that you're an employee at San Diego Hope hospital. A member of that heroic and compassionate health team."

The hospital.

"Yes. I work there. And—please excuse me. I really have to go do something."

"Wanda?" Aimee asked, after waiting several minutes for the nurse's aide to be located and brought to the phone.

"Yes, this is she."

"It's Aimee Curran. How's your elbow today?"

"Still bruised. But I'm here—didn't take the day off. Like *some* people."

Aimee reminded herself that she was a rising culinary star. Who needed to keep her day job. "I'm calling because of what we talked about yesterday. Remember?"

"Hard to forget."

Aimee glanced down the hallway toward the test kitchen and saw another finalist eating one of her brownies. "You haven't decided if you'll need to report it as an injury?"

"Not yet."

"Ah . . ." Aimee released the breath she'd been holding. "I'd like to come in Monday, after my shift, and help you feed your patients. For two weeks—you know, until you're feeling good as new. And until little Potter's feeling better too, of course. I want to help you, Wanda."

"I figured you might."

"I *LOOOVE* IT when you come help us, Aimee." Margie blew a noisy kiss from her wheelchair across the room. Her leg was strapped into a huge postoperative brace; it looked like a torture device. But it hadn't dampened the enthusiasm of the developmentally disabled roommate. Probably nothing could.

Lucas smiled as Margie continued her unabashed adoration of the dietary assistant.

"You're so nice," Margie cooed, "and pretty, too. Really, *really* pretty." The woman's dark eyes glittered. "Like a Disney princess! Right, Lucas?"

"Sure," he agreed, enjoying the pink flush that rose on

Aimee's cheeks as she stood beside him. She bent lower over his grandmother's dinner tray, cutting the pallid chicken breast into near-microscopic pieces.

"Um . . . thank you, Margie," she said finally, avoiding Lucas's eyes as she smiled at the still-giggling roommate. "I'm happy to volunteer to help."

Volunteer?

Lucas didn't know one Disney princess from another, but he could definitely recognize a blackmail victim. Aimee had been here four evenings now, offering to stay after her shift. Wanda Clay must have dangled that black olive garnish like it was O.J. Simpson's bloody glove.

"I thought," she said, glancing up at him finally, "if I got it into small pieces and mixed it with some of the mashed potatoes, it might be easier for your grandmother to swallow. We'll try it again when she gets back from physical therapy. I'll probably have to warm it up."

"Thanks, but I don't think it's going to make a difference." The familiar sadness crowded Lucas's chest. "The swallowing tests showed that her throat isn't affected all that much. It's more that she's lost interest in eating. In everything, I guess."

"Because of the stroke?"

"And losing my grandfather. Mostly that." He reached for the silver-framed photograph sitting beside his grandmother's Bible. There were also several paintbrushes—soft and hinting of turpentine—that he'd brought in another failed attempt to encourage her. "He passed away last summer."

"I'm sorry." There was genuine empathy in Aimee's eyes.

"That photo, it's your grandparents?" She glanced at the black-and-white snapshot in his hands. A young couple beside a bicycle, a paper-wrapped loaf of bread in its wicker basket.

"Yes. Shortly after they met."

"I thought . . ." A smile tugged at Aimee's lips. "I thought it was you. With an old bicycle and a wool cap—one of those photos made to look vintage. You look so much like him, with the height and those big shoulders." She leaned closer to point at the photo, and her scent wafted, faintly sweet, like the flowers in his grandmother's cliff-top garden. "Same black curly hair, light eyes, even the shape of his lips . . ." Aimee drew back, her expression showing a hint of fluster. Like she'd gone too far, been too personal. "Where was this taken? Looks like mountains. Big mountains."

"The French Alps," Lucas told her, more than a little flattered that she'd noticed those things about his grandfather— about him. "My grandfather was French. Louis Andre Marchal. My middle name," he added.

"Louis?"

"Andre. After his father." He glanced down at the young, coltishly beautiful woman holding on to the bicycle in the photo. "My grandmother was barely nineteen. An art student. She wanted to paint alpine wildflowers, and he offered to be her guide." Lucas shook his head. "She always says, 'Louis begged like such an adorable pest. How could I say no?' I bet I've heard the story a hundred times. They would have been married fifty-seven years this month."

"Ah." Aimee pressed her hand to her throat. "She must miss him so much."

"Yes. Enough that I'm afraid she's determined to follow him." As the words slipped out, he met Aimee's gaze, realizing it was the first time he'd admitted that fear out loud to anyone. "The doctors say she should be able to rally and improve enough to go back home. But it hasn't happened. She's losing weight, getting weaker . . ." He set the photo back down. Let his fingers linger on her Bible for a moment. "She told our pastor she's at peace with leaving this world."

"Lucas, I'm so sorry."

"It's more than that. Because . . ." He stopped, angry with himself. What was he doing? This girl had been coerced into being here. She didn't sign on for his personal information dump. If he didn't stop, he'd move right on to telling her about his grandmother's living will and—"It's not your problem," he said quickly. "I doubt very much this is in your dietary department job description: holding the hands of worried family members. Or even feeding patients."

"But I'm happy to help. Really."

"You mean to 'volunteer'?" Lucas laughed low in his throat. "I think we both know why you're here, Aimee."

Her brows pinched.

"What did Wanda do? Threaten to file a complaint against you?"

"No." Aimee crossed her arms, lifted her chin. "I wanted to help her, that's all."

"Look . . . I don't think it's right, but from what I've seen, nobody much likes Wanda Clay." Lucas glanced across at his grandmother's roommate, happily licking the last of her dietetic pudding from its container. "Not even Margie. And that says a lot. If you're a Disney princess, then that poor CNA is peddling poison apples. I'm an investigator. Don't try to fool me."

Aimee frowned. "Okay. Maybe this is related to that incident—though she never said it directly. I'm helping so Wanda can have extra time on her dinner break. She has her little dog out in the car."

"A dog?"

"A cute one. I swear, it's the only time I've seen Wanda smile. Potter needs medications for a couple of weeks. That's why she brought him with her. If I help with Wanda's patients, she can take care of her dog."

"And you avoid disciplinary action."

"Yes." The beautiful eyes narrowed. "Is that a crime?"

"No." Lucas raised his hands. "No yellow tape, no dusting for fingerprints—or pawprints. Do what you need to do. I won't stop you."

"Good." She glanced toward the door as Wanda entered the room. "For the record, I really like your grandmother. She's beautiful and strong despite her situation." Something wistful, maybe even sad, flickered across Aimee's face. "I also understand how it feels to lose someone you love."

Lucas had no clue what to say. And suddenly regretted everything he already had.

Aimee covered his grandmother's tray. Checked the water

in her pitcher. She waved to Wanda, took a few steps away, and then turned to look at Lucas again. "It occurs to me that you resemble your grandfather in another way too."

Lucas raised his brows.

"That 'pest' thing." Aimee's lips twitched. "Minus the 'adorable' part."

"I COULD ABSOLUTELY kiss you!" Aimee grinned at the farmers' market vendor, then whipped around to show Taylor a fistful of the slender cherry-red stalks. "Beautiful rhubarb, exactly what I wanted. Organic, local . . ." She turned back to the smiling vendor. "But they're so finicky to grow in Southern California. How do you do it?"

"We're up in the coastal mountains. It's a little cooler, but still plenty of sun. That's a Victoria variety, from our five-year-old plants." The fresh-faced young woman glanced at her tall and lanky husband, Aiden—Aiden and Eve of the Garden of Eatin' farm. "We mulch with our own compost and hand-tend all the crops ourselves." She smiled and patted her obviously expectant tummy. "Five more weeks for this particular one."

Aimee chuckled. "You're here every Friday?"

"Monday, Wednesday, *and* Friday," Eve assured, handing Aimee her change and a flyer for their family farm. "Like chickens to the roost."

"Perfect." Aimee slung her mother's faded rope market tote over her shoulder. "I'll need more of this wonderful stuff next Friday. I'm going to make it famous."

Eve grinned. "We'll be here. Count on it."

Aimee thanked her again, then followed Taylor as she wove through the tents, mounded displays of produce bright as a painter's palette, and a crowd of shoppers already boasting summer linen, sandals, and sunglasses. The air was a delicious mix of sea spray, kettle corn, and Moroccan grilled chicken. Aimee's stomach rumbled; she reminded herself to think vegan.

"I can see the creative wheels turning, my little 'rising culinary star,'" Taylor teased as they settled at a small outside table. "Rhubarb. Your mom's yummy recipe?"

"What could be better?" Aimee closed her eyes for a moment, enjoying the sun on her face as a light breeze sifted her hair. "Strawberry rhubarb crumble was my birthday dessert as far back as I can remember. All tangy and sweet, with buttery brown sugar–and–oatmeal topping. I'd smell it before I opened my eyes in the morning; then Mom would pretend to smack me with her baking spoon when I sneaked some." Aimee met her cousin's gaze, swallowing against a growing ache. "That last week . . . she said she only wished she could make my dessert one more time."

"Aw, sweetie." Taylor reached across the table to touch her hand.

"So now I'll bake it for her," Aimee said with a decisive nod. "And I'll decorate the crumble top with strawberries cut into little Valentine hearts . . ." She frowned.

"What?"

"Lucas Marchal. I can't even plan a garnish without seeing his face."

"Not such a bad face."

"I guess not." Warmth that had nothing to do with the sun crept up Aimee's neck. "But it's so obvious that he questions my motives." She saw Taylor's brows lift. "Okay, I'm there because I don't want Wanda to write me up—in smoke trails over the hospital roof while cackling from her broom." Aimee winced, instantly sorry. "Edward's awful joke. I shouldn't have repeated it."

Taylor's eyes were kind. "She's giving you a hard time?"

"Not directly." Aimee sighed. "I heard she's been an aide for like thirty years. But I don't think she likes her job. Or anyone there. I get the sense she's putting in the time and counting the minutes until she can retire. I think the only thing that makes Wanda Clay happy is her dog."

"I've seen her walking him and . . ." Taylor hesitated for a moment. "Wanda's faced some challenges. She hasn't kept it secret that her husband ran off and left her with a mountain of debt. It was a long time ago, but some people have a hard time letting go of bitter feelings. And dealing with unexpected loss." She took a slow breath. "I'm guessing she's holding on to all that hurt so tightly that she's forgotten how good it used to feel to help people. Be part of a team."

Aimee studied Taylor's face. "I swear—when I grow up, I want to be like you."

Taylor laughed, raised her hands. "Just don't expect me to weigh in on your hunky CSI situation. Out of my league."

"I doubt that," Aimee told her, wondering if her cousin had already managed to weigh in without realizing it. *Some people have a hard time letting go . . ."* Had she completely missed that about Lucas? She'd empathized with his grandmother's grief, but this was also about her grandson . . .

"You're suddenly lost in thought," Taylor noted, catching Aimee's attention again.

"No, not really," she hedged. "Just thinking I should go pick up some strawberries so I can do a trial run of that recipe tonight. Make sure I won't miss something important."

By three thirty, Aimee had found the recipe in her mother's old tin—filed under *B* for *birthday* instead of *S*—read it several times, and then calculated the necessary changes to convert it to an acceptable vegan dish. She popped a few of the luscious, sweet strawberries into her mouth, hulled the rest, and expertly chopped half of the beautiful and tangy-tart Garden of Eatin' rhubarb.

Finally she stilled her mother's German chef's knife and

checked the clock for the third time. And then told herself she was being ridiculous.

It was her day off. And miraculously, Wanda's as well. Which meant there was no obligation on Aimee's part to go to the hospital and volunteer her time in the rehab wing. Someone else would watch Margie make a rabbit out of her paper napkin. Another staffer would encourage Rosalynn Marchal to try a sip of juice and praise the dear lady's half-hearted attempt to use a fork with her left hand. Lucas would be there too, with concern in his beautiful blue eyes. And so much love. Anyone could see that. Maybe someone else could manage to listen to Lucas without bristling and giving in to her own stubborn pride so much that she completely missed . . . *Did I do that? Am I that self-centered?*

Aimee set her knife down beside her mother's recipe and reached for another strawberry, remembering what Taylor said. *"Some people have a hard time letting go."* She'd been talking about Wanda and her bitterness. But why wouldn't that apply to Lucas as well? Of course he was afraid he'd lose his grandmother. How well had Aimee handled the thought of losing her mom?

She groaned aloud, remembering her parting shot at Lucas. How she'd smugly called him a pest. She wouldn't blame him if he managed to avoid her until her obligation to Wanda was completed. Except that he'd trust her to oversee his grandmother's evening meal about as much as Wanda would trust her with Potter. Lucas would absolutely be there every night. Just the way he was there right now.

Aimee glanced at the clock again. Tray time. With Wanda off today, Aimee would be challenged about being there. As a dietary assistant, as a short-term volunteer . . . but not as a visitor.

Aimee gathered up the rhubarb and strawberries, put them in the apartment's tiny, aging fridge. Then she grabbed her purse and headed for the door.

CHAPTER SIX

LUCAS STRODE through the door of the hospital room, hating that he was late. He'd called and specifically instructed the part-time aide regarding his grandmother's needs but wasn't sure if he'd gotten across how critical it was to—

He stopped short, staring at Aimee Curran. In street clothes, rearranging some containers on his grandmother's tray.

"Uh . . ." He blinked, confused at seeing her there and also by the sudden uptick in his heart rate. Maybe it was something about the color of that fitted pink shirt or seeing her in those faded jeans, but she looked even more attractive than ever.

"Isn't it Wanda's day off?" Lucas managed finally. "I mean, I didn't think you'd be here to volunteer."

"She *loooves* us!" Margie chirped, waving her napkin.

Aimee smiled, a blush rising high on her cheeks. "What can I say?"

What could *he* say? After the way they'd parted yesterday—how lousy he'd acted—he figured Aimee wouldn't be back at all. Then to see her here tonight, when she didn't have to be . . .

"Officially," she continued, pointing to a red sticker badge affixed to her shirt, "I'm here as a visitor. But I told the aide I'd help with her dinner tray." She glanced at Lucas's grandmother, the woman's gaunt face in peaceful repose. "I'm afraid she didn't eat nearly enough. I wrote everything down."

"Thank you, Aimee. Really, you can't know how much I appreciate this. Especially today." Lucas dragged his fingers down his jaw. "We had new information on that abduction case, and it got complicated. Lots of media."

"I saw it on the news." Aimee's brows pinched with obvious concern. "I'm glad I could be here and—"

"Can I take the tray now?" an aide asked, arriving at the bedside.

Aimee glanced at Lucas.

"Yes," he told the aide, sudden weariness washing over him. "Let's let her sleep for now."

"Sounds good to me, sir."

"Well . . ." Aimee stood, stepped to the head of the bed,

and patted his grandmother's shoulder with genuine tenderness. "I should head home," she continued. "I have some things I need to do."

"Don't leave," Lucas heard himself say. "Please, stay awhile. We could . . ." His gaze darted from his grandmother across to Margie, talking with dramatic gestures to the nurse's aide. As if to prove this was hardly a place to socialize, the PA system announced a diabetic feet talk in the extended care department. Hospital ambience.

"It's nice outside," Aimee offered, capturing his gaze. "There's a patio. And I wouldn't mind some fresh air. They keep it so warm in here."

Lucas agreed. The longer Aimee's eyes held his, the warmer it got in this place.

He told the aide where he'd be, and they wandered outside. It was nice; he'd forgotten. Flagstone patio with several small metal tables and—beyond a low rock wall and between some palm trees—even a glimpse of the Pacific Ocean. The sunset, already as pink as Aimee's shirt, couldn't have been better if he'd picked it out of a travel brochure and had it rushed FedEx. His grandmother would take one look and breathe, *"God's having art class tonight."*

Aimee walked past the tables and sat on the rock wall.

Lucas joined her. It was quiet except for the distant blend of traffic and ocean waves. He began to feel awkward and wondered if Margie, the icebreaker, had patio privileges.

"That case you're working on," Aimee said, breaking the silence. "My cousin is an ER nurse here at San Diego

Hope, but she also volunteers as a crisis chaplain. She offered support at the candlelight vigil. I hope they find that poor woman and that she isn't . . ." She took a slow breath. "It has to be hard doing the work you do."

"Sometimes. But I like thinking that I'm helping to make sense of things," Lucas told her. "Too many things don't make sense these days." *Like my grandmother trying to die.* "Too much bad news." He saw her brow furrow and wondered what he was doing. They'd come out for fresh air, a respite, and he was—"But on the other hand, I heard you had some *great* news. Someone said you won a cooking contest?"

"I'm a finalist, one of four. The final bake-off will be in a week. Valentine's Day—my birthday, actually," Aimee added, "not that it matters."

"It should." Lucas decided pink was his new favorite color, those exact three shades: Aimee's T-shirt, her modest blush, and that incredible sunset framing it all. She looked like . . . a valentine. He cleared his throat; workday fatigue was moving him fast into sappy territory. "Competing against those other cooks must be intense, I'd think."

"Not in the same league as CSI." Despite the tease, Aimee's eyes held an undeniable spark of excitement. "It was stressful and thrilling at the same time. Like trying to do a timed math test while using a paint palette some stranger mixed up."

"Paint?"

Aimee laughed. "Metaphorically. I meant food ingredients, spices. We weren't told ahead of time what they would be. We were all given a mystery basket of major ingredients, access to the same basic assortment of staples, then were challenged to put our own unique twist into creating a dessert."

"Ah." Lucas smiled. Food metaphors—he hadn't seen that coming. There was much more to Aimee Curran than he ever figured. He was intrigued.

"Anyway . . ." The breeze blew a strand of coppery hair across Aimee's lips, and she swept it away. "There I am, analyzing the ingredients, imagining the possible taste combinations, watching the clock tick, and trying to deal with unfamiliar commercial kitchen equipment without sacrificing a finger." Her face lit with pinch-me-I'm-dreaming delight. "But I did it. I made the Vegan Valentine Bake-Off finals."

"You did." He smiled, her contagious excitement exactly what he needed right now. "And I heard you were on TV. That they called you a 'cooking star.'"

"'Rising culinary star,'" she clarified with a chuckle. "Not that I took it to heart, of course." Aimee shook her head. "Wow, the hospital grapevine's been buzzing."

"Yeah." Lucas wasn't about to admit that over the past week, he'd started to tune in whenever her name was mentioned. "But someone got it all wrong about what you cooked. It's funny, really. They said you made black bean brownies." His laugh faded when he caught the look on her face. "Wait . . . that's *right*?"

"Yes." Aimee's chin lifted. "I regret the name I chose. I should have called them 'cocoa Brazil' or 'chocolate surprise' or maybe 'guiltless indulgence.' Trust me; a thousand better ideas pummel your brain after they announce black bean brownies and seven other contestants start to laugh." She shot him a pointed look. "Like you did just now."

"I'm sorry—handcuff me. But when I heard it was brownies with beans . . ."

She raised her hand. "Doesn't matter. The fact is that the addition of the beans is what put me in the finals. I was the only one with the guts to try them as a vegan ingredient. Processed into a smooth paste with coconut oil, Dutch cocoa, maple syrup . . . They were delicious."

"And I'm an idiot. I don't cook. Ever. I know nothing about food, except that I like to eat it." Lucas shrugged. "Lately, with the caseload—and my grandmother—that usually amounts to a take-out burrito from Chipotle."

Aimee regarded him for a moment. "Black beans on that burrito?"

"Of course."

She smiled. "No handcuffs then."

Lucas sighed. "Really, I am sorry. I shouldn't have laughed."

"It's okay. I get that it sounds strange. Besides, you were already suspicious of me because of the whole olive fiasco. And . . ." She lifted a shoulder, but it did little to diffuse the sudden discomfort on her face. "And because you think I'm only coming here to volunteer out of selfishness. To save my own skin."

"Hold on. That's why I asked you to stay. I need to talk with you about that."

Lucas was quiet for a moment. Gathering his thoughts, Aimee assumed, as carefully as he sorted through forensic evidence. From what she'd learned of him, the man was methodical, analytic, and orderly. About his work, about his grandmother's needs, and even about his appearance: clean, neat, not quite geeky but definitely classic casual. Which made the way Lucas looked today—slightly rumpled, shadow of a beard, and that dark, wayward curl straying across his forehead—so irresistibly attractive.

"Look, Aimee, I was wrong to tease you about that food tray deal. It was as inappropriate as what that tech did to Wanda by making fun of her reaction. It was a cheap laugh. And even if I'd needed one that day—most days now—"

Lucas frowned—"it should never have been at your expense. Especially now that I know how serious you are about your culinary art."

My art. Aimee battled an impulse to lean over and kiss his cheek.

"And," Lucas continued, "whatever prompted it initially, I am nothing but grateful for the kindness you've shown my grandmother. And that you came here today," he went on, his voice thickening, "when you didn't have to, makes me feel even more like a jerk for those things I said to you before. I wanted to go after you yesterday, apologize then. I should have. I doubted you'd be back at all. I figured you'd rather risk the wrath of Wanda than be forced to deal with me."

"Nah." Aimee was grateful he couldn't read her mind: kissing his cheek sounded like an even better idea now. Then reaching up to touch that curl on his forehead . . . "Besides, I think we're even. I remember calling you a pest in my parting shot."

"Like my grandmother called my grandfather. Except . . ."

"Not 'adorable,'" Aimee finished, knowing she'd been completely wrong about that.

"Can't have everything, I guess." Lucas laughed. "Really, Aimee, I regret all of it."

"I don't. I loved hearing about your grandparents. Rosalynn and Louis Andre. And the way they met. It was so sweet." Aimee sighed, thinking of that old framed photo and how very much Lucas looked like that smitten Frenchman. "How he found those wildflowers for her."

Lucas nodded, a smile teasing his lips. "And *fraises des bois*."

"'Strawberries . . . of the woods'?" Aimee translated, trying to recall her high school French.

"Wild alpine strawberries. Very tiny, very sweet, according to my grandmother. And hard to come by." Lucas shook his head, his smile stretching. "My grandfather climbed for hours up a mountain to find them and then carefully carried them back in his cap to surprise my grandmother. I think it was the same day that photo was taken. She painted those berries too—here, wait. I'll show you."

Lucas leaned sideways to pull his phone from his back pocket, and his shoulder brushed Aimee's. Ridiculously, her skin tingled at the small touch.

"There," he said, pulling up a photo file. He handed her the phone but stayed close as she began to scroll through. Aimee breathed in his clean, masculine scent. "Some of my black-and-white candid shots are mixed in, but see? There are the wildflowers."

"Yes . . . that's lovely," she told him, her heart rate beginning to skitter as their shoulders touched again. "I love the colors and how her brushwork is so bold. I wasn't expecting that."

Lucas smiled. "She tends to take people by surprise."

Aimee's breath caught as she saw the first black-and-white candid, his grandparents in a garden. Much older than in the bicycle photo but still so clearly in love. She scrolled further, each beautifully intimate shot hitting her square in the heart. The couple in their kitchen; dancing on a beach; walking hand in hand down the steps of a church; sitting on a sagging-soft couch and reading side by side, with one shoulder resting against the other's. It was the essence of Rosalynn and Louis Marchal captured in shutter clicks. Forever love celebrated. "These are wonderful. You took them?"

"Over the years." Lucas leaned closer and pointed. "That one was in July, a few weeks before my grandfather died." He scrolled down for Aimee. "There it is. Her painting of the wild strawberries."

"Oh, my. It's glorious." Aimee's eyes took in the image, the thickly layered strokes—a palette knife, if she recalled her art appreciation studies. "The color of those little berries all piled up in that blue wool cap, and its texture contrasted against the white lace tablecloth . . . and look, that one strawberry, bitten nearly to the stem."

Lucas chuckled, his breath warm against Aimee's ear. "My grandfather loved to tell the story of how he climbed the mountain, picked those strawberries. And fed them to my grandmother one by one. He'd always say that their first kiss tasted of strawberries."

"Oh . . ." Aimee pressed her hand to her chest. "How romantic."

"Yes, well . . ." Lucas leaned away and cleared his throat, his expression hinting that he'd said more than he intended to. "That's a Frenchman for you."

"So they say." Aimee studied the photo again, amused by the fact that this analytical CSI tech was . . . one-quarter

French? Wildly romantic by genetics? His work in these candid photos proved an inherent passion. She met his gaze in the deepening dusk. "Your grandmother was—is—an amazing painter. And you are an impressive photographer, Lucas."

"Thank you. I . . ." He hesitated for a moment as if considering his words. "I've always wanted to publish a book, using the color photos of my grandmother's art combined with my black-and-white images. And the stories they've told me. It feels even more important now that I've lost my grandfather." Lucas swallowed. "And because things don't look good for my grandmother."

Aimee's heart cramped. "She's getting worse?"

"I talked to her doctor today. The blood tests show she's becoming dehydrated. That's why she's been so drowsy and weak. If she won't take more nourishment by mouth, they want to give her intravenous fluids. And insert something called a PEG tube. So they can feed her directly into her stomach."

Aimee grimaced, reminded of her queasy U-turn from a nursing career. She certainly wasn't going to recount her failures to Lucas. "When would they do that?"

"They can't. Unless my grandmother changes her living will. She's adamant that there be no invasive measures for artificial life support, including IVs and feeding tubes." Observable pain flickered across his handsome face. "I'm the trustee. I have to honor her wishes. If it's what my grandmother wants, I'd have to . . . let her die."

Aimee touched his hand lightly. "I don't want to imagine how hard that would be."

"I can't stop imagining it." His hand turned over, grasping hers very gently. "People keep reminding me that she's seventy-six, that she's had a good life—accomplished so much. And she had a wonderful marriage. But I've barely wrapped my head around losing my grandfather. How am I supposed to let her go too?"

"Is there other family?"

"Not really. I don't have brothers or sisters, and . . ." His lips tugged downward. "My parents prefer to not be involved. From way back—my grandparents raised me." Lucas took a deep breath, exhaled. "I sit there every night and read from the Bible. Her favorite verses about hope and God's loving plan for our lives. All the while she seems determined to wither up and die. I can't make sense of that." He met Aimee's gaze, blue eyes shadowed in the growing darkness. His thumb brushed the back of her hand. "I shouldn't be dumping all of this on you. It isn't what you signed on for."

"No," Aimee admitted, struggling to summon a small smile. "Tray delivery is pretty limited in that respect. But I understand what you're saying." Her throat squeezed, choking her voice to a whisper as she thought of her mother, of those awful weeks they prayed for miracles and watched her die. Aimee blinked against welling tears. "I know how much it hurts. How helpless it makes you feel. I . . . I'm so sorry you're going through this, Lucas." A tear slid down her cheek. "I wish there was something more I could do to—"

"Aimee, don't cry . . ."

Before she could blink, they were holding each other, a

hug of comfort and compassion, shared pain—and because it was what made sense in this moment. Aimee wasn't sure who reached out first; she didn't care. She didn't question, either, if anything more would come of it. She simply closed her eyes, nestled her cheek against the stubbled warmth of Lucas's, and held on.

CHAPTER EIGHT

"I DIDN'T MEAN to pull you away from hamburger duty," Taylor said, chuckling as she reached out to pluck at Aimee's mustard-splotched dietary apron. She glanced from her table, through a clutch of OB staff, toward the hospital cafeteria grill. "Though it looks like your lunch crowd has dwindled. You didn't add any scary pickle garnishes, did you?"

"Gee, thanks." Aimee tucked a strand of hair back under her paper chef cap. "I guess I needed that crack to keep me humble, and—" she covered a yawn—"awake. They had me here at five thirty to start the breakfast prep. At least I get to go home early." She breathed in the salt-on-grease aroma of

French fries and onion rings. "Another thirty-two minutes, not that I'm counting."

"Go home early to fret over your first-place recipe?"

"No." Aimee smiled at her cousin. "My test run was really good last night; no problems adapting Mom's original recipe. I switched out the butter for a high-quality vegan spread, used organic sugar, and . . ." She lowered her voice and glanced around, feeling like an idiot to even imagine someone might try to steal her recipe. "I added some freshly grated nutmeg and orange zest. And a teeny splash of Grand Marnier. Might capture some overachiever points with the judges."

Taylor grinned. "I'm so proud of you, kiddo. You really want this."

"I do." Aimee thought again of her brother and her father, moving on with their lives. Taylor too. Aimee didn't just want this new career as a chef; she *needed* it. The contest was a week from today. Everything depended on her winning. Her testing proved the recipe would work. As long as she had everything prepped and ready and there were no last-minute problems.

"So I go to the farmers' market on Friday morning," Taylor confirmed, "get the best berries I see, and pick up the rhubarb from Aiden and Eve's biblical fruit stand. And take it all to your apartment."

Aimee frowned. "I'm not so sure now."

"But you said the recipe went perfectly. And it's your lucky birthday dessert."

"No, I didn't mean that. I'm making the strawberry rhubarb crumble. It's my wheezing, antique refrigerator I'm not so sure about." Aimee shook her head. "I think it's about to go on the fritz again. My butter looked too soft this morning. And my landlord takes forever to get a repairman out. I don't want to take chances."

"We'll keep the fruit in my refrigerator, then. It's practically new, with humidity-controlled fruit bins and all that fancy stuff."

"Thanks, but your place is too far away. The contest starts super early on Saturday. I think I'll have you bring the fruit here to work. I'll get the okay to keep it in the dietary fridge, pick it up Saturday morning on my way to the contest kitchen. Every speck of the work is done there in front of the judging team, from the initial chopping and measuring to my final strawberry valentine garnish." Butterflies fluttered in Aimee's stomach. "I need everything to go exactly right. No surprises."

"Well," Taylor said, glancing toward the grill, "it seems you have one anyway." Her green eyes glittered. "Over there, rising culinary star—you have a lunch customer. And he's looking this way."

Aimee turned and felt her cheeks flame. Lucas. She returned his smile, offered a be-there-in-a-second gesture. Then glanced at her cousin. "I'd better—"

"Go; scoot," Taylor told her, clearly enjoying the little scenario. "I'm on my way back to the ER. And if I had to make a diagnosis right here, I'd say that guy looks seriously hungry."

Aimee hurried behind the grill counter, wishing to high heaven she wasn't wearing the goofy chef cap or an apron that looked like it had played two rounds of paintball . . . and that her face would cool down. If this kept up, she'd need the fire extinguisher. *It was a hug, nothing more.*

"Hey there," Lucas greeted her over the stainless steel counter. "I heard you were chief fry cook."

"Not exactly chief," she admitted, noticing that he was freshly shaved today, with no clothing rumples or rogue curls. But the same compelling eyes. Aimee tried to ignore a tingly memory of how it felt to be held in his arms. "Donny's here somewhere, probably going over receipts. I'm his assistant." She managed a teasing smile. "That would be 'sous-chef' if the ambience didn't have sirens and stat pages for labor and delivery."

Lucas laughed, then held Aimee's gaze long enough to unsettle her again. "So . . ." His eyes swept the magnetic-letter menu. "Can I get a burger?"

"Sure." Aimee reached for the freezer drawer.

"Wait. Make that one of those veggie burgers."

"Those are black bean burgers."

Lucas smiled. "All the better."

Aimee's pulse did a skip. "Anything with that?"

"Sweet potato waffle fries and . . ." The blue eyes captured hers. "Coffee with the sous-chef, maybe? Later?"

"Um . . . sure." If this kept up, Aimee could try out for the middle school pep squad. Her heart just accomplished a backflip. "I'm off early today. In about half an hour."

"Great. And it's my day off. So unless I get called in, I'm free too."

The veggie burger sizzled as it hit the grill. "Won't your grandmother be expecting you?"

"I've been kicked out. She says I'm an insufferable bully whose weapon of choice is a fork."

"Ah. You got her to eat something?"

"Barely two bites. But almost four ounces of the liquid supplement. Mixed-berry flavor—you don't want to know what she said about that stuff. Anyway, I told her I'd give her a break. And have coffee with you. She liked that—said maybe there's hope for me yet."

Aimee smiled despite the ache in her throat; the loving and playful relationship between Lucas and his grandmother—and the threat to it—prodded memories of her mother.

"There's that place down the road," Lucas continued, raising his voice over the *sputter-hiss* of his frozen fries meeting the cooking oil. "Nemo's. Great coffee, but lousy acoustics and packed like a sardine can. I thought I could grab coffees and bring them back here. And we can walk down to the overlook? I should stay fairly close since I'm supposed to get word about a meeting with one of my grandmother's doctors."

"That's perfect," Aimee assured him, with some relief. She wasn't dressed for anything that resembled a date and wasn't ready to start her imagination trotting down that path anyway. Rhubarb and strawberries were all she had room for this week. Along with some take-out coffee. Definitely room for coffee. "I'll finish up here while you eat your burger. Then I'll get out of this uniform and this ridiculous chef hat."

Lucas raised his brows. "The hat is part of the uniform? I thought it was some new fashion trend. I was going to offer you a pair of crime scene shoe covers to go with it and—"

"Careful." Aimee brandished the cooking spatula. "*My* weapon of choice."

CHAPTER NINE

"It's poisonous?"

"Only the leaves," Aimee explained, obviously unaware how amazing she looked with that coastal sun mining the copper in her hair. "The rhubarb stalks are what you eat. The curly green leaves get tossed."

"Unless you're on the chef's hit list."

Aimee shook her head, causing gold to meld with the copper. Her smile over the brim of her coffee cup made Lucas's pulse hike. "Never talk cuisine with a crime scene guy."

"The only time I ever tasted rhubarb was when I was a kid. I thought it was red celery. And smeared it with peanut butter." He grimaced.

Aimee laughed. "Bitter as all get-out. That's why you add sugar." She lifted the glazed scone he'd bought with their coffees. "But probably not more than in these, because I'm mixing the rhubarb slices with fruit—strawberries. Natural sugar."

"The bitter with the sweet." Lucas nodded, gazed out over the spectacular view. Even after a lifetime in San Diego, he never tired of seeing that blue ocean beyond the sand, hearing the soul-soothing sound of the waves. "I'm sure there's some sort of life metaphor there." He met Aimee's eyes again, remembering, like he had late into the night, the sensation of holding her close. "Today I'd rather just think about the sweet. So, rhubarb, sugar, strawberries, and . . . ?"

"Nice try. But no chance." Her eyes narrowed a fraction, and Lucas realized they were the exact color of the sea behind her. "You think I'm going to give you the recipe? How do I know you're not a culinary spy? I'm not about to reveal my secrets."

It was no secret to Lucas that this woman managed to stir emotions he thought he'd set aside. Had no time, or need, for. But holding her last night, seeing her now, only proved his grandmother's often-repeated theory: *There comes a time when you see with your heart.* A week ago he'd seen a beautiful and stubborn young woman working the angles to get herself out of a bad situation. But then he'd seen her kindness, her dogged determination, intelligence, humor, and—

"Not going to admit to recipe espionage?" she asked, prodding Lucas from his thoughts.

"You're safe with me," he told her, glad she couldn't guess

that he'd started to wonder what it would be like to kiss her. Brush that coppery hair away from her face, draw her close, and . . .

"Out of respect for my 'art'?" Aimee asked, the teasing gone from her voice. "You said that about my cooking, called it my 'culinary art.'"

"Yes. I think my grandmother helped me to see a lot of things through that lens. She always talked about spiritual gifts. She said we all have them—God-given talents—and that part of our work here on earth is to discover them and use them for good. She thinks of her painting in that respect. And tells me that my eye for photography is a gift too."

"I agree. On both counts. Though your contemporary olive work was not the least bit inspired." She chuckled, brushed scone crumbs from her lips.

There it was again, the thought of kissing her. *Get a grip, Marchal.* "Does it feel that way to you, too? Cooking, I mean. That it's your calling?"

Lucas didn't expect Aimee's reaction, certainly not a sudden welling of tears.

"I'm sorry," she said, swiping at her eye with the coffee napkin. "I'm fine. It's just that cooking was a huge part of my relationship with my mother."

"No need to apologize. She . . . That's what you meant yesterday, when you said you knew what it felt like to lose someone?"

"Mom died ten years ago. Ten years on Valentine's Day."

Lucas flinched. "She passed away on your birthday?"

"My sixteenth. She was sick for a while, but I don't think you're ever prepared for . . ." Aimee found a smile. "Mom was a school nurse. She always kept an eye out for kids who needed some extra TLC. And food. You should have seen the sack of homemade power bars and fruit she lugged to school. She was an incredible cook, and I was her sous-chef. I think my first bib was an apron." She sighed. "Kitchen time with Mom was the best."

"That recipe for the contest—it's hers?" Lucas deduced.

"Strawberry rhubarb crumble was my favorite birthday 'cake.' I could always count on it. And some daphne."

"Daffy? Like . . . the duck?"

"*D-a-p-h-n-e*." Aimee spelled it for him. "The February birthday flower. She'd find one and tuck it behind my ear, from the very first birthday I can remember. It's pink and white, sort of delicate, and smells like heaven. It's from a shrub that only blooms this month. I guess it's very finicky to grow." Aimee shook her head. "Like rhubarb in Southern California. Thank heaven for the Garden of Eatin'."

Lucas was quiet for a moment, watching her sea-color eyes and thinking there was so much more behind them than he'd ever guessed. "And now, on your birthday, you're fixing her recipe. For the Vegan Valentine Bake-Off."

"Yes. To honor her. And because the grand prize is full tuition for culinary school. I think she'd like to see me do that." Aimee took a breath. "I've been a little slow at finding my calling. And now all of it—the contest, my birthday, the tenth anniversary of losing her, and that dessert—feels like it was all supposed to happen. Like God had a hand in it." She met Lucas's gaze. "Does that make me sound like a crazy person?"

"No." He resisted the strong urge to pull her close, hug her like he had last night. Or maybe Aimee had reached out to him first; Lucas still wasn't sure. He only knew that it had felt right. Felt that way now too. "I don't think it sounds crazy at all. I do believe in a divine plan." He smiled. "And my grandmother would give a big *amen* to that."

"My mother too." Aimee peered out across the ocean. "You're talking with your grandmother's doctor today?"

"Her geriatric psychiatrist. Or I should say, the one that was assigned to her. My grandmother had plenty to say about that, trust me."

"Why a psychiatrist? Unless I'm being too nosy."

"No, it's okay." Lucas fielded the familiar stab of pain. "To evaluate her for dementia or clinical depression. Find a reason for her refusal to eat and come back after the stroke."

"Is dementia possible? I mean, your grandmother seems so clear."

"She does—is—from everything I can see. I think the psych component is part of a standard evaluation in these cases." He hated that his stomach had gone sour. Best to change the subject. "So . . . this dog of Wanda's, what kind is it?"

"A corgi named Potter. Old, from what I can tell. And really friendly." Aimee smiled. "I thought he was going to topple off the tailgate of Wanda's SUV to get to me. Her best friend, looks like."

"My grandmother loves dogs. They had an old beagle until a couple of years ago. My grandfather always talked about surprising her with another one. But . . ." Lucas thought better of restating the obvious. "I'd go out and buy her a dog today if I thought it would help."

"You always hear that animals are good medicine."

They were both quiet for a while, watching the waves in the distance. A gull soared overhead, his lone cry unanswered.

Lucas shifted his weight, drew in a breath. He told himself to just say it. "If things heat up on the abduction case I'm working, the way the authorities think they will, I'll probably be doing some overtime. Hustling between evidence gathering and the hospital. And you've got work, plus whatever you need to do to get ready for that contest."

Aimee's eyes met his, and Lucas almost lost his nerve.

"I mean, it's a hectic week for both of us. And you're probably already doing something for your birthday weekend. But—"

"No."

"No, what?"

"I don't have any other plans for the weekend. My father will call on Saturday—he lives in Orange County now. And my brother will text, probably two or three days late." Aimee shook her head. "First-year medical student at OHSU, Oregon. He doesn't even remember his own birthday. My cousin's working swing shift all weekend. So even if I win, I'll probably just be happy dancing at home by my—"

"I want to take you to dinner," Lucas said in a rush. "Sunday, if that works. I promise I won't pay any waiters to embarrass you with a birthday song. Nothing like that." Either his heart was hammering his ears or a tsunami was about to wipe out San Diego. He was out of practice with this kind of thing. "I like you, Aimee. And I thought it might be good to see each other away from the hospital. You know?"

Her cheeks were his new favorite color again. "Yes."

"Yes, you know? Or yes, you'll come to dinner with me on Sunday?"

"Both."

He stared, the tsunami becoming a warm eddy. "That's . . . great. That's—" his pocket buzzed—"my cell phone. Excuse me a second."

"Sure."

He read the text and then checked the time. "I need to get back to the hospital," he explained. "The doctor wants to talk with me."

"I'm ready." Aimee grabbed her paper trash and coffee, reached for her purse. "I'm sure, like you said, that psych exam was simply routine. I don't think they'll find a problem."

"Right," Lucas said as they started back up the road to the hospital. "Routine."

He thought about taking Aimee's hand, but it was probably too soon for something like that. Besides, would she want anything to do with him if she knew the truth? Today's psychiatric exam wasn't routine. Lucas had asked for it. If his grandmother was found incompetent, it could explain her decisions regarding her advance medical directive—the refusal of IVs and feeding tubes even as temporary measures. Her health was declining. Was Lucas really supposed to stand by and let that happen? Especially if today's exam showed that Rosalynn Marchal wasn't as "clear" as Aimee thought?

A wave of guilt made his gut tense. *Am I hoping for that?*

CHAPTER TEN

"Picking up my paycheck. Not here to work," Wanda explained. "But Potter wanted to walk around the grounds and see people. Didn't you, buddy?" As if to prove her words, the little dog whined and stretched his leash toward Aimee, tail waving like a Veterans Day parade flag.

"Hey there, fella." She knelt on the hospital sidewalk, rubbed the dog's velvety ears as he stretched up to give her a lick. "You look like you're feeling better."

"One more week on the medications." Wanda shifted the leash from one hand to the other, and Aimee caught a glimpse of the bruise on her elbow. It was changing colors, almost an olive green now, Aimee thought, then quickly shoved any reminder of olives aside.

"Then he can stay at home while I work," Wanda added, smiling down at her dog. Once again Aimee was amazed at the transformation in her features. Like that moment the Grinch's heart grew. "Though I think he'll miss the chance to make friends. He's a schmoozer."

"You know," Aimee ventured, chuckling at the corgi's blissful response to a chin scratch, "I'll bet the rehab patients would get a real kick out of meeting Potter. I can't imagine anyone not smiling when they see this guy. And you always hear that dogs are good therapy." She risked a glance up at Wanda, expecting the terse twitch of the woman's lips.

"Rules."

"I've seen patients in the extended-care wing have pet visits," Aimee countered, standing again. A thought struck her. "Mrs. Marchal and her husband lost their dog a few years back. Her husband planned to get her a new one, but . . ." Aimee saw by the pinch of Wanda's brows that she understood the widow's loss. Not the same as her own ugly situation, but she'd suffered too. "Maybe meeting Potter would perk her up," Aimee continued. "And of course, Margie—"

"Needs no perking—*please*!" Despite the aide's attempt at a grouchy smirk, there was an inkling of amusement in her weary eyes. Wanda glanced down at Potter. "I suppose I could slip in the side door, say I forgot something at my locker."

"I suppose."

"Well . . ." The aide reached down and lifted the little dog into her arms. Then shot a pointed look at Aimee between his oversize ears. "*If* I do it, and if I get in trouble, I'll say it was your idea."

"Deal."

Aimee walked across the parking lot to her own car, thinking this was the second deal she'd entered into with this nurse's aide. Both of them a bit of a risk, but maybe some risks were worth taking. Like the baking contest. And . . . She smiled. *Accepting a date with Lucas Marchal.*

✳   ✳   ✳

"It's a cliché, I know," the psychiatrist told Lucas as she rubbed her glasses on the hem of her blouse, "but this really is such a small world." A dimple appeared in the rosy roundness of one cheek. "I have a Rosalynn Marchal oil hanging in my office. I won the bid at a Humane Society auction a few years back. It's an ocean study. The most amazing azure blue, with those two whitewashed chairs on the beach . . . Everyone comments on it. *Peaceful* being the key word."

Lucas nodded; he could use some peace in his small world right now. "Did my grandmother . . . ? Was she able to talk much?"

"She's weak." The doctor glanced toward the doorway of the visitors' lounge as if to assure their privacy. "But we talked. About painting, actually—marvelous for me, since I learned a bit more about my purchase—and then about your grandfather. His illness and her stroke on the heels of that." The psychiatrist slipped her glasses on and met Lucas's gaze directly. "I wouldn't be discussing this without her permission."

"I know that. I respect it. I . . . love my grandmother."

"It shows." The doctor's eyes were kind. "And you're very important to her as well. She doesn't see a conflict between her love for you and her decisions regarding her medical directives."

"Choosing to give up and die?" Lucas knew he sounded blunt.

The doctor was quiet for a moment. "I can understand how it might feel that way. And that her living will puts you in a very uncomfortable position."

"Tell me about it." Lucas's lips compressed. "She seems mentally clear to you?"

"She does. Your grandmother's given this a lot of thought, and not just recently. Though I have the sense that her losses have reinforced what she's always felt was true: that, when the time comes, she's not leaving this world as much as she is 'going home.' I'm sure you know that her faith is a huge source of comfort. And peace."

Lucas dragged his fingers through his hair, struggling to form the words. "Did she say she wants to die?"

"No." The doctor sought his gaze, empathy in her eyes as she repeated, "No. She simply said that, right now, life on earth has lost its flavor. And that heaven is calling."

Lucas frowned. "Well, if you ask me, heaven's got the

wrong number—and I'll do everything I can to find some 'flavor' my grandmother likes. If I have to hire Baskin-Robbins to do a drive-by."

"I hear you." Once again the doctor's expression was full of warmth. The dimple reappeared. "And she told me to expect that kind of reaction. She says that you're a 'science guy,' and you've got to map things out on a spreadsheet to make sense of them. She thinks you still need to learn that there comes a time when you—"

"See with your heart," Lucas said, finishing the thought. "I've heard that a few times before." He drew in a deep breath and released it, trying to convince himself that this was good news. A positive report from a doctor in the midst of too many bad ones lately. "Did my grandmother say anything else?"

"That you shouldn't forget to water her garden."

When Lucas got back to his grandmother's room, he was astounded to see Wanda Clay there. In street clothes—and holding a dog in her arms.

"He loves me!" Margie squealed, giggling as the corgi nudged her pudgy arm with his nose. "See, Lucas? Potter thinks I'm very, very special. He wants my leg to get well so I can hold his leash and—"

"I forgot something in my locker," Wanda mumbled, meeting Lucas's gaze across the room. "I was on my way out. Just stopped in for a minute, that's all."

"Well . . . thanks." He glanced toward his grandmother's

bed, saw her smiling. "Looks like your dog made some friends."

"Always." Wanda jiggled the dog in her arms, and Lucas swore her gruff voice managed a cootchie-coo. "My little man is quite the social butterfly. Aren't you, baby?" Then her terse expression returned. "I'm going now," she muttered, heading for the door.

"Bye, Potter!" Margie raised both hands, waggling her fingers. "Nice to meet you—come back!"

Lucas shook his head as he walked to his grandmother's side. Her Bible was in her lap, and he found himself questioning the mercy in a divine plan that would take both of his grandparents so close together. He could find no peace in that.

"You had a visitor," he began.

"Two." His grandmother's eyes, to prove what a fool he was, were sharper, clearer than ever. "A darling dog. And my grandson's hired gun." She smiled before he could sputter a guilty apology. "Very nice woman. With fine taste. She owns one of my paintings."

"So she said." Lucas glanced toward the bedside table. "Your paintbrushes. Did the aides put them away?"

"I asked them to put the brushes in a sack. So you could take them back to the house."

Lucas's heart stalled. "But I thought you could use them in occupational therapy, while you're learning to do things with your left hand."

"Here." His grandmother reached out, took hold of his

hand. Her skin was soft, thin as the tracing paper he'd used in grade school. Her fingers squeezed his. "*This* is what I want to do with my left hand. I don't want to talk about how many bites of food I took, how much I weighed this morning, what my blood tests showed . . . or how I'll earn a gold star if I take just two more steps with that wretched metal walker." She shook her head and sighed, the snowy braid grazing her sharply prominent collarbone. "I want to talk about *you*."

Lucas lifted her hand to his lips, praying she didn't want to talk to him about funeral homes. "What do you want to know?"

"Tell me what you're doing. Outside of this place."

He shrugged. "The usual. I'm expecting some overtime this week."

"Not at work. I meant, what are you doing for your life?"

"My life?" Lucas repeated. The truth was, he had very little life outside of work and this room. "I'm eating, sleeping, playing a little basketball, watering your flower beds, and . . ."

"And?" His grandmother hunched forward, her eyes squinting a bit as if she were taking aim at a clay pigeon thrown high in the sky.

"Well . . . when I had coffee with Aimee Curran today, I invited her out to dinner. On Sunday evening." Lucas smiled, unexpected warmth spreading across his chest. "I like her, Grams."

"Ah . . ."

There was an almost-imperceptible shift in his grandmother's gaze, but Lucas caught it. She'd glanced at the framed photo: his grandparents, the day of their first kiss. She sank back against the pillow and sighed. "That's exactly what I wanted to hear."

"HOLD OUT YOUR HAND," Taylor chided. "Prove it. I think I see a little nervous twitch."

"No way." Aimee extended her hand and smirked at her cousin. "No trembles. No nerves. Steady as a rock—or should I say steady as a surgeon with a scalpel?"

"Let's not." Taylor grimaced. "You don't want to know the things I've seen."

"You're right. I'm the one who hit the OR floor." Aimee maneuvered the loaded tray cart a little closer to the wall as a clutch of respiratory therapists jogged by, responding to an overhead page to the ICU. "But really, no worries. I've got things under control for the contest. I'm feeling really good about this. Hopeful." She smiled. "About a lot of things."

"I see that."

Taylor's knowing expression made Aimee's stomach dip. It was a new, giddy gymnastic move she'd perfected the past several days.

"Dinner with CSI guy Sunday night?" her cousin asked.

"That's the plan." Aimee sighed. "Unless all these new breaks in the abduction case bring him in to process new evidence. Lucas isn't officially on call, but . . ."

"I get that. But thank God that woman escaped her captor—my heart was breaking for her family and friends. She's finally safe. And if the information she's given leads to an arrest, that will be frosting on the cake." Taylor wrinkled her nose. "Excuse the dessert metaphor. Considering."

"No problem. But that reminds me: I was right; my fridge *is* dying. I could poach eggs in the vegetable bins. I brought my vegan butter to work this morning and tucked it in the dietary cooler. Tomorrow morning you'll bring the strawberries and the miracle rhubarb straight from the farmers' market to me here. I'll add them to my refrigerator stash, safe and sound. Then I can whiz by and get them Saturday morning." Aimee smiled. "I'm bringing my mom's favorite spoon, the orange plastic one with the happy face cutout."

"I remember it." Taylor lifted a brow. "Hey, tomorrow's your last day of bondage to Wanda, isn't it?"

"Right, but . . ." Worry crowded in. "I wish I were leaving in a better situation. I'm afraid things haven't been improving with Mrs. Marchal."

※　※　※

"Hospice?" Lucas shook his head, certain he'd heard the discharge planner incorrectly. "You don't mean like what they do for people who . . . want to die at home?"

"I meant that hospice care could be an eventual option," the woman explained, her dark eyes meeting his. "If your grandmother doesn't want to return to the hospital and her health continues to decline, we can arrange for nurse visits and a home health aide."

"But she beat the pneumonia, and the therapists said it was possible she could regain some strength in her leg. At the very least, be mobile with the walker. And learn to use her left hand." Dread tried to choke him. "She was supposed to get better."

"We all want that, Mr. Marchal. But unless your grandmother agrees to prescribed medical interventions . . ."

"You mean the IVs and the feeding tube." He glanced across the room. A lab technician was trying yet another vein to draw his grandmother's blood. Her frail arms were black-and-blue. "I'll talk with her again and try to change her mind."

"If she's not going to accept further treatment, we can't keep her here. It isn't medically warranted. The only option would be the extended care facility."

"Nursing home," Lucas breathed. "She won't go for that."

The social worker captured his gaze. "She wants to go home."

Lucas had gone out to the patio to get some air when Aimee found him. Just the sight of her—hair free of its band and tumbling over the collar of her uniform, those beautiful, caring eyes—brought a peace he hadn't been able to find all day. Her smile hit him square in the heart. "Hey," he said softly. "Must be dinnertime."

"Your grandmother's tray should be there in a few minutes. I think they switched it out to full liquids tonight." Her brows drew together. "What's wrong?"

"They didn't try to take her for physical therapy today. She's too weak. And she's lost another two pounds. That's eleven in two weeks." For the first time, Lucas found no comfort in the sensible order of numbers. "They're starting to talk about hospice."

Aimee pressed her fingers to her throat. "Lucas, what can you do?"

He shook his head, looked toward the doors to the hospital. "They drew blood again. I'll hear about that tomorrow, I guess. And according to the social worker, the rehab team is going to reevaluate my grandmother on Monday. If things haven't changed—and if she hasn't changed her mind about life support measures—there's no medical reason to keep her here. She'll insist on going home." His throat closed. "To die."

"No. Oh no . . ." Aimee grasped his forearm, her eyes intense. "That's not going to happen. We're going in there right now. We'll double-team her—you handle the soup-spoon; I'll man the juice straw. I'll distract her with tales of my worst kitchen bloopers while you slip her some lime Jell-O. We can do this, Lucas. I promise."

He smiled, overwhelmed by gratitude and the sudden urge to kiss her. "Sounds like a plan."

She nodded, her lips twitching upward at the corners. "We'll flip a coin for Margie."

"Margie?"

Aimee grinned. "I promised her a finger-puppet show if she ate her vegetables."

CHAPTER TWELVE

DESPITE YESTERDAY'S BRAVADO with her cousin, Aimee couldn't deny the truth: she was getting jittery about the bake-off. *Tomorrow.* Her stomach did a swan dive. She stilled the dietary department's chef blade, gazed down at the fingers on her right hand: each nail polished in a different color, the thumb in "Natural Blush." She'd realized, late last night as she re-rechecked her ingredient and tool lists, that her fingers—chopping, measuring, whisking—would be on camera, in close-up. For the whole world to see. Since she had no idea what would look best, she'd tried several colors, then managed an awkward series of selfie videos of her hand in action. But even so, Aimee still wasn't sure which—

"Are you going to use that knife, Curran, or just *think* those tomatoes into neat little slices?" Donny, the grill chef, chuckled, his beefy hands planted on his hips. "I could sure use a stack for my burgers, one way or the other."

"Sorry," Aimee told him, feeling her face turning the shade of her thumb polish.

Donny smiled. "We're all going to be rooting for you tomorrow, kid. You're gonna do fine."

"Thank you." She gripped the knife, pretending her fingernails didn't look like a Skittles spill. "I've got things under control. And sliced tomatoes coming your way, pronto."

"Great." Donny took a step away, then turned to look at Aimee again. "So what are you going to do after cooking school? Work your way up in some of our local restaurants? Or—" one dark brow rose toward his paper cap—"become a top chef on one of those fancy cruise ships? Maybe open your own place? What's the big dream?"

"I . . ." Aimee stared at him, her mind a complete blank. *What's my dream?* Was it possible she'd never thought beyond—?

"No worries." The chef raised his palms. "Didn't mean to put you on the spot. You're young. Plenty of time to find your calling." His grin exposed a gold-rimmed tooth. "First things first, Curran: knock 'em dead tomorrow."

"Right." Aimee drew the knife through the seeded tomato, sneaked a peek at the wall clock. Taylor would have left the farmers' market by now after getting the strawberries and the rhubarb. She'd have put them in the insulated bag and would be driving straight to the hospital. Aimee had already cleared a spot for them in the dietary refrigerator and prepared a paper towel–lined dish for the ripe organic berries. She'd hand-lettered a half-dozen little signs saying, *Aimee's fruit—please don't touch.* In English and Spanish. She smiled, remembering the French word for *strawberry . . . fraises.* And Lucas's romantic story about his grandparents.

They'd managed to coax Mrs. Marchal into taking more than seventeen ounces of fluids from her dinner tray last night, difficult because she seemed especially drowsy. At one point, she even choked a little on the soup. It had brought back too many memories of Aimee's mother in those last, sad days. But still, it was worth it to see some of Lucas's worry recede. He was cautiously optimistic that there would be no need for the doctors to approach his grandmother with the issue of intravenous fluids and feeding tubes; he thought by Monday she'd pull out of this slump on her own. The hope in his eyes had touched Aimee's heart. And though yesterday had been her last shift working for Wanda, she still planned to stop by tonight and—

"Aaagh!" Aimee yanked her hand back from the blade in pain and disbelief. Stared at the blood. Her left index finger, dripping.

"No . . . no." She grabbed a towel, hurried to the sink, and forced herself to hold her finger under the water stream despite the immediate sting. Aimee grimaced, made herself take a quick peek: a slice into the fingertip, blood welling again and making it hard to tell how deep it was. She squeezed the towel against it, her mind tumbling. She'd have to go home; the hospital wouldn't let her work around food with a wound. Would it be a problem with the bake-off? Would she be disqual—?

"Aimee?" Taylor stepped into the kitchen, the market tote bag over her shoulder. "What's wrong?"

"Cut myself—can't believe it. I'm afraid to really look."

"Let me see." Taylor set the tote down and moved toward the sink. "You don't have to look; just let me have it."

Aimee kept her eyes on the hopeful market bag. *Please, Lord . . .* "Is it bad?"

"No." Taylor pressed against the wound with a clean part of the towel. "Sorry; I'm trying to get it to stop bleeding. It's a slice, pretty shallow. Not any place where we need to worry about tendons or nerves." She caught Aimee's gaze. "You're good with your tetanus?"

"Last fall." Aimee hated that she'd begun to tremble. "Will it need stitches?"

"I doubt it." Taylor gave her a reassuring smile. "Some eager-beaver intern might want to try, but I've taped up my own cuts that were bigger than this and they healed fine. It will need a cleanup, maybe some Steri-Strips to close it."

"How about that glue stuff?" Aimee asked, beginning to relax.

"Yes, Dermabond might work. You could ask the doc."

"Oh, good. Because stitches and bandages would show. On camera." Aimee waggled her uninjured and brightly polished fingertips. "The contest is being taped for TV. And I definitely don't want to look like the kind of rookie who can't even slice a tomato without hacking herself up. Everything needs to be absolutely perfect and—"

"Aimee . . ." Taylor winced as if her own finger were sliced. "The Garden of Eatin' farmers weren't there. I couldn't get the rhubarb."

CHAPTER THIRTEEN

C'MON, CALL ME . . . Aimee stared at her maddeningly silent cell phone and drummed her fingers—including the freshly glued one—on her small, seventies-vintage kitchen table. Then she took a slow breath and prayed. *Please, Lord. It's my future. Make this happen with a new recipe.*

Everything depended on getting official contest approval for a substitute dessert. After all, there were baskets of beautiful strawberries waiting at the hospital, and Aimee had a spendy stockpile of vegan butter, nutmeg, organic sugar . . . and a secret weapon: her mother's recipe tin. There *had* to be a winner in there. Aimee would bet her life on that. And she'd find it as soon as she got the green light from the Vegan Valentine Bake-Off coordinator. Nothing would happen without that, and the clock was ticking toward the start of the contest. She'd left a message on the coordinator's phone, let herself believe it could happen. Even that fragile hope was far better than how discouraged she'd been barely an hour ago.

After the urgent care PA glued her finger, she and Taylor had split the list of all the local farmers' markets and driven off in different directions. A futile hunt to find the AWOL Aiden and Eve. They questioned the vendors in all the booths without success. Everyone was surprised that Garden of Eatin' was a no-show; nobody knew why. They all suggested trying to call the farm phone number.

Right. Aimee frowned at the farm flyer lying on the kitchen table next to her. There had been no answer at the farm; she'd left three messages. Then she'd tried to find an alternate source for local organic rhubarb. Not one city market had it. Frozen fruit would get Aimee laughed out of the contest kitchen, but who could make strawberry rhubarb crumble without rhubarb? She'd imagined the embarrassment of telling her family and friends that she'd been disqualified and been certain she'd be doomed to defending olive garnishes for the rest of her life, when the obvious solution occurred to her: she'd find a new, last-minute but completely brilliant dessert idea. All Aimee needed was—

Her heart stalled as her cell phone rang. Then it did an unrelated, but athletically worthy, somersault: *Lucas.*

"Hey," she said, keeping an ear tuned for the call-waiting beep. "What's new?"

"We caught the kidnapper—you haven't heard?"

"No . . ." She glanced at her glued finger and then at her mother's recipe file, not sure if her current situation was an adequate excuse for checking out of the real world. "It's been a little hectic on my end. Does this mean you're working the scene?"

"Two scenes—two camps where he held that woman. Way up in the woods. I'm going to be here for most of the evening. And I don't know when I'll be able to visit my grandmother. They moved her reevaulation up. It's happening tomorrow morning."

"On a Saturday? Why?"

"Because . . ." Lucas hesitated, obvious concern in his voice. "Those last lab tests showed further dehydration and early signs of kidney failure."

Aimee winced. "Oh no . . . I'm so sorry to hear that."

"It's why she's been so weak and sleepy." He drew a breath. "They took more blood today to compare the numbers. I told them we got her to take more fluids, so maybe it's changed. But they still plan to see her in the morning. And recommend that she accept IV fluids, maybe a temporary feeding tube until things turn around. Everything depends on her decision. I'll be there in the morning, but I really wanted a chance to talk with her ahead of time. Tonight."

"And you're stuck there." Aimee sighed, feeling his frustration.

"I thought you might sit with her for a while. Work your magic with the juice straw and maybe encourage her to consider an IV. Would you do that? When you're finished with your shift in dietary, of course."

"I'm not at work; they sent me home. I had a little accident—cut myself."

"What? Are you okay?"

"Yes," Aimee assured him, feeling like an idiot all over again as she glanced down at her glued-together finger. "It's just a small slice. No stitches. But they said I shouldn't work with it."

"Makes sense." It sounded like Lucas sighed. "I guess it will be awkward, physically, to try and manage—"

"It's not only that," Aimee interrupted before he could mention his grandmother again. Guilt tried to arm wrestle her growing anxiety. Why hadn't the coordinator called? "There's a problem about tomorrow. The contest," she explained. "I couldn't get the rhubarb. The Garden of Eatin' people weren't at the farmers' market and aren't answering their phone. The farm is somewhere up in the coastal mountains, and there's no other source for organic, local rhubarb. I have a call out to the contest coordinator to get permission to make a substitution." She rested her hand on her mother's recipe tin. "And then I'll have to find the right recipe and convert it to vegan ingredients. Then do a test run in my oven. And—"

"Sounds like you're too busy," Lucas broke in. Something in his voice suggested he'd heard more than enough.

"I'm really sorry," Aimee told him, guilt getting the upper

hand. His grandmother's kidneys were in jeopardy and she was whining about rhubarb. Of course Lucas would see it that way; he couldn't understand how much Aimee needed to—"I'll call dietary," she offered in a rush, "and talk to the woman who's taking over the tray delivery for me. I know her pretty well. Maybe I can convince her to stay awhile and encourage your grandmother to drink her fluids. And then if you talk to the evening aides . . ."

"Already did that. I do it *every* day, Aimee. You know that." There was a muffled groan. "I wasn't trying to put you on the spot. I thought you were already at the hospital. It's just that I know my grandmother likes you . . ."

"I like her too, Lucas. A lot." Aimee hated that they were having this conversation over the phone; she couldn't read his expression, see his eyes. "I wish I could help, but I'm probably going to be up half the night getting the recipe right and—"

"I get that. Look, I've got to go. The team's waiting."

"Sure. I'll check in with you tomorrow, after—"

"Bye."

Aimee disconnected, closed her eyes for a moment. She reminded herself that she wasn't equipped to offer the kind of help Rosalynn Marchal really needed: medical expertise. The kind of skills that her humiliating failure at nursing school proved she lacked. She was no more than a glorified tray deliverer who'd been coerced into—

Aimee's cell phone buzzed; her heart leaped to her throat as she answered.

"Aimee Curran?"

"Yes," she breathed, recognizing the accent of the contest coordinator, the same man who'd encouraged her in the semifinals. "This is she."

Please . . .

"I got your message. A pity about the rhubarb. I must tell you that it's highly irregular to substitute a recipe. Especially mere hours before the competition. It would be up to the judging team to accept it, and I certainly won't bother them tonight."

"I can understand that, sir." Aimee's shoulders sagged. She was failing again. "I do appreciate your returning my call and—"

"It's irregular, but not entirely unheard of in this particular competition. And of course, the recipe would have to comply with the same vegan, organic, and local requirements. I would suggest that you come prepared to make this substitute dessert. Arrive thirty minutes earlier than the scheduled time."

Aimee's breath caught. "You mean there's a chance?"

"We'll present your proposal to the judging team." The coordinator chuckled. "As Jacques Pépin has been known to say, 'Cooking is the art of adjustment.' Is that not so, Miss Curran?"

"Uh . . . yes, absolutely," she agreed, clueless about the quote, sure her voice was squeaking like a mouse, but still so very—"I'm grateful. So grateful for this. Thank you."

Aimee disconnected, nearly giddy with relief. She'd been

given a chance and she wasn't going to blow it. Tomorrow she'd win the baking contest, secure her admission to culinary school. The beginning of her future.

Her brow furrowed as she recalled what the grill chef had asked her today: *"What's the big dream?"* Donny had said that she was young, had plenty of time to find her calling. And she had found it. Of course she had. Food—being a "rising culinary star" on the fast track to becoming a chef—that was Aimee's calling. And despite today's stumbling blocks, she was back on track. On her way forward.

"Mom . . . ," Aimee said aloud, seeing her mother's lucky spoon among the tools she'd gathered for the contest. She raised the orange plastic implement, smiling back at the silly, cutout happy face. "I'm going to make you proud. I promise."

She set the spoon down and reached for the recipe tin, lifted the lid, and began searching through the index cards. They were faded and dog-eared, some smudged with blotted food stains, and all in her mother's so-familiar looping cursive. A few had stick-on gold stars. Two hundred recipes or more . . . ten times that many precious memories. Aimee's throat tightened. She'd so wished to be able to use the rhubarb recipe. Valentine's Day, her birthday, and the dessert her mother always made: it had all seemed so perfect.

Her heart cramped. Practically perfect—a sprig of daphne flowers behind her ear would have made it truly perfect. But Aimee still had the local strawberries and a second chance now. The answer was here somewhere.

Please, God. Help me find exactly the right recipe.

CHAPTER FOURTEEN

LUCAS FLICKED ON the truck's headlights and continued down the mountain. It was getting dark, and by the time he got back to San Diego, his grandmother would be asleep. Still dehydrated and still in a stubborn mind-set to refuse life support measures. He'd have to go see her in the morning, get there ahead of the medical team and try to talk her into changing her mind. What were the realistic chances of that happening? Why—when it was so important—couldn't he be even half as effective in helping his grandmother as he was in his career?

He glanced toward the equipment lying on the seat beside him: digital camera, lenses, tripods, bindle paper, biohazard bags, the latent print kit, tweezers and forceps, flags, seals, flashlight . . . and boxes for collecting weapons. His jaw tightened as he recalled snapping photos of ropes and duct tape, presumably used to bind the abducted woman. Thank God the suspect had been apprehended before he harmed someone else. Lucas liked knowing he'd play a role in bringing the man to justice by providing the carefully gathered and documented evidence already headed for the crime lab, then probably a courtroom. He liked that he helped to make logical sense of painful chaos, bringing order after tragedy.

If only he could accomplish a fraction of that with his grandmother. Maybe he could have, if Aimee . . .

No. He gripped the steering wheel, reminding himself that he'd done all the brooding he was going to over that. It wasn't fair to blame Aimee. She had no obligation to him or his grandmother. She'd already done far more than necessary to help, even beyond the payback to Wanda. She had every right to pursue her dream. Lucas took a slow breath, remembering their conversation as they sat overlooking the ocean and drinking their coffee. She'd talked about her mother, said that following a culinary career would continue something important they'd had together. Aimee wanted to honor that. She'd said, too, that she felt like "God had a hand in it" because the Vegan Valentine Bake-Off was taking place on the tenth anniversary of her mother's death and Aimee planned to prepare the same dessert her mother always made . . . for her birthday. His stomach sank. Tomorrow was Aimee's birthday and she couldn't make that special dessert.

He slowed the truck, pulled to a stop on the shoulder, hating himself. He'd practically hung up on her—what a jerk. He glanced at the clock on the dash, trying to remember what she'd said about that organic farm. With the crazy name . . . Yeah, *Garden of Eatin'*.

Lucas pulled out his cell phone, opened his browser, and tapped in the name. Aimee said the rhubarb farm was "up in the coastal mountains." That it was anywhere near here was a long shot. And worth a try.

✳ ✳ ✳

Strawberry cobbler, strawberry pie . . . Strawberry Fields Forever cake?

Aimee pulled the pink-smudged index card from the recipe tin, laid it atop the others, and checked the clock. Nearly seven thirty now. She'd have to run to Trader Joe's to grab more vegan buttery spread. And practice berries—the farmers' market strawberries were at the hospital, safe from her gasping kitchen fridge. Then she'd have to whip up the recipe, do the test bake, and pray it worked; there wasn't time for flubs. And then . . . Aimee lifted her hand, frowned at the mismatched polish. She still had to fix that, too. It had been so much easier when a nail polish choice was the biggest problem.

Aimee's eyes swept to the clock again. The hospital dinner trays would have been taken away by now; the friend in dietary had said she'd planned to sit with Mrs. Marchal, but things got hectic and they were short-staffed for kitchen cleanup. Hopefully the rehab aides had gotten Lucas's grandmother to eat. He said he'd talked to them. *"I do it every day, Aimee. You know that."* She flinched, remembering the tone of his voice over the phone. He was disappointed, frustrated. But so was Aimee. If she didn't find the right recipe . . .

She thumbed through the rest of the *S*s, moved on to the *T*s—there could be a strawberry tart or torte . . . but there wasn't. Aimee told herself to stop, settle for the cake named after an old Beatles song, go to the store, and start baking. But . . . *it doesn't feel right.*

She flipped through the *U*s, the *W*s, found nothing in the *X* slot, decided yams were yucky with strawberries, pushed past the empty *Z* tab, then started to close the recipe tin and—

What's that?

In the back of the tin were two sheets of spiral notebook paper, folded into quarters. Not index cards, but . . . Aimee smiled as she saw the gold stars her mother had embellished the sheets with. Tried and proven-winner recipes. But the first one wasn't a recipe at all. It was her mother's handwritten notes for her food ministry, a service she'd provided for fellow church members as long as Aimee could remember. Long enough that at least a half dozen of these people had since passed away.

She scanned the list of food recipients, her mother's notes. Mrs. Campell, she'd penciled, had had a hip replacement, loved sweets despite her diabetes. *Bring light fruit parfait and a new sweet romance novel. Cowboys . . .* Mr. Foster lost his wife the year before and was becoming more reclusive. His appetite was "finicky," but he liked Swedish turkey meatballs. Aimee smiled at her mother's addendum: *Bring a treat for Scottie dog, ask about him. Mr. Foster will relax and eat a little more.* Aimee chuckled. Alice Wheaton had gout, loved chiles rellenos San Jose—*bring Beano. And avoid talk of politics.*

Her throat tightened at the next entry: Melanie Carson, single, first-time mother. Laid off from her job. She could hear her mother's sweet voice in the note: *Bring cheesy chicken and rice and some of that almond lotion she admired. Tell her she's an amazing mother and show her the baby photo of Aimee. Remind her that, even as a mother, she's still God's precious little girl.*

"Mom . . ." Aimee set the paper down, choked by sudden tears. Miranda Curran's notes said it all, revealed her heart. Aimee had planned to take one of these recipes and adapt it to win a contest, while her mother had adapted recipes to *people.* Used her passion, her skills, to bring a smile, boost a spirit, and make a difference, one person at a time. Now that was a spiritual gift, a calling.

Aimee lifted the remaining sheet of paper. Not in her mother's handwriting this time. A faded, printed page. Maybe something her mother photocopied, titled simply "The Recipe":

Take 2 heaping cups of Patience
   1 heart full of Love

2 handfuls of Generosity
Sprinkle with Kindness
Add plenty of Faith

Mix well and spread over a period of a lifetime and
serve everybody you meet.

Aimee read it again as a warm tear slid down her cheek.
She pressed a hand over her heart, closed her eyes, breathed
in the scent of daphne flowers, and heard her mother's laugh,
the sound of her happy-face spoon scraping the side of a
mixing bowl. Her mother's gifts of love. Taylor had nailed it,
only two weeks ago. When Aimee told her about the contest,
how she planned to adapt her mother's recipe to fit the vegan
venue, Taylor reminded her that *"Aunt Miranda was all about
'stirring in the love.'"*

Aimee wiped at a tear, astounded and at the same time
peaceful—and so very certain. She'd sat right here, on the
eve of the contest, her birthday, and the anniversary of her
mother's death, and asked God to help her find exactly the
right recipe. He couldn't have said it more plainly. Patience,
love, generosity, kindness, faith, and . . .

". . . serve everybody you meet."

Aimee pushed away from the table, hefted her purse from
the chair back, and hustled out the door. Then put her car in
gear and headed to the hospital.

CHAPTER FIFTEEN

"I'm glad you called," the breathless Aiden Owens told Lucas. "I was going to sit down and try to return some messages now that things have settled down some. And Evie and our son—" his voice cracked—"are out of danger."

"Danger?"

"Because of his early birth," the Garden of Eatin' co-owner explained. "Sorry; how could you know that? But it's been crazy hectic here at the hospital. And absolutely awesome. His name is Wyatt Cornell. After our grandparents."

"That's great," Lucas told the man, thinking this was the last thing he'd expected. "Congratulations . . . to all of you."

"Yeah. Thanks, man. I'm still wrapping my head around it." He laughed. "And you're probably looking for produce."

"Rhubarb," Lucas confirmed. "It feels weird saying this, considering, but it's kind of an emergency." He relayed the situation briefly, surprised to find that the man remembered Aimee. But then again . . . *how could you not?*

"And the contest is tomorrow?"

"Yes, starts really early in the morning. Aimee's one of four semifinalists."

"We saw the TV clip and were really happy for her. It was gutsy to go with the black bean brownies. But I guess it didn't click that she needs our rhubarb for the finals; or maybe Aimee did tell us, but . . ." Aiden sighed. "Wyatt happened. I'm sorry, but we're way out in La Mesa."

"And I'm up in the mountains. On my way home from a work site."

"Mountains? Where?"

Lucas told him, suddenly daring to hope.

"Awesome!" Aiden whooped. "You're only twenty-five minutes from our farm. Turn left at the mileage sign—our wooden sign is just beside it. The road is paved most of the way, then turns into gravel. It dead-ends into our place."

"Someone there? A farmhand or . . . ?"

"Nope. Just the collie. No worries; she only growls to hide the fact that she's a complete sissy."

"So I can go there now?"

"Right. Got a flashlight?"

"Sure. And a knife—if I need it." Technically Lucas had

been in possession of two knives today. One was sealed in an evidence box now, but this new dad didn't need to hear that.

"No knife," Aiden told him. "You never cut rhubarb to harvest it. That's important. But you'll need that flashlight, and you'll have to follow my directions to find the right field and choose the best stalks."

"I'm listening," Lucas assured. "Is there a place I can leave some cash or—?"

"Nah. This one's on me, friend. Tell Aimee we're rooting for her, and we wouldn't mind if she mentions the Garden of Eatin' to the TV folks."

"I'll do that. Thanks. Hey, this is really great," Lucas added, touched by the man's kindness. "Tomorrow's Aimee's birthday, and she's sort of doing this contest in memory of her mother. The rhubarb dish was something special between them."

"I hear you. And I'm glad we could be part of that. I don't believe in coincidence. Me catching your call just now and you being in that area—sounds like a God thing to me."

"Yeah, maybe so." Lucas thought once again of Aimee's words: *God had a hand in it.*

"Now," Aiden said over the sound of an infant's mewling cry, "let's get you up there."

In thirty minutes, Lucas was at the farm. Or to be more exact, he was trudging in darkness up—and up—the rutted deer path that led to the farthest, most mature, rhubarb patch. After climbing over the chained and padlocked gate the proud new father had forgotten to mention. Fortunately Lucas had worn hiking boots to collect evidence at the crime scenes, and there was a decent amount of moonlight. He was grateful, too, that the collie was as friendly as Aiden had promised, though the geese—guarding the unexpected gate—weren't at all. They'd hissed like serpents in Eden and were still managing a menacing waddle up the path behind him.

"Almost there?" Lucas asked the collie, stopping to aim his flashlight up the path. A cricket chorus joined the hisses. Lucas squinted in the darkness. Aiden had said there would be a small marker designating the mature field and . . . "Ah, there."

He stared the geese down, then followed the collie the remaining dozen yards. Pale moonlight shone on the rhubarb field, sizable green mounds scattered like dome tents at Scout camp. Lucas had snagged a large evidence bag from his kit and shoved a few pairs of plastic gloves inside it. He'd forgotten to ask if "poisonous leaves" meant there was a problem with touching them as well. This off-road adventure would be pointless if he passed out from rhubarb toxicity and was finished off by homicidal geese.

He stopped at a green clump, snapped on the gloves, and focused his flashlight beam. Shiny red stalks, about an inch wide—he was in the right place. Now to . . . Lucas knelt, grabbed a stalk, and gave it a twist at the base, the way Aiden had instructed. It broke off cleanly. He smiled, blocked the collie as she tried to lick his face, and twisted a second one, then a third. He slipped them into the evidence bag. Easy. He'd been told to take no more than four per plant. Aiden thought a dozen stalks, about a pound, should be more than enough for strawberry rhubarb crumble.

Aimee.

Lucas had tried to call her several times, but the cell coverage was bad out here. He wanted to let her know he had the rhubarb, and he wanted to say he was sorry for how he'd been on the phone. Guilt jabbed again. She'd sounded anxious, concerned. And he'd blown her off the minute he'd determined she'd be of no use to him. For his plan. His need to control it all—make sense of his grandmother's situation in the same way he deconstructed a crime scene. Tidy, organized, palatable.

Lucas twisted another stalk, then gazed across the moonlit field, up at the sky. Stars had begun to appear. He took a deep breath of the fresh, loam-scented air and thought of his grandmother. Her garden, her art, her strength . . . and her deep faith. Her humor and gentle wisdom had been a gift to him all these years. *"See with your heart."*

Maybe he'd been so busy trying to control what was happening with her—to save himself from grieving another loss—that he couldn't see the truth: she *was* being "called home." Maybe his stubborn need to hold her here was selfish and unfair. Unrealistic. Maybe, like Aimee was trying to do for her mother with that birthday dessert, Lucas ought to be thinking more of honoring his grandmother by respecting her decisions.

Even if it meant letting her go.

"Lord, please . . ." He bowed his head and whispered around the deepening ache in his throat. "Help me to accept what I need to."

CHAPTER SIXTEEN

AIMEE REACHED San Diego Hope's rehab unit just after the aides prepared the patients for sleep and dimmed the hallway and room lights. Margie was already snoring, a valentine teddy bear hugged tightly against her chubby neck. It was hard to see, from the doorway, if Mrs. Marchal was still awake. But even in the scant light, she looked fatigued and drawn. As Aimee approached, she could tell that someone had applied moisturizing balm to her lips, giving them a faint sheen, and her long hair lay over one shoulder, brushed and secured with a blue ribbon. The tray table was pulled close, her Bible and the French Alps photo within reach of her unaffected arm.

Aimee saw the water pitcher on the bedside stand and wished she knew if Lucas's grandmother had taken any of her dinner. She took a slow breath, remembering her mother's most important "ingredients." *With love, patience . . .*

Mrs. Marchal's eyes opened, then widened as she recognized Aimee. "How . . . delightful." She glanced toward the darkened windows. "It's late for you to be here, isn't it?"

"I'm adapting my schedule. To make time for things that really matter." Aimee smiled and pulled a chair close. "Like seeing you." She reached through the bedrails, gave the woman's arm a gentle squeeze. "How are you today, Mrs. Marchal?"

"Depends on who you ask." The woman sighed. "Those doctors, with all their useless talk of tests, therapy plans . . . If they had a paint palette, it would be nothing but black and gray."

Aimee thought of Lucas's photos of his grandmother's art. "If it was your palette, what color was this day?"

Mrs. Marchal tipped her head, clearly amused. "Paint my day?" Her slow smile was much like her grandson's. "Is this a clever new plan guaranteed to have me jogging the halls and ordering pizza delivery? Did Lucas send you on a mission of mercy?"

"Not exactly," Aimee hedged, feeling guilty all over again. "Pizza wasn't mentioned—or paint." She smiled back at the woman. "But I'll admit, I'd be happy to tell him I found a way to coax you into drinking a tall glass of that berry-flavored supplement."

"Berry?" Mrs. Marchal shook her head. "By no stretch of the imagination. And I still have quite a good one, even if my grandson would prefer to prove that I've lost my mental faculties." She rubbed the weakened fingers of her right hand. "Along with everything else."

"I don't believe that," Aimee told her. "Lucas has nothing but respect for you. And so much love. It's just that . . ." She hesitated, choosing her words. There were boundaries even on a mercy mission. "I think I know how he feels, Mrs. Marchal. I lost my mother when I was sixteen, ten years ago tomorrow. I knew it was coming and that only a miracle could change things. I prayed for that miracle, right until the end." Aimee's throat constricted. "I'd still give anything to have more time, even one day with her."

"Yes." Mrs. Marchal glanced at the silver-framed photo.

"Lucas doesn't want to lose you," Aimee said, lowering her voice as an aide peeked through the doorway. She met Mrs. Marchal's gaze. "He's doing everything he can because, even if he's a grown man, he still needs his grandmother."

"Ah . . . I see. Of course . . ." Mrs. Marchal lay back against her pillow, closed her eyes.

Several minutes passed. Silent, except for Margie's muffled snore and the occasional sound of staff voices down the hallway. Just when Aimee was certain she'd fallen asleep, she spoke again.

"Rembrandt Perm Red," she whispered, a wistful look on her face. "And Aliz Crimson . . . No, perhaps Quinn Red instead of the Aliz. Mix it a little."

Aimee scooted the chair closer. "Are those paint colors, Mrs. Marchal?"

"Oils. The palette I'd use for real berries." She rubbed her weakened fingers again, then lifted her left hand as if making brushstrokes. "French Vermilion and Burnt Scarlet can be lovely. I like a glaze, but . . ." The invisible brush swept the air in fluid, unhesitating strokes. "The layers must be dry. It takes time if you want the berries to look beautifully real."

Aimee thought of the photo Lucas had shown her. Layered blues and reds . . . His grandfather's wool cap filled with—"What kind of berries are you painting?" she asked, barely above a whisper.

"Strawberries." Mrs. Marchal lowered the imaginary brush, and her gaze moved to the framed photo on the tray table. "*Fraises des bois*. Mountain strawberries." She took a breath, let it out slowly. "Louis climbed hours to pick them for me. So small. But so . . ." Her eyes closed a moment, and a smile teased her lips.

Aimee leaned closer. "Sweet?"

"Yes." Mrs. Marchal lifted her fingers to her lips, her eyes soft and her expression almost luminous. A tear slid down her cheek. "They taste . . . like heaven. If only I could . . ."

Strawberries.

"Wait. Don't move. Stay right there," Aimee stammered foolishly, her thoughts racing as she slid from her chair. "I'll be right back. I'll hurry."

It took her ten minutes to find the evening supervisor, three more to convince the woman to open the dietary door, and another few minutes to lift the sack of farmers' market strawberries—complete with Don't Touch signs in two languages—from the refrigerator. That she jogged back to rehab without crushing any of the berries was a complete miracle. The first of two miracles, she prayed.

"I brought you something," she rasped, pulling her chair close to Mrs. Marchal's bed again. "I have something for you."

Aimee reached into the sack, retrieved a basket of Rembrandt Red berries. The scent—sweet as heaven—filled the air scant seconds before two fat berries rolled from the basket and plopped onto Mrs. Marchal's hospital gown.

"Oops."

"You're pelting me with strawberries?" Mrs. Marchal chuckled, her fingers closing around one. "That's your newest plan, Aimee Curran?"

"My plan . . . and my paint palette," Aimee told her, waving the basket slowly under her nose. The scent wafted like sun-warmed hope. "More red for both of us. What do you think, Mrs. Marchal?"

"I think . . ." Lucas's grandmother brought the berry to her lips. Tears shimmered in her eyes. "I think if we're going to sit up half the night eating strawberries together, you should probably call me Rosalynn."

CHAPTER SEVENTEEN

"Miss Curran withdrew her name from the competition," the man explained in a German accent, his spotless white cook's clothing identifying him as an official even without the name badge. "She said something quite important had come up."

"Important?" Lucas shifted the bulky evidence bag. "Did she say anything more?"

"Only that she was sorry for any inconvenience." The man peered at the bag in Lucas's arms. Pale dawn light through the contest kitchen windows caught the ruby color of the stalks. "That's very lovely rhubarb."

"Uh, yeah . . . Well, thank you for your help."

"Please tell Miss Curran that I wish her well." The man

smiled. "I have a hunch we can expect great things from that young lady."

Lucas said good-bye, then tapped Aimee's number into his phone. It went to voice mail the same way it had last night. He checked the time and decided it was too early to swing by her apartment and completely wrong to abuse his resources to track down an address she'd never given him.

"She said something quite important had come up." What did that mean? Had she simply given up on the baking contest because of the rhubarb? It didn't sound like Aimee.

Lucas shelved his concern, drove on to the hospital instead. Hopefully his grandmother was awake and there would be time to talk with her before the rehab evaluation team came by. After those insightful moments last night—while being hissed at by a goose patrol in a rhubarb patch—he'd decided that his only priority was to be his grandmother's advocate. He'd offer loving support of her wishes. Even though he was still holding out hope that this morning's blood tests would show some improvement. . . .

"It's Lucas!" Margie cheered as he crossed the room's threshold. "You're in time for the party. It's been going all night!"

He chuckled, waved, took a few steps in his grandmother's direction . . . stopped and stared. She was sitting in a wheelchair, right arm in a sling, left hand holding a large plastic cup, from which she was sipping with a straw.

"Juice," she told him, setting the cup on the tray table next to something that looked like an empty stack of those green plastic fruit baskets. And maybe one of her paintbrushes?

"Don't look so surprised." Her smile teased as if she'd bested him at skeet. "I was thirsty."

"I . . ." Lucas's heart climbed toward his throat. He wasn't imagining it; there was color in her cheeks and her eyes were clear, bright. "Did they do the blood tests?"

"No." His grandmother waved her hand. "I told them to go away. And I canceled that meeting with the doctors."

"That's right. She sure did." Wanda Clay walked toward the bed, offered a smile that made Lucas wonder if he was hallucinating from rhubarb toxicity. The fact that her corgi was trotting behind her only increased his suspicions. He was toxic or dreaming.

"I'm confused," he admitted. "What's going on here?"

Wanda tossed a knowing look at his grandmother. "Rosalynn talked with the dietitian, and we're trying some new things—starting with breakfast. Your grandmother's feeling a lot better."

"Because of our party!" Margie crowed, waving one of the green fruit baskets. "Everyone had strawberries, even Potter. And everybody's feeling better now. All because of Aimee."

"Aimee?" Lucas asked, his confusion complete. "What—?" He stopped midquestion as his grandmother pointed. He turned to look, and his heart stalled.

"Hi," she said, walking toward them. Her hair looked sleep-tossed, clothes sort of rumpled. "Remind me to bring a hairbrush next time." Her gaze met Lucas's, and the familiar blush rose in her cheeks. She took a soft breath. "Good morning."

"Good morning," he managed, the whole tableau beginning to come together in his head. "I tried to call you last night. This morning too. I got your rhubarb. The Owens baby came early; that's why they weren't at the market. But they let me go in and pick—"

"You did that?" Aimee's hand pressed to her chest. "You went there and got it?"

"Yes. And when I couldn't reach you, I decided to go to the contest kitchen this morning. But they said—"

"I wanted to be here," Aimee told him, a small pucker of her brows asking Lucas to say no more. She turned to smile at his grandmother. "We made good use of the strawberries, didn't we, Rosalynn?"

"We did. Aimee learned a bit about painting, and I came to know some wonderful things about her mother, and that today is this dear girl's birthday."

"On Valentine's Day!" Margie chirped. "Aimee's birthday and Valentine's Day, and she stayed here *alllll* night to help Rosalynn feel better. Oh!" She pressed her hands together, eyes lighting. "You should give Aimee a kiss, Lucas. To say thank-you and happy birthday and—"

"Margie . . ." Aimee shot the roommate a pleading look.

"Happy birthday," Lucas said, tempted beyond reason and not even caring that everyone, including his grandmother and Wanda's dog, was watching. He'd never wanted to kiss any woman more than he wanted to kiss Aimee Curran right this moment. "And thank you, Aimee."

"That's nice," Margie coached. "Now go ahead and—"

"You're welcome," Aimee blurted, reaching out to offer a handshake. "Really, I'm glad I came. But I should go home now and get some sleep."

"I'll walk you out to your car," Lucas told her, his pulse hiking at the warmth of her touch. "I have all that rhubarb in my truck. I'd have no idea what to do with it."

"Right . . ." Aimee cast a wary eye toward Margie, slipped her fingers away. "Okay. Let me grab my purse."

She did that, and they walked outside, each quiet with their own thoughts. Lucas got the rhubarb from his truck and handed it to her, knowing Margie would be disappointed by the lack of romance.

"An evidence bag?" Aimee asked, meeting his gaze for the first time.

"It's what I had. You're lucky there are no feathers or peck marks." Lucas smiled. "Adventures in the Garden of Eatin'." His breath snagged as she reached out to touch his arm.

"Thank you, Lucas." Aimee's eyes grew shiny with tears. "That you did this for me . . . it means more than I can say."

"You did more. Far more." He ached to pull her close. "You gave up the contest, your *dream*, to help my grandmother." Lucas glanced toward the hospital. "I came here this morning to find her sitting up and eating, when only last night I decided I had to accept her choices. I prayed I'd find peace with that."

"I think we both learned some important things last night."

"Yeah." Lucas took a step closer, glanced down at the

fruit-stuffed evidence bag. "Nothing like poor planning—
hug a woman and squash some rhubarb."

Aimee smiled. "As much as I like that idea, I . . ." She
stifled a yawn. "I need a shower and a nap."

He didn't want to let her out of his sight. "That dinner,"
Lucas said quickly. "Sunday—tomorrow. Are we still on?"

"Sure. But . . ." Aimee's eyes captured his over the evidence bag. "Maybe we could get together later this evening
for a while too. It's my birthday, and I just got an idea."

"Sounds good," Lucas told her, thinking nothing could
beat Margie's idea. "I'll spend some time with my grandmother and then call you later?"

"Yes. Around three o'clock would be good." Aimee hugged
the rhubarb stalks closer. "I should be ready by then."

CHAPTER EIGHTEEN

"It's . . . beyond words," Aimee breathed, still mesmerized by the view. "When I suggested having dessert by the ocean, I never imagined this." Her gaze swept from the sunset-pink clouds and azure water to the graceful branches and blooms beyond the driftwood gazebo high on a cliff above the sea. "Your grandmother's garden is . . ." Aimee shook her head and smiled. "Completely the way I'd expect it to be. It's amazing because Rosalynn Marchal is an amazing woman."

"I thought you'd like it."

"I love it."

Aimee's heart skittered as Lucas's blue eyes met hers over the small shell-embellished table. Strings of dainty bulbs cast specks of dancing light over his crisp white oxford shirt. A collection of wind chimes tinkled on the breeze, mixing with the faint strains of classical music coming from Rosalynn's tiny alfresco art studio. There wasn't a more perfect setting for a birthday, a more wonderful way to celebrate it. Aimee smiled as Lucas raised his fork to his lips, savored another mouthful of her strawberry rhubarb crumble with something akin to a deep, blissful moan.

"I've changed your childhood memory of rhubarb?" she teased.

"Beyond that—I've forgotten the geese."

She laughed, still touched that he'd done that for her. Driven so far, walked up that dark path. So like his grandfather, climbing the French mountain to pick—

"The strawberries make it perfect," Lucas told her. "Sweet with the sour. And all this crumbly oatmeal topping . . . It's your mother's original recipe?"

"Right down to the creamery butter. The only adaptation is . . . *me*, what I want to do with all she's taught me. She didn't coach me to be a 'culinary star.' I didn't see that until last night. Now I know what I'm supposed to do."

"You're going to talk with your supervisor tomorrow?"

Aimee nodded. Lucas was referring to what she'd told him earlier: she wanted to become a registered dietitian. She planned to ask her department head about the required course of study for that profession. And also about the Hope medical system's educational scholarship program. For some reason, she felt like it would all come together this time.

"I'm excited," Aimee told him, feeling goose bumps rise. "I know this is what my mother would have wanted. My chance to make a real difference in people's lives."

"You're already doing that. With my grandmother. She said she'd take her paintbrushes to OT this week. And—" he shook his head—"you've made a difference with Wanda Clay. I wouldn't have taken bets on that. But she was grinning like a kid at Disneyland today."

"I know." Aimee smiled, remembering it. "She can hardly wait until Potter is officially a certified therapy dog. She's already talking about visits to the other Hope hospitals. I think Potter's going to remind Wanda why she was called to nursing in the first place—to help people."

"Another thing God had a hand in?" Lucas asked, reminding Aimee of her words back when they were first getting to know each other.

"I'd say so." She nodded. "Absolutely."

Lucas reached across the table, traced his finger across the back of Aimee's hand. "And then there's Margie. Now that woman has a plan."

Aimee's face warmed. "Yes, she does."

"She'd be happy to know I'm having dessert with her favorite princess."

Aimee wrinkled her nose. "Probably best not to tell her. Besides, you promised: no valentines, no birthday fuss. I won't lay that double whammy on anyone."

Lucas was quiet for a moment, holding Aimee's gaze. The brief silence was filled with the distant sound of ocean waves and the tinkling wind chimes. Vivaldi's *Four Seasons* floated from the windows of Rosalynn's studio.

"I do have something for your birthday," Lucas said finally. A smile quirked his lips. "I promise it has nothing to do with hearts and cupids. It's something small, but a big part of the reason I brought you here."

"Now I'm intrigued." Aimee was glad he'd kept hold of her hand. Just that small touch was a valentine all in itself. "What is this gift?"

"You'll have to walk with me." Lucas stood and reached out to take her hand again. "Over there. We'll be able to see the sunset better too."

He was right. They stopped near a little bench just beyond the studio, in a section of the garden that was a Monet canvas of spring flowers: irises, tulips, daffodils, and snow-white dogwood. They looked out over the sea, gone rosy-gold and purple as it yielded to the sunset. Aimee's heart sank as Lucas let go of her hand. Right now, his touch, his kind heart, were the only gifts she needed.

"What are you doing?" she asked, squinting as he plucked at a chest-high shrub a few feet away.

"Getting your gift," he told her. "Which apparently requires a pocketknife. Unlike rhubarb. Hang on."

"Okay." Aimee smiled, perplexed, until the sweet and so-familiar scent wafted on the ocean breeze. It took her back to every birthday she could remember. "Lucas, is that—?"

"Daphne. Your birthday flower." He stood in front of her, holding the sprig like the fragile, heaven-sent beauty it was.

"I had no clue it was growing here. But you told my grandmother. And she told me."

"Oh, Lucas. This is . . ." Aimee's voice cracked. "Nothing could be better."

"Good. Hold still." He reached out, tucked the daphne behind Aimee's ear. Then traced his fingers very gently along her jaw. "It's a pretty flower. But you are far more beautiful. And you've made a difference in my life too. I hope that continues—I want it to. Happy birthday, Aimee."

Lucas took her face in his hands—carefully, as if she were the flower now—bent down, and touched his lips to her cheek. Then leaned back a little to study her face. Waiting, Aimee suspected, for her permission. She smiled, thinking it might scare him to death if she cheered him on Margie-style. She leaned a little closer, lifted her face, half closed her eyes.

Lucas's hands slid toward the back of Aimee's head, his fingers buried in her hair. He drew her into the kiss. Lips warm, gentle, a little tentative at first . . . then, when she responded, far more thorough, claiming her mouth fully. Aimee slipped her arms around Lucas, kissing him back. She wasn't sure if the humming in her ears was her heart or the Pacific Ocean.

"Well . . ." Aimee took a breath and tried to calm her racing heart—to no avail. She tilted her head, drinking in Lucas's beautiful blue eyes. And thought of another couple long ago. "So," she teased, kissing the corner of his mouth, "do I taste like *fraises des bois*?"

Lucas laughed, shifting his strong arms to hike her closer

against him. "Maybe. But I'm the analytical type. I think I'll need another sample."

"That depends."

"On what?" There was the smallest pinch of doubt between Lucas's brows.

"On whether or not we are officially valentines."

Lucas grinned. "The double whammy? You're pulling that card?"

"Of course. She who wears the daphne sets the course."

"In that case, bring on the chubby cupids." Lucas chuckled, his lips already nuzzling her throat. "I'm not worried about arrows. I've survived rhubarb geese. And . . ." His tone grew serious. "I think this is only the beginning for us, Aimee."

"I'm good with that," she whispered, despite the fact that her heart had just bested Vivaldi, string by glorious string.

Everything feels right finally. Thank you, Lord. Thank you.

Aimee wove her arms around Lucas Marchal's neck and returned his kiss, very certain that this happy beginning had all the right ingredients.

STRAWBERRY RHUBARB CRUMBLE

Preheat oven to 350 degrees.

Mix together the following ingredients and put into an 8 x 8–inch ungreased pan:

- 3 cups fresh strawberries, hulled and halved
- 3 cups chopped rhubarb
- 1 tsp grated orange zest
- ¼–½ cup sugar, depending on sweetness of berries

Then mix together until crumbly:

- ½ cup flour
- ⅓ cup rolled oats
- ½ cup brown sugar
- ¼ tsp ground cloves
- ¾ tsp cinnamon
- ¼ tsp freshly grated nutmeg
- ⅓ cup melted butter (may substitute vegan margarine)

Sprinkle crumble mixture over fruit. Bake at 350 degrees for forty to fifty minutes, until golden. Enjoy!

ABOUT THE AUTHOR

CANDACE CALVERT is a former ER nurse and author of the Mercy Hospital series, the Grace Medical series, and the new Crisis Team series. Her medical dramas offer readers a chance to "scrub in" on the exciting world of emergency medicine. Wife, mother, and very proud grandmother, Candace makes her home in northern California. Visit her website at www.candacecalvert.com.

ALSO BY CANDACE CALVERT

Crisis Team series

By Your Side
Step by Step (coming January 2016)

Grace Medical series

Trauma Plan
Rescue Team
Life Support

Mercy Hospital series

Critical Care
Disaster Status
Code Triage

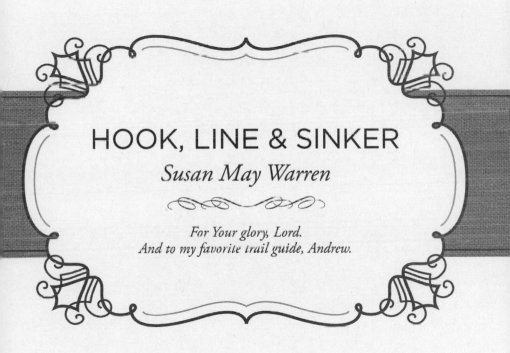

HOOK, LINE & SINKER

Susan May Warren

For Your glory, Lord.
And to my favorite trail guide, Andrew.

CHAPTER ONE

ROSS SPRINGER KNEW he was going into the drink the second Abby Cushman stepped up to the mark, fixed those intelligent blue eyes on the bull's-eye, and let the beanbag zip. *Thwack!* Home run as usual, and Ross landed with a splash in the icy water.

He launched out of the bath with a gasp.

"Did you make her mad?" His bull-sized friend Bucko wore a smirk when he handed Ross a towel.

Ross swiped his face, watching the only girl he'd ever loved strut away. "That's her default expression around me, Buck."

Bucko's eyes danced with tease against his dark face. "You mean I've discovered a female that doesn't swoon and drop into a heap when you walk into the room?" He feigned a horrified look.

Ross threw the towel at him. "How are we doing on funds?"

Bucko shook his head as Ross climbed back onto the platform and scanned the gym. The crowd for the ministry fund-raiser swelled, a loud hum bouncing off the bleachers, the upraised basketball net, and the announcer's booth. Still, he'd have to take a dousing if his group hoped to fill the coffers for next year's events. Ross's evangelistic ski trip to Spirit Mountain in Duluth had netted more fun than funds, and he hoped to leave a legacy as the leader of New Life other than the guy who drained the pot.

Who was he kidding? Even if they lured the entire Bethel College campus, they wouldn't earn enough to pull them out of bankruptcy. Ross sat on the platform, chilled to the bone, feeling like an idiot in his cutoffs and doggy-dried hair. He'd led the New Lifers right into the red. Even if he'd organized the largest youth evangelistic events in college history, handing out blankets and lunches to more street kids than they could count, his leadership would be forgotten faster than the five o'clock news.

So much for his final hurrah. Super senior Ross taking the reins of the New Lifers to resurrect the family name . . . only to grind it to dust. This time next year, he'd be driving one of his father's meat delivery trucks while a new star yanked New Life out of the undertow of debt.

His parents' unspoken prophecies would finally see fulfillment. He'd never be the man Scotty would have been. Even if

Scotty didn't become a famous preacher, he'd had the smarts to take over his father's business as suburban butcher turned businessman. Someone respectable. Someone who didn't fail his second senior year and run the New Lifers into the grave.

Someone Abby could love.

Perhaps even someone God could use for His eternal plans.

Ross smiled, trying not to let despair seep through his expression, and scanned the room, hoping to attract some business. His gaze stopped on Abby—big surprise. He hadn't been able to delete her from his line of vision all year, and even now, with their once-beautiful relationship frayed beyond repair, he felt the familiar rush of grief.

If it hadn't been for his foolish heart buying into campus gossip, she might just be smiling in his general direction, turning his insides to jelly instead of knots. She laughed with her friends, and he imagined the sound of it—hot and sweet, like burning syrup on his heart.

"Ross, get ready!" Melinda stood at the line, a grin on her face, her cornrowed hair piled atop her head. "I have great aim."

"Prove it!" Ross waved his hands, and she botched her first throw. "Double or nothing, Lindy!"

Melinda surrendered another ticket. "Sweet thing, I've been waiting to dunk you since last summer." She wound up like a big-league hurler and pitched the beanbag. Ross heard it thump a second before his bench released.

The water gulped him, and this time he settled on the

bottom. The carnival organizers had thrown in a batch of plastic goldfish, and they whirled around him in spastic circles.

He sprang out of the water with a gasp.

Melinda splashed at him, laughing. "Got ya!"

Ross splashed her back, feeling buoyant for the first time in weeks. No, maybe years. Melinda screamed and jumped away. Bucko tossed Ross a towel as he climbed out of the pool.

"I got an idea." Ross could hear excitement in his voice. And why not? Maybe, just maybe, he might be able to resurrect this pitiful ending to what might have been a stellar senior year and a bright future.

"Yeah?" Bucko pushed Ross toward the platform. "If it includes me getting wet, the answer is no."

"Fishing, Bucko." Ross climbed to his perch. "We're gonna go fishing."

❊　❊　❊

Abigail would dunk him again if payback didn't feel so good. She veered a wide path around the tank on her second time around the gym.

"You about ready to head home?" she asked Laurie, her roommate and fellow grad student. If it weren't for Laurie's dousing of guilt, Abigail would be poring over her doctorate thesis right now—a Greek translation of the book of 1 John.

"You need some cotton candy. Some meat on those bones."

Laurie hooked Abigail's elbow and wove them through the crowd.

Laurie's words stung. Exactly what Abigail needed—another reminder about her all-bones-no-curves body. Just because she happened to like vegetables and exercise didn't make her a candidate for fattening up from her friends.

Besides, she'd long ago given up trying to add curves and liked herself this way.

Well, sorta.

As Abigail stood listening to her friend order for her, she noticed a sizable group flocked around Ross, hypnotized as he hard-sold some idea—probably a crazy, albeit fun, one. The lingering satisfaction of dunking him evaporated when she saw that his burnished blond hair had dried to an enticing, curly mop. A few renegade chunks flopped into those mischievous brown eyes that still had the power to wrap her heart into knots and make her forget her real name.

Abigail Cushman. Not Abby. Not his home-run gal. Especially not Babe, his lucky charm. She turned away before tears burned her eyes. Why had she let Laurie talk her into attending this event?

Well, it wasn't as if she could skip the ministry fund-raiser. The Sojourners, the Bible club Abigail founded two years ago, had their own contest—guessing the number of jelly beans in a vase. But by the looks of the line in front of New Life, the Sojourners might as well divide up the spoils and head home. More bodies, mostly girls not yet vaccinated against Ross's charm, pushed to hear his voice.

"C'mon," Laurie said as her gaze landed on the object of Abigail's torments. "Let's see what's up."

Oh, sure, draw closer to the flame. Abigail shook her head when Laurie wheedled into the crowd and deliberately turned her back, hoping to escape Ross's catchy enthusiasm. "A fishing contest. Up north in Deep Haven. A purse of nearly five thousand dollars."

Abigail cocked an eyebrow. Five thousand dollars? That kind of cash would pay for a new shipment of Bibles for their sister group in Ukraine. She turned, caught Laurie's eye.

"We can even divide into teams, get sponsors, and run our own mini contest," Ross exclaimed over the mounting fervor.

Well, New Life could divide into teams. But the Sojourners had a grand total of six members. Over the past year, thanks to Ross's ski trip, the Sojourners had lost most of their roster to New Life.

But fishing? As in scaly bodies, hooks, and worms? Abigail shuddered. No thank you.

Except . . . She glanced at Ross. He mounted his dunking platform, standing on it like a politician, whipping his crowd into a frenzy. Fishing! Fun! Fund-raising! He bounced on his feet while he spoke, squishing water from his flip-flops, his trademark footgear that had started a yearlong trend on campus. She had the urge to grab another beanie and sink him.

Just like he'd done to her heart.

"Let's do it," Laurie said. "It would be fun. Maybe we can even recruit new blood."

New blood. From New Life. Abigail instantly felt sick

for allowing the thought to tug at her. They were all in this together, weren't they? Neither the Sojourners nor the New Lifers had the corner on evangelism. Still, watching the tide grow as if Ross were some sort of movie star—and it didn't hurt his reputation as campus catch when he turned on that million-watt smile—sharpened Abigail's competitive edge. One last fight to prove to herself, her college, her family . . . to Ross . . . that she wasn't the dowdy, all-brains-no-fun girl glued to her Greek book. That God could use her too.

A fishing contest.

Brains versus beauty.

And to think she'd once briefly dreamed she belonged in beauty's arms. She glanced at Laurie. "Yeah, maybe. Find out what you can."

Laurie melted into the crowd, smitten by Ross's magical power.

Abigail shook her head, dumped her cotton candy into the trash bin, and headed back to her apartment.

CHAPTER TWO

"You want to take a bunch of unseasoned college students on a fishing trip to raise money?"

Ross looked up from his studies into Melinda's soul-spearing brown eyes. "Yep."

"Then I'm going to state it loud and clear so we're moving to the same music." Melinda leaned over the lunch table, her red fingernails clicking. She looked like a Hawaiian princess in a turban and orange floral-print muumuu. "I don't touch fish. I don't cook it, clean it, or pull any ugly hook out of its mouth—noway, nohow."

"Noted."

"And the no-touching rule includes worms, leeches, and any other kind of gross and slimy fishy-type bait."

"Got it." Ross glanced at his Greek book, painfully sure that even if he hot-glued his head to the pages, he hadn't a hope of imprinting the words onto his brain for his final exam.

"You feeling okay?" Melinda sat beside him and pressed her hand on his forehead. "You're not sassin' me."

Ross hung his head in his hands. "I've wised up. You know everything, Melinda."

His words only half kidded. Nearly finished with her master's in child psychology, Melinda had a job lined up at Elisha's Room in New York as a youth counselor for the homeless, a job Ross would give all the teeth in his mouth for. He'd nearly landed the position, highlighting his two-year stint after his junior year serving with Youths in Crisis in Mexico in lieu of a diploma. In the end, however, they wanted brains as well as savvy. Something he obviously didn't have. He already felt like the class dunce, being three years older than every other senior.

It seemed downright unfair that his desire to reach the lost youth of the new millennium would require a bachelor's degree.

Melinda laughed, her eyes sparkling. "Such a smart boy. Well, I don't know how you got the dean of students to jump aboard your idea nor how you talked the Wellbridge Group into offering a matching grant to the winner's purse. That's a fine bit of fund-raising, Springer."

"Finesse, my dear Lindy," Ross said in his most-likely-to-succeed tone. She didn't have to know that he'd called his father with a proposal to fund the contest and received a direct line to the Wellbridge president, a personal friend of Ronald Springer. For now, his father was in the dark, and Ross was still in his good graces. But then again, what choice did his father have, really? He had one son left on whom to pin his hopes.

"And you know how to fish, right?" Melinda asked.

"Piece of cake." Ross closed his book. His eyes felt crossed, and the pitch-black filling the cafeteria windows didn't help. "Speaking of food, is the café open?"

As Melinda glanced at the clock, Ross spotted Abby sitting across the room. She rose, tucked her bag over her shoulder, and started toward the door. Her gaze didn't even skim him.

He remembered the day he returned from Mexico. She actually glowed—her eyes, her smile, her entire being—when she saw him. His throat thickened. She looked stunning today in light-brown dress pants and a sleeveless white top. Tall, elegant. Perfect. She was tan—probably from all those hours sitting on the lawn studying—and the sun had raised the highlights from the depths of her brown hair.

It nearly turned him deaf as Melinda continued her monologue.

"So we get up there on Wednesday and fish until Sunday? Where are we going to sleep? After last summer, I swore off tents, thank you. What about Noah? Does he know we're . . . ?" Her voice faded.

Ross glanced at Melinda. She'd caught him watching Abby leave through the double doors.

"Still nursing regrets?"

He forced a smile. "I don't know what you mean."

"It's not a sin to like her, you know. Even if she was Scotty's girlfriend."

Ross opened his mouth, intending to deny his feelings.

But Melinda smiled and touched his hand. "Just because he's dead doesn't mean you have to stop living."

✻ ✻ ✻

Laurie strode into the library looking like she'd reeled in the winning walleye. "I got everything we ever need to know about fishing." She plopped her backpack onto the table with a smack and began pulling out books. "*Fishing from A to Z. The Quintessential Fisherman. Bait and Lures Encyclopedia.*"

Abigail picked up one of the books. "*A River Runs Through It?*"

"That's recreational reading to get us in the mood."

Abigail sighed. Her synapses must have been misfiring when she'd registered the Sojourners for the contest. Just because a few old members surfaced from the dusty rosters didn't mean their ranks would swell or that they had a prayer of winning. She pushed the books away. "I don't know, Laurie. I haven't the foggiest idea how to fish."

"So?" Laurie pushed the book back. "Miss Straight-A Student can't learn? Girlfriend, you are the one who told me that anything I needed I could find in a book." The wind had teased Laurie's kinky reddish-brown hair but left a nice glow in her green eyes. "C'mon. It'll be fun. Remember fun?"

Uh, actually, no. Abigail hadn't had fun since the day she spent with—

"And I hear that they're having other contests too. Like the largest walleye, northern pike, and the most crappies." Laurie raised her eyebrows as if Abigail had the slightest idea what she was talking about and should be impressed.

"Crappies?"

Laurie dug out a slightly crumpled green flyer from her backpack. "And they're having a cook-off. Best shore lunch batter."

"Gross."

Laurie's face fell. "Please? I know it'll be fun. A final fling."

"Our only fling."

"Yes, but final. As in, I'm going home to Sioux Falls and you're going—"

"No, I'm staying here. They offered me an assistant professor position."

"What?" Laurie's voice rose, eliciting a chorus of hushes. She leaned closer.

Abigail smiled. Just when she'd decided life wasn't fair, that she'd have to move home and listen to her parents wax eloquent about her sister's handsome, accomplished fiancé, she'd been rescued. *Thank You, God.* She'd begun to wonder if the Almighty even knew she was down here. She certainly wasn't making an impression so far. "Assistant professor. Greek and Hebrew department."

Laurie high-fived her. "Way to go. Guess you'll be tutoring all the summer school flunkies then, huh?"

Abigail shrugged. As long as she was employed. And busy. Preferably too busy to let the wedding invitation, now shoved deep inside her Greek verbs dictionary, do serious damage to her self-esteem. Too busy to be hurt that her sister had asked her to be a personal attendant rather than a bridesmaid.

Just because God had given her beautiful, talented younger sister an adoring fiancé who relegated Abigail to an afterthought in the wedding party didn't mean He'd forgotten her, right? Twenty-eight wasn't too old to find the perfect man—even if it felt like that at Bethel Bridal College. Except she wasn't looking. She liked her life, her dedication to splicing ancient languages and discovering God's treasures within His own words.

"So that means you'll be tutoring Ross," Laurie said through Abigail's thoughts.

Abigail blinked at her. "What?"

"Word has it he failed his Greek final."

Abigail kept her face stoic. "Interesting."

Laurie glared at her. "Why don't you just tell him the truth and end this charade?"

What truth? That he'd skewered her heart the day he walked out on her at Scotty's funeral? Or that he'd stomped their relationship to a pulp a month later when he accused her of loving Scotty instead of him? Or that he hadn't once, not in a year and a half, mentioned the fact that he'd declared his love? Had he been lying to her even then?

There was a reason she preferred her books to men. Her Greek book didn't make her want to hide in a closet and cry.

"What charade?"

"Oh, please." Laurie shook her head. "The guise of grieving girlfriend. You and I both know that you never loved Scotty the way you love Ross."

"Shh." Abigail leaned close, her voice tight. "Oh, thank you for that news. I was just waiting for the right time to announce to the entire campus that I was hanging around Scotty to get to his brother."

Laurie went white, and Abigail felt sick. Despite her sarcastic, arsenic tone, every word was horribly, bitterly, unforgivably true.

Scotty had been a friend—not a boyfriend, but it looked that way. Only Scotty knew that she accompanied him home on the weekends not to visit her family or even to study with him, but to attend Ross's baseball games and bankrupt him in Monopoly. Around Ross she didn't need the academic accolades to feel special, didn't have to carry a book like a portable friend. Around Ross, she didn't feel like an afterthought. In fact, she'd believed that perhaps she'd been Ross's main thought.

At least until he took Scotty's place on the campus hotshot list.

"I'm sorry," Abigail said softly and touched Laurie's arm. "I'm just—"

"Hurting." Laurie took her hand. "Let's go to the contest. Maybe in Deep Haven, away from the campus, you'll find a way to make peace, if not friends."

Abigail dredged up a smile and the smallest of nods. But she knew the truth now, even if she hadn't then. Ross wasn't the thirteen-year-old boy she'd fallen for when she'd socked him in the eye with a baseball. She'd never be able to keep up with this charismatic Ross nor muscle through his harem.

Most of all, she wasn't about to love a man who considered her only one of his adoring multitudes.

CHAPTER THREE

"A FISHING CONTEST in the woods of Minnesota." Ross stepped out of his SUV. The fresh air of Wilderness Challenge, a camp nestled in the northern Minnesota landscape, loosened his taut nerves. "I can nearly smell the fish just waiting to jump onto my hook."

"You're gonna have to unpack first." Bucko tossed a sleeping bag at Ross, hitting him on the shoulder. "Hello? Stop smelling and join your team please."

Ross ignored him and headed toward the lodge. "Noah?" Last summer, camp director and youth pastor Noah Standing Bear had answered God's call to drag inner-city kids to the life-changing terrain of the forest. Ross served as a counselor during its first season. His chest tightened at the memory of trying to teach street-hardened kids the truths of the gospel.

They'd barely escaped with their lives.

"Noah?" he called again.

The screen door to the lodge squealed open, and the subject of Ross's thoughts tromped out to the porch. Noah grinned and wrapped his huge grip around Ross's hand. The Native American, the size of a small grizzly, might look like he could scare a kid into salvation, but God had gentled him into a man with the touch of Christ.

"You made it." Noah surveyed Ross's motley group of wannabe fisherpersons, now unloading their sleeping bags, crates of food, and donated fishing tackle. "Are you ready for this?"

"I hope so. You're going to give me pointers, right?"

Noah made a face. "Pal, if you're depending on me, you're going to be eating peanut butter. But don't worry. I hooked you up with a champion fisherman. He should be here anytime."

Noah waved to Bucko. "I have to take off tomorrow morning for a meeting in the Cities. You'll have to hold down the fort." He gave a one-armed hug to Melinda. "You're looking mighty fine, Lindy."

The fact that Noah could make Melinda, a woman who'd spent her youth shrugging at colorful remarks from the hoodlums in her school, blush told Ross that Noah could still turn a girl to mush. Why couldn't Ross do that? Sure, he had no shortage of friends, but the girl he really wanted was about as susceptible to his compliments as a sunbaked Egyptian brick.

Noah turned to Ross. "Okay, I housed the fellas in the A-frame and the ladies in the cookshack. Even with the other group, there should be plenty of room."

"Other group?" Ross felt slightly ill.

Melinda frowned. "Uh-oh. I forgot. I gave the Sojourners Noah's number. It only seemed right. They're such a small group."

"They're the competition." Ouch. He didn't mean to sound petty, but still, weren't they trying to win?

"They're fellow fishermen. We're here to have fun, right?" Melinda gave him a one-eyed frown that could make a weak man tremble.

Ross nodded.

She smiled slowly. "Oh, I know what this is about. Listen, she probably won't even show up. I can't imagine that fishing is her sport."

Ross closed his eyes and shook his head. "Oh no, Lindy. Anything she can beat me in . . . that's Abby's sport." Behind his eyes, he saw Abby laughing, the sunset to her back, tease in her eyes as she choked up on the bat and prepared for a grand slam. "No, making me feel like loser scum is her absolute favorite thing to do. She'll be here. Or I'll clean the outhouses for the entire week."

* * *

"Are you sure you're not lost?" Laurie leaned over the Rand McNally atlas on her lap, her nose nearly touching the page.

"I think we were supposed to turn back at the little bear holding the Gunflint Trail sign."

"Until he's six-foot-something and waving semaphores, I'm sticking by the directions Mr. Standing Bear gave me."

Laurie shook her head. "You gotta learn to let go, live the wild life."

"Oh yeah, right. With a quarter tank of gas and the sun nearly gone? No thanks."

Abigail hung an elbow out the window of her rusty Honda and let the snappy Lake Superior air tangle her hair. The scenery had the magical ability to snare her tension and leave her feeling strangely emptied. New. Similar to the smell that emanated from her gear—a sleeping bag, tackle box, and hiking boots. She'd even found a fishing vest and filled it with a tidy list of supplies—clippers, Polaroid glasses, insect repellent, a fishing knife, and a compact Windbreaker—everything Wally at the SuperSports shop had suggested after their "fishing basics" class.

She glanced in her rearview mirror. The other carload of Sojourners—three ladies and a guy named Simon—was glued to her tail. In her backseat, the stacks of bookmarked how-to fishing books had scattered onto the boxes of MRE lunches and Tuna Helper. She'd also surfed the Internet and found a shore lunch batter recipe that just might make the judges' mouths water.

If she decided to enter the contest, of course.

Excitement felt like a fresh breeze through her soul. Her professors, the dean of students, and even the campus newspaper had adopted Ross's fishing idea as if he were the maestro of marketing. Still, after delivering her Greek thesis, she'd hunkered down and absorbed the advice of fishing masters and for the first time thought, yes, perhaps she could win this contest. Maybe not haul in a muskie but land a keeper that would prove she could keep up with the New Lifers and stop her paltry group from disintegrating.

She'd started Sojourners with a desire to see students learn the Bible, believing that a solid knowledge of the Scriptures gave power to evangelism. However, the New Lifers seemed to attract students like walleyes around a school of juicy cisco, despite her exegetical efforts.

She couldn't deny the lurking fear that two days into this excursion she'd find Laurie and the other members of her group singing "Kumbaya" around the New Lifers' campfire. Leaving her alone at her own dying blaze, with her in-depth Bible study of 1 John, trying to have a scintillating theological discussion with the raccoons.

And Ross would be right. She had about as much charisma as a hermit crab. The girl who surrounded herself with books. Her shell of an organization would crumble the minute she vacated.

She stomped down the accelerator and saw the County Road 14 sign fly by.

Laurie pointed at the dirt road snaking up into the pine-shrouded hills. "Our turn?"

Abigail sighed, found the nearest driveway, and turned the car around, hoping that she hadn't also overshot her abilities.

She pulled into the courtyard of the Wilderness Challenge camp. The magenta sky outlined the dark lodge, save for one yellow light pooling gold on the steps. Abigail turned off the car and climbed out, amazed at the sudden calm. The crickets buzzed, and a breeze rustled the birch and pines. "Hello?"

Abigail rubbed her arms. The impulse to dive into the car and abandon this very bad idea, this leap into Ross's world, nearly possessed her legs. She had to muscle them up the steps. She paused, then opened the door.

Her heart stopped in her throat.

Ross sat at a long wooden table, a kerosene lamp illuminating his unruly blond hair. He studied a map, his long fingers tracing a line and his lips moving as he talked to himself. It took her back to a memory of his freshman year, the time she'd caught him memorizing the lineage of Christ before his New Testament survey class.

He looked up.

Her breath caught. In his eyes was a look that made her forget he'd stomped her heart to a pulp. A look that always had the power to render her weak and make her believe she alone knew the one truth that lined the secret pool of his heart.

Fear.

CHAPTER FOUR

Ross HADN'T INTENDED for the fishing contest to hook Abby. Still, his breath skipped at her outline in the doorframe of the lodge. The woman had the ability, even as a teen, to knock his heart to his knees, and that power had only intensified with age. His lamplight illuminated her shock, then the sudden armament of her emotional defenses. She looked ready for battle in a pair of hiking boots, a down vest, and her long, beautiful, dark-coffee-brown hair in braids.

He cleared his throat, hoping to swallow back any trace of her effect. "Hey."

She opened her mouth, and he braced himself. He certainly didn't deserve anything civil after the jerk he'd been following Scotty's accident. It took him nearly six months to figure out that she'd needed him and that he'd treated her with the gentleness of a boar. Even if he'd been mistaken about her feelings for him, she didn't deserve the way he drove a stake through their lifelong friendship. He'd hoped for this moment when he might—

"Is anyone here?" Laurie burst in behind Abby. "Oh . . . hi, Ross."

"Hi, Laurie. Everyone is down by the campfire. I'm just . . ." He looked at the map he'd been studying and quickly donned the good-ole-boy smile that had brought him campus notoriety. "Goofin' around. C'mon in." He stood, and his heart fell when Abby turned and walked out the door. Laurie shrugged and took off behind her.

The door slammed, and Ross stood in the quiet lodge, regret knotting his chest.

Well, he hadn't spent every waking moment of the last three weeks putting together this fund-raising fling to try to earn Abby's forgiveness.

Who was he kidding? He'd been working for an entire year to figure out how to erase his caustic words. They'd been spoken in grief. In misunderstanding. In stupidity. *Tell me the truth. You were in love with Scotty, not me.* Even now, listening to his voice and seeing her crumpled face in memory made his stomach churn. *I should have known better.*

He took a deep breath and gathered the map. He heard Abby's voice outside, giving directions to her friends, shortly drowned out by others. It seemed the entire New Life crew abandoned the campfire to help the Sojourners unpack. Ross snuck out the back door and down to the empty campfire pit. A loon's call echoed, and the smell of burning wood drew him close. He stared at the flames, mesmerized.

"You okay, Ross?" Noah sat on the third tier of the ring of benches, with his feet propped up. He wore a flannel shirt, his huge arms hanging over his knees.

Ross shrugged. "Just regret."

Noah hummed. It invited exposition. Ross sat, his back to Noah, staring at the blanket of stars. "Do you ever feel trapped? Like you're watching your life from the outside, wishing you'd made different choices?"

Behind him, Noah murmured understanding.

Ross took a deep breath. "Don't you wish you could just start over? Be someone different?"

"I did." Noah moved to sit beside him. "Remember who you're talking to." He gave a wry grin. "I'm still trying to outrun my past." He glanced at Ross. "Is this about your brother?"

Ross sighed. "Let's just say that my life derailed the day he died. And now I don't know where to get back on."

Noah picked up a stick, pushed it through the coals. "You're feeling lost?"

"I'm feeling like I'm in someone else's body. The things I want to do, I don't do, and the things I don't want to do, I do."

"That's a pretty common problem."

"No, I'm serious, Noah. I say these things and I think, *Don't say that.* Or I see her standing there, and more than anything I want to throw myself at her feet and tell her how sorry I am."

"Her?"

Ross looked away. Her. The only person who made him feel like he wasn't second best. Until, of course, he discovered that he was. "That didn't come out right."

"I think it did." Noah's stick caught fire, blazed. "What are you sorry about?"

For betraying a friendship that had made him feel brilliant and wise and exactly the person he was supposed to be? "For not being Scotty."

Yes. He was most sorry for not being the one man Abby truly wanted.

✳   ✳   ✳

Why had Abigail ever thought she could drive a boat, find the perfect fishing hole, bait her hook, cast, and reel in a keeper? She stood outside the knot of students, listening to Noah Standing Bear outline the rules for the contest, her heart sinking into her boots.

"You'll be fishing in teams of two or three. Each night, you can enter your largest fish for an official weigh-in. We'll keep track of each team's totals for each species. On Sunday, the appropriate prizes will be awarded, contributed by your school's donors; then the total weight will be submitted to Deep Haven's contest."

Abigail mentally calculated the parameters. They could

enter six walleye, three northern pike, six smallmouth bass, six largemouth bass, and one muskie, with a minimum size limit of forty inches. The thought of hauling in a fish that just might bite her gave her the willies.

"We'll eat the fish you don't enter into the contest," Noah continued. "The rest will be marked and put on ice for validation by the Deep Haven judges."

Fish for dinner each night? Yes, she enjoyed an occasional walleye fried in butter, but . . . Abigail exchanged a look with Laurie, glad she'd brought along granola bars.

"You'll each be assigned a fishing boat, courtesy of Trout Lake Outfitters. You'll have to stay on the Trout Lake chain of lakes; we don't have ample trailers to haul you all over the Boundary Waters. At the Trout Lake landing, you'll find a bait shop with leeches, crawlers, and minnows."

Laurie wrinkled her nose and grimaced at Abigail.

"Weigh-in is at seven each night. If you pull in after that, your catch is ineligible." Noah motioned to a sturdy-looking man standing behind him. "Pastor Dan Matthews from Deep Haven will be running the show. Any questions or complaints can be directed to him. I know we're getting a late start, but you have three days to get your catches in, and the clock starts now. Happy fishing."

A low murmur broke out as the crowd loosened.

"What now?" Laurie asked. She looked particularly "fishy" this morning in an angler's hat complete with lures, insect repellent, and wet wipes shoved into the loops around the brim.

Abigail waved to Simon and the three other Sojourners

who seemed to be gravitating toward a New Lifer's strategy huddle. "Listen, gang, I studied the map and I think we need to break into groups. We don't have the numbers the New Lifers do, but we have smarts." Out of her peripheral vision she caught Ross with his usual entourage of fans, dressed to kill in a pair of Levi's and a brown sweatshirt that turned his hair to gold. "We must be specific if we hope to win. Heather and Becky, you fish walleyes. They're going deeper this time of year as the day gets hotter. Simon and Esther, you fish bass. You'll find them by the reedy areas. And Laurie and I will hunt down the northern."

Her little group gaped at her like she'd spoken Dutch.

"Did you pay any attention to Wally at SuperSports?" Abigail asked, dodging a wave of panic.

Esther nodded. "Enough to know that I haven't the foggiest idea what I'm doing. I thought we were going to come out here, sit around with a pole and a minnow, and fellowship." Her gray eyes widened. "But you want us to catch something?"

Abigail looked at her team. "Uh, no. Actually, I want us to win."

Heather gave an incredulous huff. "No, seriously, Abigail. We haven't a prayer of winning. Look at those guys."

The New Lifers did seem outfitted for combat, each armed with a small tackle box and a conventional fishing pole as they headed down the trail to the Trout Lake landing. Laughter drifted back to the horrified Sojourners.

"Don't let them scare you. We have great equipment. Wally outfitted us for everything. We have twenty-pound rods with fifteen-pound test lines, about thirty different kinds of lures—crank baits, poppers, chuggers, plastic worms, spoons, spinners, and jigs. Plus, we actually know what we're doing. I distinctly remember spending one evening with you all tying blood knots, surgeon's knots, and haywire twists and an entire day of hands-on practice, digging hooks out of the foliage. Heather, you were nearly beheaded by one of Simon's casts! Most importantly, I sent each of you a detailed map of Trout Lake, outlining how to read the water and where to find the fish. Please, please tell me that you paid attention!"

Heather gave a wry smile, but her gaze tracked the last of the New Lifers tramping up the path. "I thought . . . well, we were just going to have fun."

Abigail's fear took a swipe at her public-relations skills and pitched her voice high. "No fun. We're here to fish!"

Even Laurie stared at her as if she were possessed.

Abigail turned away, weak with frustration. Oh, joy. Ross was watching her from his pickup. He'd draped a green poncho over one arm and held his fishing rod like a spear, looking every inch a forest warrior. Her heart lodged in the center of her throat. Then he smiled. The kindness in it swept tears into her eyes. Even as a child, his smile could dupe her into feeling they were in a room alone. She yanked her gaze away, angry at the feelings churning in her heart.

The Sojourners had abandoned her, heading up the trail with their tackle and fellowship. She watched them go, despair a sinker on her heart, dragging her to the bottom. *Good girl, Abigail. Way to win friends and influence people.*

CHAPTER FIVE

A DAY OF ANGLING never failed to find that quiet place in Ross's soul. The golden sun parted the water like the road to El Dorado, and Ross closed his eyes to the lap of waves against his boat, listening to the plop as fish surfaced or the echo of laughter across the lake. Deep inside, he knew that even if the New Lifers flopped, his idea was a winner.

The sun bronzed his face and heated his bones as he listened to Bucko recount the date he'd had with Melinda. At the same time, he couldn't help dreaming of the look he'd seen on Abigail's face this morning. Surprise. Vulnerability. He'd inadvertently stepped into a private, painful place and slipped a smile under her defenses.

And for a moment, she'd smiled back.

It had put the first blink of sunshine into his day.

The second had been the old geezer bobber-fishing near the boat landing.

"Whatcha huntin'?" The man, predictably dressed in a pair of high-top boots, loose-fitting khakis, a faded flannel shirt, and a cap with the name of a grain company, edged over to the boat and eyed Ross's tackle.

"Anything I can get." Ross loaded in the box of crawlers he'd picked up at the bait shop. "Walleye, maybe."

The man chuckled. "Stay along the weed beds and fish crawlers while they're fresh. Then, if the sun gets too hot, switch to a crank bait and send it deep. Your walleye are going be following their prey—the cisco and tullibees—and you want to be on their tail."

Ross nodded.

"The thing about walleye is that they're lazy fish. You gotta go where they're hanging around waiting for a snack."

Ross thanked him as he pushed away from shore, grateful that, although Noah's expert had failed to show, God had provided a guide. Just maybe the Almighty would help Ross piece together the shambles of his college career before he began his fruitless future. He only wished he could be the man God needed to answer the calling in Ross's heart.

Ross landed two beautiful walleyes within the hour. And the three crappies, two smallmouth bass, and a decent-size northern only improved the day.

The stringer line scraped now and again against the boat.

"Melinda told me you and Abigail have a history." Bucko spit out a burst of sunflower seeds. They floated on the water.

"You gotta lean back and get more breath if you want good trajectory," Ross said, cramming a fistful of seeds into his already-raw cheek.

Bucko grinned, looking like a squirrel with his wad of snacks. "Quit dodging. I see you two. You get near each other and I can smell enough fuel to power the space shuttle. I'm afraid to see what would happen with some sparks."

Ross played with his line. "She's an old friend of the family."

"I've got one!" Bucko jerked hard, setting the hook, then stood and started reeling. "Grab the net!"

Ross watched as the big man played the line, then helped him net the catch, a pretty northern.

Bucko seemed to have forgotten his question, but Ross's memories lingered as he waited for his own lucky strike. Abigail in braids, playing kick the can in their neighborhood, tagging him free and setting his spirit alight with those playful eyes. Of course, even then, he worshiped her. After all, she was Scotty's age, and she'd never given a serious look in his direction.

Until junior high, when suddenly she showed up for his Little League games, even hanging around for batting practice. "Hey, Abby, betcha can't hit it over my head!" he'd called, backing into center field. She'd delivered a shiner that swelled half his face. He never regretted it nor the sympathy in her eyes. "Don't hold back on my account," he teased, and when she kissed him on the forehead, he nearly cried with the rush of emotions. "You're my home-run gal, huh?"

No, Bucko didn't need to know that in his sixteenth summer, he dubbed her the Babe, his batting buddy and secret good-luck charm. She'd been a freshman in college, coming home on the weekends with Scotty to visit her family. And secretly him. Those were the days when he didn't ponder her motives, just enjoyed the fact that she attended his three-season events—football, hockey, baseball—and lived for the sweet smile she gave him, whether he won or lost.

When he attended Bethel, following in Scotty's massive footsteps, Abby was there to wave at him across campus. Yes, she usually had Scotty in tow. But by then Ross suspected he and Abby Cushman were more than friends.

Even when he'd spent two years in Mexico, up to his elbows in despair, hunger, and street kids, Abby had been on the other end of the e-mails and occasional letters to add sunshine to his often-dark world. He'd returned with hopes, dreams.

Then, that Christmas, those dreams materialized.

"She's a beaut, huh?" Bucko asked as he held up his northern.

"More than I can ever imagine," Ross said and spit out a wad of seeds as he swept Abby from his mind.

✳ ✳ ✳

Abigail stood with her crew, feeling their stares peeling skin off the back of her neck. So she hadn't made any friends today, prowling the lake like an angry coach. But after all their training, shouldn't they take the contest seriously? Weren't they here to win?

Abigail shut out the indictments screaming in the back of her brain and watched the weigh-in. The New Lifers, of course, more than hauled in their daily catch and were sorting out which trophies to enter in the official contest. Abigail stared at their stringer, feeling slightly ill. They had three smallmouth bass, a decent-looking largemouth, two northerns, and a beautiful walleye that Abigail was tempted to eat. The MRE she'd choked down for lunch lumped like nuclear waste in her stomach, and she'd give about a zillion dollars for a decent Caesar salad and garlic bread.

"Sojourners, are you ready to weigh in?"

Abigail stepped up to the porch, where Pastor Dan reached for her stringer. "Is this it?"

She must have given him a pitiful look because he smiled. "Not a bad-looking walleye here."

Abigail watched as the numbers registered. She didn't linger long at the scoreboard.

Her Sojourners had already scattered to change clothes. Abigail trudged toward the cookshack, turning over the day's events. Yes, she'd forgotten her sunblock and burned her nose, but other than that, she'd fished to perfection. At least she thought she had. She searched for the right spot, with reeds or submerged trees, started out with a slow troll, and fished the hole when she'd had a bite. She'd picked her bait, catching the two northern on a black-and-white spoon.

In the late afternoon, she'd even managed to relax. Until, of course, she saw Ross speeding across the lake, the wind parting his hair. He had his sleeves rolled up, and those muscular arms raised a memory that felt like a stab.

She'd been skunked the rest of the day.

The door to the cookshack whined as she opened it.

The Sojourner girls were at their bunk, changing into shorts and T-shirts.

"I'm starved. Do you mind if I whip us up something for supper?" Esther asked. "I don't think I can look at a fish."

Abigail nodded, thankful that the Ethiopian exchange student could work miracles with a couple pounds of meat. "Then after supper, I think we should strategize. I have a few ideas—"

"The New Lifers are having a baseball game after supper," Laurie said, gathering her frizzy brown hair into a ponytail.

"Baseball?" Abigail leaned against the bed frame, feeling suddenly very, very tired.

Laurie tugged on her tennis shoes. "Yeah. Do you know how to play, Esther?"

"Even if she doesn't, Ross said that he'd teach her. Besides, it's just for fun." Heather coated herself with perfume.

"Ross organized this?" Abigail sat down and pulled off her hiking boots. Even her bones ached, an ailment attributed to sitting in a metal boat all day. Oh, to have some meat on her body.

"Yeah, he caught up with me while you were weighing

in." Heather shook her head. "That man has a smile that makes me forget my own name."

"I know," Abigail muttered.

Laurie shot her a grin. "Come and play with us. It'll be fun."

Oh yeah, about as fun as pulling out my fingernails one by one.

"Yeah, sure."

As the door closed behind them, Abigail flopped on her bed and buried her face in her pillow. The last time she'd played baseball with Ross it had been in the dead of winter, over a year ago. They'd been shoveling his driveway, and he'd lobbed her a snowball. She'd sent it shattering with her snow shovel. Which led to a snowball fight that still had the power to make her smile on her darkest day. Especially the part where he'd tackled her, held her, and let the dusky light hide them behind a snowbank.

It was there, caught in the dizzying smell of his aftershave and the intoxicating look of adoration in his eyes, that Abigail knew.

She loved the little brother of her best friend, probably since he was a punk kid chasing her around the house during kick the can. For sure since she'd blackened his eye on the baseball field and cheered number 23 through four years of football, hockey, and baseball. And now that he was back from his two-year ministry stint, tanned, all grown-up, and tall enough to hold her in his arms, she'd fallen for him hook, line, and sinker.

And Ross loved her too. She'd read it between the lines of his letters, in his lopsided smile and the way his eyes filled with her reflection. He'd even mumbled it as he leaned down and touched her lips with his. He'd been gentle, perhaps a bit afraid, but as the shadows blanketed them and his kiss became exploring and more confident, she forgot that she was three years older and decided that her heart belonged to Ross Springer.

Of course, three mere weeks later, Scotty smacked into a tree at Vail and Ross stepped into his shoes, morphing into Ross, New Life leader, boy wonder.

She'd lost her Ross the day his big brother was lowered into the cold earth.

Baseball, indeed. Suddenly, more than anything, she yearned to remind the guy of everything they'd had . . . and lost.

CHAPTER SIX

BASEBALL AND FISHING. Two harmless pastimes that, in Abby Cushman's hands, became all-out, fight-or-die battles.

"Batter up!" Ross stood at the mound of their makeshift baseball diamond in the middle of a field and tried to hide the fact that he felt thirteen again. A heady thrill rushed through him as Abby picked up a bat and sauntered toward the plate.

Home-run Abby up to bat. He wondered if he'd be able to pitch when every muscle in his body felt as tight as a fifteen-pound line playing a muskie. "Ready, batter?"

She measured her stance, balanced her weight, then lifted the bat and stared him down. It whooshed him back about a decade. She'd tied her brown, glossy hair in a ponytail and pushed up the sleeves of her blue Bethel sweatshirt. Her thin arms still rippled with strength, and her face set in a grim line.

"Come on, Abigail!" someone shouted from the sideline.

No. C'mon, Babe. My home-run gal. Pop it into the trees. He swallowed hard and forced a grin, wondering if she too remembered the day she'd given him a shiner or the night he'd tossed her a snowball pitch, and she'd decimated his heart with a kiss that still made him a little weak.

"Ready, pitch," she called and choked up on the bat.

He wound up and sailed a slider right past her.

She jerked, then glared at him. "That took off skin, 23!"

He nearly missed the throwback. She'd called him by his number.

She planted her feet, adjusted her weight. "Gimme a fastball."

Was she baiting him? He glanced toward the first baseman, meeting Melinda's gaze. She was all grins.

He wound up. A beautiful curve, fast and inside.

Abby swished. Oh, did it make her mad. He could nearly see smoke spiraling from her ears as she took a practice swing. He winced, glad he wasn't at the other end of the bat. Again, Abby was going all out to win. Only, what was she aiming for? Hoping to remind him of a sweet and precious friendship that meant more to him than it should have? He didn't care. Abby was in his line of sight, and if she wanted a fastball, he'd deliver.

"Okay, homer, this one is for you." He knew he'd just bared his heart and didn't care. Finally. He and Abby. One-on-one. *Thank You, Lord.*

Fastball, down the middle, a perfect strike. Abby connected with a bone-splitting crack.

The baseball line-drived past his head and over second, hit the ground, then bounced wickedly on the uneven ground.

"Run, Abby!" He hoped the New Lifers didn't hear him cheering his lungs out.

Abby tossed the bat and took off. She still balled her fists when she ran, still tucked her head down like a charging bull. Seeing it made him ache.

She rounded first to a screaming crowd while the New Lifers scrambled after the ball. Bucko, out in left, ran after the still-bouncing ball and leaped on it. Abby sailed past second and floored it to third.

Run home, Babe! Ross backed up toward home, his mitt high. "Bucko, over here!"

Bucko threw a hand-smacking sizzler, and Ross caught it without flinching as Abby rounded third. He whirled and bolted for home.

He heard her breath when she hit the dirt, arms out, and a second later he tagged her in a dive and roll.

Silence, heavy breaths, then—

"Safe!" Melinda yelled, abandoning first to ump at home. She grinned down at Abby. "Girlfriend, you sure can hit 'em!"

Ross sat up, breathing hard, feeling like he'd peeled off a layer of skin from his back. Abby had an ugly scrape on her chin and weed burn down her arms, but she smiled at him in triumph, lifting her chin.

Ross shook his head. "That's my home-run gal."

To his utter shock, her smile crumbled, and tears filled her eyes. Then, as the crowd cheered their hero, Abby jumped up and sprinted toward camp.

What an idiot. A downright fool!

Abigail ran into the cookshack and slammed the door, her heart threatening to continue the race, hop in her Honda, and floor it south.

What had she been thinking? Home-run gal. She was a glutton for punishment, marching up to the plate and toying with Ross like they were old friends.

They *were* old friends. As in past tense. Worn-out. Thrown away. Abigail sank to the floor. Then why did his smile feel like fire ravaging her chest?

Her shoulders shook as her emotions wrung out into her hands. She'd been possessed by some errant emotion, one that had her believing she was immune to Ross's smile. Even worse, she'd heard him cheering as she ran the bases, and for a brief second, she'd longed for Ross to truly mean the words he'd spoken. *My home-run gal.*

She should abandon this farce and return to Bethel, to the safety of her off-campus apartment and her solid future wrapping her brain around Greek conjugations. She wasn't made to be a part of Ross's multitudes. Especially if she was going to burst into tears every time he made her feel one of a kind.

"Abby?"

His voice, soft like a breeze, filtered through the door. She stiffened. Maybe if she was very, very quiet—

"I know you're in there. Please open the door."

She cringed. "No. Go away." *Do your mocking out of my earshot, please.*

"No. We've been avoiding each other for too long. I want—no, I need—to talk to you. Please."

The pleading at the end of his voice made her traitorous heart jump to attention. Her voice too. "What do you want to say?"

"Open the door."

And let him see her red, blotchy face? No thank you. "I guess we don't have anything to talk about."

"No, wait. Yes, we do. I—"

She imagined him, one hand resting against the door, rubbing his forehead on his upper arm, then touching it to the door. She even heard a faint bump. "I'm . . . Well, I just want to say I'm sorry."

Her throat tightened.

"I know I hurt you. I was young and stupid and . . . well, hurting. I am so sorry. Can't we just, you know, put it behind us?"

Abigail gritted her teeth, but tears leaked out. "I was hurting too."

"I know," he said quietly.

And with that admission, the grief returned. Scotty's funeral. The Cushman family lined up behind the Springers, the way Karen Springer held Abigail like a daughter, the shame of knowing she never loved Scotty the way everyone wanted her to. She felt she ought to feel torn asunder, so she buried herself in studies and let the gossip swirl around her. Scotty's girl, they called her, and she couldn't deny it without marring Scotty's precious memory. Instead, she claimed a table in the far side of the library, avoided Ross like the flu, and tried to find a way to tell him the truth without looking like a two-timing hussy. And then late one night when everyone hustled in after a basketball game to smuggle in some last-minute studying, she'd heard a voice that she knew better than her own.

"Hi, Abby," he'd said softly, and she'd seen hurt in his eyes. "Tell me the truth—you were in love with Scotty, not me." As she stood, scraping up words, he ran over her silence and delivered a one-two punch that shattered her heart. "I guess it's true. Now that Scotty's gone, the fun's over. I should have known better."

His pain, raw in his voice, took her breath away. She stood, gape-mouthed as he stalked away, muttering his final blow. "I hope you and your Greek book live happily ever after."

"You didn't let me explain," she said now, still inside that painful moment.

"I'm so, so sorry, Abby. I shouldn't have said that. I should have recognized that you were in mourning. I didn't want to admit how much Scotty meant to you."

Abigail frowned. "He was my best friend."

"I know. Now I know. Then, I was . . . jealous. Confused." She heard another thump and imagined him putting his hand on the door. Inside the cabin, dark shadows shrouded her in anonymous protection.

"But I see now how terribly I treated you. I am so sorry. Please, Abby."

Abigail took a deep breath, feeling raw and wrung out. She wiped her face and opened the door. He stood in the darkness, his slumped shoulders betraying the pain in his voice. "It's okay, Ross. I forgave you a long time ago."

She heard his quick intake of breath and quickly sandbagged her heart. "But my name is Abigail. Not Abby. Not Babe and especially not your home-run gal."

She heard him stand in silence a good five minutes before he turned and shuffled into the night.

Day two. First Annual Fun and Fund-Raising Bethel Fishing Contest. And Ross already felt like a loser. He loaded his tackle into his fishing boat, acutely aware of the cold mist rising over the lake and the chill that rattled his bones. The sun hid behind the eastern clouds, preferring to dent the morning with pale light instead of a full invasion. The weather matched his mood. Dismal. He'd slept about three hours, flogged by accusations and regret.

He'd accomplished his goals. He'd apologized to Abby and had been granted forgiveness. He should feel free.

Instead, he felt bludgeoned by the unflinching truth. Abby didn't want him. Never had. Still saw him as the kid who tried to impress her by lettering in his high school sports or trouncing her in Monopoly. The one sweet kiss they'd shared felt suddenly, cruelly like pity.

"You're up early."

Ross nearly jumped out of his rain poncho when an elderly man, looking like a wilderness accessory, emerged from the drizzle.

"Trying to catch the big ones," Ross mumbled as he recognized his grizzled educator from the day before.

The man edged over to the boat and eyed Ross's tackle. "Catch 'em walleye?"

"Uh, yeah, thanks. You gave good advice." Ross loaded in his tackle box.

"Whatcha huntin' today?"

"Bass, maybe." Ross shrugged, uncaring. Being out on the water would keep him from hopping in his car and fleeing from the woman he could never have.

The man chuckled. It sounded like the low rumble of distant thunder. Or maybe it was thunder. Ross eyed the sky.

"Bass like grub worms unless the sun comes out. Then switch to plastic jerk bait. Most of all, look for the change in landscape, cuts in the bank, cover of any type."

Ross nodded.

"If it gets to raining good, check out the streams heading into Bear Lake. Bass like to hide around the boulders. Most importantly, don't give up."

"Thanks."

The man tipped his head and trudged up the road toward the parking lot. Ross watched him go.

Bucko emerged from the trail, lugging supplies. "Who was that?"

"A local. Gave me some fishing pointers."

Bucko moved toward the boat and climbed in, loading his tackle. "We'd better get going. I saw Abigail and her troops behind us."

"She's up early."

Bucko raised one dark eyebrow. "Yeah, well, according to Melinda, who I talked to while grabbing breakfast, Abigail spent the night crying. You know anything about that?"

Ross closed his eyes, feeling sick. "I guess I opened a few wounds last night at the baseball game."

"Speaking of, how's your knee?"

"Painful, but I'll live." He'd managed to strain his knee diving over Abby's body.

"You were in stellar form. I have to admit, I've never seen you so dedicated."

Ross pushed his boat out, climbed in, and used the oar to push it to deeper water. Through the mist, he saw Abby and her team emerge onto the landing. She stood there like some ethereal being, thin and regal, watching him float away.

Ross swallowed the regrets lining his throat as he pull-started the motor.

❋   ❋   ❋

Abigail had a wet, wretched day. Aside from the rain that deluged her from nine to noon, she'd caught three bluegills, one tiny walleye, and a smallmouth bass that cut her when she held it down to unhook its mouth. She'd forgotten her gloves in the cookshack, along with her map of the lake.

Which meant she spent half the day fishing for northern in a prime bass location.

She caught, however, plenty of glimpses of the man she was trying to forget.

As Simon motored them back to camp, rain lashed her face and blew against her rain outfit. Cold seeped in like a bacteria, starting a shiver deep in her bones. She'd trade in all her fishing gear plus her entire set of Bible Knowledge Commentaries for a warm bath and a thick USDA prime-cut sirloin.

Instead, she looked forward to fish or perhaps granola bars or, if she threw herself at Esther's feet, some sort of gourmet Ethiopian cuisine.

Abigail helped tie up the boat, took her catch, her tackle, and her dead minnows, and headed back to camp.

She had her head down, fighting the wind, and almost plowed over the old man sitting by the trail, bobber-fishing as if it were a bright, sunny day.

"Howdy, missy!" he said, and she jumped, nearly leaving her teeth behind.

He had bushy white eyebrows and deep-set brown eyes that glinted with humor. "You okay?"

Well, no, actually. Not only did she have a paltry catch and feel like a mangy alley cat, but she hadn't been able to dodge Ross's heart-tearing apology for the better part of five minutes all day. Or night, for that matter. "I'm fine, thank you," she lied and began to move past him.

He cleared his throat. "'Some people fish all their lives without knowing it is not really the fish they are after.'"

"Excuse me?"

He chuckled, and the sound rippled under her skin. "Henry David Thoreau. I was just wondering if you caught what you were hoping for." He smiled kindly, then began to hum. It sounded like an old hymn.

Abigail stared at him a moment before she trudged back to camp.

The weigh-in sent her spirit into an abyss. She slogged back to the cookshack and dug out her track pants, wool socks, a sweatshirt, and a down vest. She was beginning to feel like she might get warm sometime around next Christmas when Laurie stuck her head into the cabin. "Oh, you're back. Great. We're having fellowship in the lodge. C'mon and get a bite to eat."

Abigail flopped on the bunk, feeling like an overcooked noodle, but Laurie grabbed her hand and wrestled her to her feet. "You'll feel better."

Two cups of hot cocoa later, she had begun to feel her toes. She sat alone at one of the long lodge tables, but the sound of voices and laughter finally drew her like honey. Ambling over to an overstuffed chair in the shadows, she sat and watched Ross strumming his guitar and leading the group in worship. She could see Scotty in him, in the natural charisma that flowed from all Springer blood.

Scotty didn't have Ross's kindness, the way he reached out and touched someone's shoulder or threw back his head and laughed with an accepting humor. He'd been a born leader of the New Lifers, but Abigail couldn't help but flinch at the way he'd lead from the top down. Type A, demanding. Type B Ross had a way of weaving people into agreement with his smile and enthusiasm. And somehow, hidden in the shadows, listening to him lead the group in singing and prayer felt comforting, even soothing. She could perhaps even dream that they'd stayed friends, more than friends . . .

Abigail awoke curled in the ratty lodge armchair to the low, popping crackles of the dying fire. Moonlight spilled through the windows, the sky clear after being emptied.

As her eyes adjusted to the milky light, she made out a body standing over the fire, both arms braced against the mantel. She huddled under the afghan some kind soul had spread over her and intended to simply close her eyes and feign slumber.

Except a low groan escaped as the man buried his head in his arms.

Ross.

Her heart noticed immediately and began to hum. Well, she could either sneak out or stay huddled, hoping he didn't spot her.

Watching him, shoulders slumped, ensconced in the posture of defeat, she had the crazy urge to go over and fold him in her arms. He looked so much like the athlete who'd nearly punched a hole in his school locker after losing state finals that it took her breath away.

And she realized why she couldn't look at him without aching, why she burned every time she saw him surrounded by his congregation of adoring women.

He'd become Scotty. Scotty, the student council president. Scotty, the superachiever, the straight-A student, the seminary star.

The Ross she knew was quiet. He liked playing the guitar, beating her in board games. His life goal had been to become a youth counselor. This Ross was a class leader milking his good looks, his Springer smile. She didn't know this new and improved Ross.

If she was honest, she'd admit that jealousy had settled deep in the recesses of her bruised heart. There'd been a time when he smiled for her alone, swaggered up to bat with one eye on her cheering in the stands. Now his gleam turned on for any girl on campus. Under Ross's teasing, she'd felt beautiful, not bony and daring, not dull.

She'd dreamed that they belonged together.

Now he belonged to everyone.

As if sensing her thoughts, Ross walked over to the window, picked up his guitar, and strummed. The soft sounds grazed over the raw, wounded places in Abigail's heart, and she emitted a sad moan.

Whoops. She clamped her hand over her mouth.

Ross turned. His gaze found hers, and in it she saw sorrow. "Oh, hi. I didn't know you were still here." Which implied, of course, that he'd seen her earlier. For some reason this lit a blaze down Abigail's spine.

"Hi."

He put down the guitar. "Been a long day. Catch much?"

She shook her head.

"Me either. Got skunked."

"Don't worry. A few of your other team members managed to put some fish on the boards. You're still ahead."

Did he flinch? As if the fact that the New Lifers were trouncing her made him feel . . . guilty?

"Are you okay?" The words spilled out before she could rein them in.

He looked out the window at the moonlight spilling over the wet ground. "Yeah. Just . . . tired."

For some idiotic reason, her eyes filled. "Me too."

CHAPTER EIGHT

ROSS WATCHED HER, a lump rising in his throat to block his airway. Sleep had disheveled her hair, and she looked like a waif wrapped up in a holey afghan, but with the moon touching her face and the texture of kindness in her eyes, she'd never looked more utterly, heart-stoppingly beautiful. It raised an errant memory that spilled out.

"Do you remember the time when we went on that canoe trip? I think I was fifteen. My dad hooked us up with that guy who dragged us to the Quetico National Forest outpost on the Minnesotan/Canadian border?"

In Abigail's eyes, he saw her scrolling through the past to the windswept day they'd ridden in the NFS boat. Of course, she wouldn't remember that he had longed for that day for nearly three months, couldn't wait to spend a week paddling through the forest, identifying birds or fighting her for control of the canoe. He didn't care that she was eighteen or he just a freshman. Only about the way the wind entwined her hair, the way she seemed to see him anew each time she looked at him. He lived for her laughter, and the fact that more often than not she stayed over even after Scotty went out, challenging him to a one-on-one basketball match or killing him in Scrabble, told him the feelings he nurtured were mutual.

"I remember you wore the same pair of fatigues the entire week," she said, a smile tugging her mouth.

"And you forgot to hang our food pack and nearly sacrificed our rations to a bear."

"You and Scotty chased him away," she said, laughing. "You just had to sleep under the stars. I worried about you every night."

"You did?"

She tucked her cute nose into the afghan.

He sat down on the sofa across from her, his pulse wild. "Do you remember when we camped at Bradley Lake? You dumped our entire bottle of water purifier in the lake?"

She glared at him, then nodded slowly, and her gaze went to his forehead. "That's where you got hurt. What were you doing exactly?"

He felt himself blushing. "Boulder problems."

"Oh yeah. Climbing up the face of a cliff without a rope." She pointed to her head with one of her fingers, still ensconced under the afghan. "I'd say you had boulder problems."

He laughed and she giggled. Under the blanket of late-night silence, it felt soothing, even hopeful.

"I've never been so afraid as when you ran up, blood running down your face." Her smile vanished. "You were almost killed."

Ross remembered her small scream, the way she put her hand right over his wound, and the expression of sheer fear on her face, a look still buried in his heart.

He leaned back, lifted his hair. "Still have the battle scars."

She shook her head but lowered the afghan, and he saw she was smiling. "I thought we'd have to call in the National Rescue Service for your mother."

"Good thing you had that first-aid kit."

What she didn't know was that he'd wanted to impress her. To show her that, while Scotty might be the leader of the pack, smart and intelligent, Ross had the guts to live life on the edge. He'd wanted her to see him as older, bolder, braver.

And in the end, he had proven he was the family clown. Suddenly, he just wanted to flee back to the lake and find a nice, deep hole and hide.

"You looked like such a tough guy. I think Scotty was jealous."

"Yeah, well, it would have been the only time."

She frowned at him. "Hardly. Scotty was always amazed at your ability to think on your feet. You saved us that trip—we would still be roaming the Canadian forest if you hadn't figured out how to spot the portages."

"It just took a little bit of patience and study."

"No, it just took you." Her gaze felt like it could swallow him. She'd drawn up her legs and now put them on the floor, looked over her shoulder, then leaned close.

"But, Ross . . . who are you now?"

✳ ✳ ✳

He opened his mouth—whether to answer, she didn't know because a crash sounded in the lodge kitchen.

Her heart jumped into her throat. "What was that?"

Ross had already started for the source.

Abigail scrambled out of the afghan and ran after him. "Ross, be careful!"

She dodged the back swing of the hanging door and scooted in two steps behind him, nearly running up his spine when he stopped.

She peeked over his shoulder. "Oh no!"

The freezer door stood half-open, water dripping off the bottom. The supply of Sojourners' fish collected for the Deep Haven contest lay spilled across the kitchen floor. "Who would do this?"

She grabbed a towel and began to scoop up the prizes, holding her breath as she stacked them back into a now-soggy cardboard box. Her mind reeled as Ross poked his head out of the back door, looking for suspects, and called, "Anyone out there?"

Only the campus heartbreaker.

She couldn't help the habitual cynicism.

"Are they all there?" Ross squatted beside her, and she felt painfully aware of his closeness, the smoky, woodsy scent in his clothes. What was he doing in the lodge so late when everyone else had left? The question rose like the redolence of foul play. Would he really keep her busy her while someone sabotaged her catch?

"I think so." She should know better than to let him, even for a moment, whittle her down with sweet memories. They couldn't rewind time. She knew what he thought of her. Even if he apologized for his words, deep in his heart he believed that she was a woman who could count her friends on one hand, known for her ability to keep the library lights burning.

Could she help it if she had a degree to earn? Especially after Ross's cruel words, it seemed she'd morphed into the very person he'd proclaimed. Was she the only one who noticed that she didn't have her sister's beauty or Ross's magnetism? Her assets rested between her ears, and she didn't intend to waste them. Still, she had to admit that his words speared her soul. She felt . . . prickly. Unattractive. And deep inside, she wondered if God could really use a person who spent all her time conjugating verbs. Even so, she had her future carefully mapped out—assistant professor to senior professor and eventually an overseas teaching assignment. By that time Ross would have a large, energetic following as an inner-city youth evangelist.

Their future was about as likely as she was to haul in a fifty-pound muskie on her feeble crank baits and fifteen-pound test line.

Still, it had comforted her to sit in the moon-bathed lodge and listen to him enjoy their past. As if he too missed it.

She shook herself free of that thought and put frost into her voice. "Are you trying to sabotage me?"

"What?" He finished loading the fish, then shoved the box into the cooler and closed the door. He turned, and the hurt on his face made her ache to her toes. She turned away, but he touched her chin and forced her to look at him. "Sabotage?"

She stepped away from his grasp. "I know you'd do anything to win."

"No. I wouldn't. I thought you knew me better than that."

She shook her head. "I used to. But—I don't think I know you at all." She stomped out to the fire, grabbed her afghan, and dragged it to the kitchen. She not only didn't know him; she didn't trust him.

"What are you doing?"

Abigail wound the afghan around her shoulders and slouched down, her back to the fridge. "Standing guard."

His laugher made tears edge her eyes. Oh, sure, now she was the funny, weird girl saving her fish. The campus crackpot.

Well, at least she didn't pretend to be someone she wasn't.

He crouched at her feet. "Abby, I'm not out to steal your fish. No matter how much I want to win." He was fighting a smile, and it made her want to wallop him.

"I'm staying here."

"No, you're not." Without warning, he scooped her up

and marched her out to the fireplace. "If you want to keep an eye on me, you'll do it in here where it's warm." He plopped her onto the sofa.

She sat up, fury burning her stomach. How dare he?

He flopped down in the opposite chair. His expression told her that her words had wounded as he stared into the fire. She sat there, pulse roaring, and saw the Ross she'd loved and missed. The Ross without his adoring fans; the humble, quiet Ross.

The Ross who made her feel special. Cherished. One in a million.

"I'm sorry, Abigail." He leaned back, closed his eyes. "I know that I'll never be Scotty, but please, give me some credit."

Never be Scotty? But she didn't want Scotty. She wanted Ross.

"What are you talking about?"

He opened one eye. "Nothing. Don't worry. Tomorrow's the last day of the contest. After that I'll be out of your life forever. You'll never have to set eyes on me again."

Her throat burned. Then, without another word, she got up and stalked out before she burst into tears.

CHAPTER NINE

If Ross wanted to win the fishing contest, he'd have to net the big one. The muskellunge. The New Lifers had reeled in the daily limit in each category, and while none of their catch would qualify as the "mother of all fish," they had some decent weights. A muskie would seal their entry.

Ross sat in his boat, the early morning sun hot on his neck, and fiddled with a cinch knot. The grizzled voice of the old geezer he'd seen again this morning played in his mind. When he'd mentioned his prey—muskie—the man's eyes lit up.

"Find the edge of the milfoil, when there is a transition to sand, then use that black-and-silver crappie-looking spinner you got in your box."

The fact that Ross found it an hour later had him wondering just how much the phantom angler knew about his gear.

He cast, let his line fall ten feet down, praying it didn't snag on weeds, and began playing it. Without Bucko in the prow, his thoughts tangled in last night's events.

He wasn't Scotty. Never had that truth so twisted like a six-inch buck knife. Abigail would have never accused Scotty of stealing her fish.

Then again, Scotty would have never taken the New Lifers fishing. He would have sold candy bars or launched a telemarketing campaign. Scotty relished order, not fun. Perhaps that's what made him a star leader whose light still hadn't dimmed.

A loon called forlornly, picking up Ross's mood. As he'd led singing last night, he'd watched the final pages of his life turning. There was no dishonor in driving delivery trucks; it just felt like defeat after his dreams of doing something with eternal significance. But unlike Scotty, he didn't have the brainpower to match his dreams.

He should have been the one to hit the tree. The bitter thought made him shudder. He missed Scotty so much that at times it felt like an open wound. And his attempts to fill the guy's shoes felt like homage. Or grief therapy. Whatever.

If only he knew who God wanted him to be. Abby's words churned in his soul. *Who are you now?*

Answer: Ross Springer, Greek flunky, senior dropout.

Wouldn't Abigail Cushman, PhD, be impressed when she heard that?

Ross's throat burned when he looked into the bruised sky. *Who am I, God? I'm not Scotty or Abby, but I want to be used by You. Show me how, please.*

Dark clouds tumbled overhead, mirroring the tumult in his soul. Well, maybe he could land a whopper. His final hurrah.

Ross flicked his line back to cast and knew he'd done it wrong the second he snapped his wrist. He released the spinner too soon; the line played out behind him and hooked his shoulder blade.

He gulped in a breath, blinking back the sting. Oh, super. He'd landed . . . himself.

What a hero.

He reeled in the slack and attempted to reach the wound but only managed to lodge the hook deeper. Pain shot through the top of his head.

He could return to camp, but oh, wouldn't that be fun?

Or . . . he heard a motor. Shading his eyes, he made out a lone fisherman trolling along the weedy shoreline. He squinted and his heart fell. Abigail. Up early. Of course.

God certainly had a sense of humor.

Well, she already thought him a fool, didn't she? And she did have the golden touch when it came to outdoor mishaps.

He started his outboard and headed toward eternal humiliation.

✳ ✳ ✳

According to every book Abigail had read, muskie liked deep, weedy areas, "prop wash," and fat cisco spinners. After inventorying her insignificant entry, she had one hope of bringing home a prize—landing the alligator-jawed progeny of the freshwater.

She'd slept little and wasn't surprised when Laurie groaned and turned over on her lumpy mattress, shrugging Abigail away. Well, she hadn't seriously thought the Sojourners would stick with her to the bitter end, had she?

She refused to acknowledge the truth. Nor the fact that most of her group had plans to go hiking today with a New Life contingency. So much for recruiting new members.

Tugging on her line with one hand and manning the outboard with the other, she mentally cast her day into God's hands. She'd missed her morning quiet time, but the words from the psalm—was it 25?—Ross read last night lingered in her mind. *"O Lord, I give my life to you. I trust in you, my God! Do not let me be disgraced, or let my enemies rejoice in my defeat."*

Abigail closed her eyes. *Lord, the New Lifers aren't exactly my enemies, but I do feel disgraced. What did I do wrong? Please help me be the leader You want me to be. Help the Sojourners to grow. And please, Lord, help me catch a fish.*

The memory of the paltry Sojourner catch made her shudder. How could she have accused Ross of thievery? The hurt in his eyes dug a hole in her chest. *I'll never be Scotty . . .*

She gasped, even as her line gave a tug. *Never be Scotty.* But he wanted to be. With a painful whoosh she understood. She'd seen fear in his eyes. Could it be that he wanted to be Scotty because he really believed the campus rumors that she'd been in love with his big brother? Was he afraid he'd never measure up to Scotty in her eyes?

How could he believe that after she'd spent the better part of her life cheering him on?

Maybe because she'd never contradicted the rumors.

Oh, Ross. She didn't want a man who had to be smarter, faster, braver than her. A man who made her feel second best. She wanted Ross—the man who made her believe his world started and stopped on her smile. That he could do anything with her on his side.

Someone with a 4.0 grade point average should have seen the truth in his red-rimmed eyes, his raw accusation. She felt as sensitive as a north shore agate.

Her line jerked again and she slowed, turned.

But in her wake she saw not a muskie but Ross, waving as his boat sped toward her. She blinked back her tears and gave a feeble wave. What did he want?

He looked devastatingly handsome with his windblown burnt-gold hair, those brown eyes, a wry smile. He reached out and grabbed her boat. Swallowed. The expression on his face snatched the breath right out of her chest. "Abby, can you help me?"

He angled his shoulder at her. She winced. A hook, one of those wicked-looking crank baits with the fuzzy ends, dug into his shoulder blade. She smiled, feeling strangely giddy. "Come here, hero. I'll unhook you."

He tied his boat to hers and climbed over, maneuvering like a man in pain.

"How did you do this?" She examined his wound. Her class in basic fishing had included a lesson in hook removal. SOP said to push it through the skin on the other side, clip the barb, and slide it out.

He reddened. "Bad cast."

"I guess." Pushing one of the tri-hooks through the meat to the other side looked like an agonizing journey. "I think I can use this new technique they taught me." She didn't add that she'd mutilated a pig's foot in the process. But the last two times the hook had slid out nicely. "Give me a second."

"You have all day. I'm not going anywhere."

She didn't comment. The way he sat in her boat without his masses . . . well, it raised an impulse to hold him hostage. To scroll back time and enjoy the friendship of their youth. Rifling through her tackle box, she found some line and clipped off a long piece. Tying it at the base of the hook's J, she hoped to apply leverage and slide it out. "Wanna bite on some leather?"

"Oh, very funny. Just . . . do it."

"Hold very, very still." She wound the leverage line around her finger and angled it down, pushing the base of the hook into his flesh. He grunted. She closed her pliers around the eye and, moving fast, twisted the hook out of his shoulder.

An awful, gut-churning sound came out from between his gritted teeth.

"I got it!"

"Yeah, I think you might have taken out all the muscle in my shoulder too. Ouch, Abs, that hurt." But he was grinning, and his eyes shone.

She put her hand over his bleeding wound. "You should get back to camp and bandage that up."

But he wasn't listening. "Abby, your line!"

She whirled and grabbed her pole just as it toppled over the edge into the water. "I got something!"

She jumped to her feet, yanked on the line, and set her hook. "Ross, grab the net!"

She heard him laughing. He leaned over the side as if hoping to spot her catch. Meanwhile, the fish fought her, ripping the reel from her fingers. The line zipped out as she tried to stop it.

"Help!"

Ross seized the rod, stopped the spill of line. "It's still hooked." He reeled, making meager process. "Abby girl, I think this is a homer!"

Standing there, gripped in the adrenaline, memories assaulting her without mercy, she couldn't help it. She kissed him on the cheek. The impulsiveness of her act made her blink, but when he turned, a surprised grin on his face, she grinned back.

"Get the net, Babe," he said in a sweetly roughened voice. "You're going to have a trophy tonight."

CHAPTER TEN

ABBY HAD LANDED her trophy fish. Ross grinned as she muscled her twenty-plus-pound muskie to the lodge, along with her beautiful stringer of prize northern. The woman had outfished, outsmiled, and outjoked him, and suddenly he didn't care that his shoulder felt like pulverized flesh or that his ego had been mulched along with it.

A perfect day. Every nerve sizzled with the pure joy of rekindling their friendship. As if sitting in a motorboat in the middle of Trout Lake had given their relationship safe haven. Abby emerged from her don't-get-near-me shell and spent the day teasing him, laughing at his jokes, igniting hope deep in his heart.

"I've missed you, Abby," he'd said at one point in the early afternoon, after she'd whipped up a gourmet shore lunch. The woman had a virtual tackle box full of surprises. He'd told her so, and she'd blushed, a color that only made her downright delicious.

Oh, how he'd wanted to unravel the meaning behind that blush and the reason she'd run out last night after he apologized for not being the man she wanted. But he feared destroying this magical day with their brutal history.

Seeing her standing on the porch, knowing that after today she'd go on to her perfectly outlined, intellectual life, and he to his blue-collar job, made him ache.

"Twenty-seven pounds, eight ounces, forty-three inches," Dan announced. "Caught on a fifteen-pound test line?"

Abby nodded, glowing past the tan on her face.

Ross whooped along with the rest of the New Lifers and Sojourners.

They put her muskie on ice and added her catch to the totals, which, unfortunately, still left the Sojourners woefully below the weights of the New Lifers. But was the New Lifers' catch enough to land the grand prize in the Deep Haven fish-off?

The campfire crackled and shot sparks into the night. Noah Standing Bear, back from his Minneapolis errand, stood in the front of the group looking like a road warrior in a black T-shirt and jeans. Ross noticed Anne Lundstrom, the camp's EMT, sitting on the bench. The woman carried an aura of wisdom and strength in her hazel eyes. He supposed after last summer's incredible save, she'd always be among his unsung heroes.

"Congratulations on your successful week," Noah said. "As I promised, I invited a professional fisherman to speak to you. I'd like to introduce you to the Reverend Maynard Draper. Retired evangelist and hobby angler."

Ross watched as the man who'd managed to point him to every fishing hole and even knew the contents of his tackle box strode from behind the benches. He carried a fat, worn Bible and smiled in a way that hinted he knew their secrets.

The campfire sent fireworks into the night. The night sounds filled the shocked silence a moment before Reverend Draper cleared his throat. He had a voice to match his face— gentle, wise, and slightly roughened around the edges.

"The greatest fisherman said, 'The Kingdom of Heaven is like a fishing net that was thrown into the water and caught fish of every kind. When the net was full, they dragged it up onto the shore, sat down, and sorted the good fish into crates, but threw the bad ones away.'" He chuckled. "I've seen your catch. And I know that you kept everything you hauled up, hoping to make your limits. Tomorrow at the weigh-in, you'll find out the results. But you've already done your job to the best of your ability."

He closed his Bible. "I've enjoyed watching you this week." He pointed to Ross. "This guy fished for anything he could attract with his bait. But the angling queen here—" he grinned at Abby, whose eyes widened—"she was deliberate about her technique, casting for northern and muskie." He winked at her. "Nice catch, by the way."

Ross warmed at her grin.

"The point is, they both caught fish. Using different bait, different methods. Neither was better." He opened his Bible and read a verse Ross knew well. 'Come, follow me, and I will show you how to fish for people!'

"Jesus doesn't ask us to fish only with crank bait or live minnows. He tells us to fish. In every account of fishing in the New Testament, when Jesus tells them to cast their net, they haul up a mother lode. Our job isn't to narrow down the bait; it is to be obedient with the fishing.

"God wants to use all of you, with your different skills, techniques, and passions, to fish for the Kingdom. He'll sort out the fish. He wants you to be obedient in the casting of your nets.

"I'm encouraged by the example of Peter and Andrew, the first fishermen. Andrew was quiet. He didn't have his brother's passion. But he didn't need it. Once he introduced Peter to Jesus, the spark ignited."

He smiled, and Ross saw truth in his eyes.

"Use your gifts—cast your net. Then trust Jesus to make you fishers of men."

✳ ✳ ✳

Abigail sang the final chorus of the praise song, feeling as if, when Ross looked at her, she just might be the only person under the grand canopy of stars.

If only Ross wasn't destined for inner-city New York after graduation. She'd heard he had applied for the position at

Elisha's Room. And who wouldn't hire a man like Ross, a servant zealous for the salvation of teenagers? If only she could buy into his method of evangelism, team with him. But she had her own path. She'd worked for this future, hadn't she? Spent a small lifetime studying for her PhD in Greek.

God couldn't ask her to abandon her life goals, her expensive education, for love.

Love?

Warmth rushed through her. Oh yes, she still loved Ross. So much it took her breath away. She longed for his smile in her direction, for the way he made her feel beautiful, smart, and like the only woman who really knew him.

What was it he said this afternoon? *I've missed you, Abby.* The sincerity in his voice stirred—no, downright ignited— the embers she'd tried to pack into a cold ball.

Maybe, just maybe, if she told him the truth, they could figure out a future. Hadn't their relationship survived a two year stint on opposite ends of the northern hemisphere?

She waited, huddled on her bench as the students dispersed. It bothered her just a little how Ross spent time with each student, investing in each conversation with animated enthusiasm. But then again, wasn't that Ross? A leader who touched people one by one.

She'd asked him what happened to him. The answer raised gooseflesh like a cold gust of lake wind. Her old Ross hadn't changed—he'd grown into a man of God, a fisherman God could use. No, he wasn't Scotty. Scotty would have beelined to the next item on his to-do list the moment their fellowship time ended, driven by his goals.

Sorta like . . . her.

Abigail bit her lip as regret sliced through her. No wonder the New Lifers had burgeoning attendance, and the Sojourners barely managed to scrounge up enough brains for a lively discussion. Yes, the New Lifers could still use serious Bible training, but they had a corner on relationships that the Sojourners—no, she—could learn from.

The first lesson was authenticity. Ross had it in spades. This, in a word, reeled her in and told her why Scotty had never invaded her heart. With Scotty she felt like an add-on.

Ross made her feel essential. Beautiful. Brilliant.

Then he turned her direction and smiled. As if he'd known she was waiting for him. Her heart did a flip and landed at her toes.

He ambled over to her, his guitar slung behind him like a medieval troubadour's. "Good sermon, huh?"

She nodded. Cleared her throat. *C'mon, intellect, don't fail me now.*

"I found your thief, by the way." He smiled, but she felt shame boil in her chest. "A raccoon. Tracks all over the kitchen this morning and outside in the mud. We figure someone left the freezer open, and he couldn't help but figure out a way in." He shrugged. "Sneaky guy."

"So it was you, then." She waggled her eyebrows at his confused look. "Sorta the way you snuck aboard my fishing boat today." *And back into my heart.*

"Hey, that was a real wound—"

She laughed. He looked so perplexed, so suddenly afraid. The expression spiraled right to her courage and bolstered it. She forced out the words she'd been dying to say for over a year. "Ross, I was never in love with Scotty."

His smile vanished. He went white and looked away. She touched his forearm, wanting to take his hand. "I know everyone thought I was, but I never, ever loved him . . . well, at least not the way . . . I . . . love . . . you."

Her voice betrayed her and hid in her swelling throat. But Ross's gaze turned to her, searching for the truth. He reached out for the bench, slowly sat, as if his knees threatened collapse. "You love me?"

She tried a verbal yes, but only a nod emerged.

He smiled and, with it, caught up her heart in a passionate sweep. "Oh, home-run gal, I love you too." He pushed her hair behind her ear, wound his hand into it. "I . . . I've loved you since I was thirteen years old and you flattened me with a line drive."

She might as well surrender to the tears pricking her eyes. He wiped one away with his thumb. His eyes roamed her face, her eyes, her lips. And then he leaned close and kissed her. Softly. Exactly how he had kissed her the night he'd tackled her in the snow. Only this had a much greater effect.

She put her hands on his chest, balling his sweatshirt in her fists, and hung on. A lifetime of longing, of heartache, of love flooded into the moment, and she kissed him with a passion that surprised them both, from his wide-eyed expression.

A low, mischievous smile slid up his face. "Where have you been all my life?"

She grinned. "Right here. Cheering you on."

CHAPTER ELEVEN

THE FISHERPEOPLE of Bethel College pooled their catch and entered it in the Deep Haven contest. Sojourners and New Lifers, together on one entry. As Pastor Dan weighed their entry, Ross knew.

They'd won. Not only the trophy, but a new beginning. The Sojourners would enrich the New Lifers' ranks, fortifying their passion for relationships with a knowledge of Scripture. New Sojourners would reach beyond the borders of their campus and out into the world.

Even if Ross would never be a part of this new blaze, he'd know he'd been among the first sparks.

Fanning to flame the work Scotty began. Perhaps God intended that all along.

Abby hoisted the trophy and the crowd cheered. Her gaze landed on him, and he nodded, hoping she could see love in his expression.

If only he were smarter. He longed to believe her when she said she never loved Scotty. But Scotty hadn't flunked out of his senior year. Scotty went on to seminary and right now would have been taking a pastorate and doing great things for God.

Ross hadn't been thinking with a clear head when he'd taken her into his arms last night. He couldn't bring her home, away from the dreams for which she'd sacrificed so many years of study. He couldn't give her a rich ministry life, a setting where her gifts and skills could flourish.

So he hadn't revealed his dismal future.

Dread tightened in his stomach as she descended the stairs and threaded through the crowd and into his arms.

"Well done, Abs." He held her tight, unable to let go. Burying his face in her soft hair, he drank in her smell, something floral and clean, thanks to the shower she'd taken at the municipal pool. "You won it for us."

Her beautiful blue eyes held such sweetness that it made him want to cry.

"Are you headed back to Minneapolis today?" He sounded like he had a cold.

She nodded. "Wanna meet me at the cafeteria for a burger tonight?"

He looked over the top of her head at Melinda and Bucko, who had veered off from the group and were walking hand in hand down the boardwalk. "I'm headed home."

"Oh, well. Okay. I guess you gotta pack for New York, huh?"

He smiled, pushing her hair behind her ear, loving the feel of it in his fingers. "You're a great fisherperson, Babe. God has gifted you in so many ways. I'm so proud of you. I just know you'll do great at Bethel." He smiled, a flimsy barricade between his words and a breakdown in the middle of the street. "I'll see ya round."

"Oh." The look on her face tore right thought his chest. "I see. Okay."

She turned away, and he nearly ran after her. *I'll try again! I'll be more than I am!* But he'd decided last night at the campfire that if God wanted him to drive a meat truck, he'd do it faithfully, casting his nets along the way.

He watched Abby join Laurie and the rest of her Sojourners. When she looked back in his direction, he stalked toward his car and out of her life.

✳ ✳ ✳

The drive to Minneapolis had to be the longest of Abby's entire life. She watched the landscape whoosh by, the pine and birch forest turning to meadow south of Duluth, then to suburbs as they trekked into the Twin Cities. By the time Laurie pulled up to their tiny off-campus apartment, Abby knew she couldn't hold in the tears one minute longer.

Ross didn't want her. She'd unlocked her heart, let him take a good look, and he'd walked away. Obviously her love wasn't enough for him. Her love, her smile, her personality. Dull. Uninspiring. Then why had he told her he loved her?

She dragged her luggage, the trophy, her sleeping bag, and tackle into the apartment. Piling it in the middle of the room, she flopped down on the sofa and flung her arm over her eyes.

Laurie closed the door behind her. Abby heard the foot-falls across the carpet, knowing she'd been less than fair in giving her friend one-word answers for two hundred and fifty miles, but she didn't want to uncover her heart for Esther's prying eyes.

Feeling Laurie touch her legs, Abby gave a peek. Laurie sat at the end of the sofa, face pinched. "Okay, now it's just us. Tell me what happened."

Abby closed her eyes, gulped a deep breath, and spilled out the wretched story. "And then he just walked away." She shook her head. "What's with that?"

A slight smile played on Laurie's face. "Girlfriend, for a straight-A valedictorian, you need to beef up on your male savvy. The guy failed his senior year."

"So?" Abby frowned.

Laurie gave a great Ricky Ricardo look of incredulity. "Work with me. He didn't get his New York gig. He's going home to deliver meat."

Abby frowned. "Then why did he walk out on me?"

Laurie grabbed her by the shoulders, looking exasperated.

"Pay attention! How's he supposed to keep up with Doctor of Greek Abigail Cushman?"

"Oh, as if my degree matters."

"Again, you need to enroll in Men 101. They don't like to look like failures in front of the women they love. He did say he loved you, right?"

Abby slowly nodded. "I feel sick."

"Yeah, well, I have a solution." Laurie stood and walked over to the counter, picked up an envelope. "I love weddings, don't you?"

Abby dived into Laurie's idea, hoping that she wasn't casting her heart at Ross's feet only to see it trampled. She even sucked in her pride and agreed to be her sister's personal attendant.

Perhaps this day could mend more than one bridge.

❋ ❋ ❋

Two weeks later, on a cloudless June day, Abby helped Alyssa into her gown. With her long blonde hair piled atop her head and her flowing white dress, Alyssa had the power to stop hearts.

"I'm so happy for you," Abby whispered into Alyssa's ear as she hugged her and discovered that she meant it. So she wasn't the bride. She could be a superb personal attendant and wrap Alyssa up in her love.

"Thanks, Abby," Alyssa said, her eyes filling.

Abby smiled and grabbed a tissue. "Don't cry. You'll

smudge." Even if Ross wasn't here with the Springers, Abby could enjoy the day congratulating her sister and applying everything God had taught her over the fishing weekend.

She'd decided she was Andrew, Peter's quiet, wise brother, helping people one by one find the Savior. She didn't have Ross's charisma, but she had a rock-solid knowledge of the Scriptures. And God expected her to use the brainpower He'd given her. Even if the Sojourners had folded, God would use the new group, with their combined strengths, to build His Kingdom. He'd use *her* to build His Kingdom.

Ross's words from Psalm 25 returned to her. *"He leads the humble in doing right, teaching them his way."* The Lord had led her and taught her through college, then grad school. And then He'd helped her not only land a prize-winning muskie but attract the attention of the campus catch.

Now she just had to set the hook and reel him in.

Buoyed by her sister's bridal glow, Abby escaped to find Laurie. The organ music swelled from the sanctuary as she exited the vestibule. She spied Laurie squeezing into a parking spot near the back.

"Your sister's a popular gal," Laurie commented as she approached.

"That's the understatement of the year."

Laurie made a face that reflected mock pain. "You two don't have any issues, do you?"

"No, we're good." Abby took her arm and marched them up to the church, scraping up her courage. Had Ross and his parents already arrived? Or would he run from this event like he'd run from their future? Her confidence took a diving leap . . . and skidded into cold fear when she located him standing next to the gift table.

He looked devastatingly handsome in blue dress pants, a royal-blue shirt, and a yellow tie. The combination had the power to turn her around and send her running. Until she saw his footgear—a pair of flip-flops.

Oh, so Ross. She couldn't help but giggle.

Then he turned and the laughter stopped.

His mouth opened, and she saw his reaction in his beautiful eyes before she heard it. "Wow."

So Laurie had been right to dress her to the nines. "Hi."

He gave Laurie a cursory nod, then fixed his gaze, 120 percent full wattage, on Abby. "You look . . ."

"*Wow* works for me."

He took her hand, swallowed. "I missed you."

Oh, good. "Me too." She took a breath. *Fish hooked. Now reel.* Music swelled through the church, and Alyssa emerged from the nursery. She caught Abby's eye and reached out with a smile. Abby smiled back and kicked her courage into high gear. "Listen, Ross, I know you failed college."

She would have done less damage if she'd kicked him in the shins. He gulped, turned a painful color. She squeezed his hand. "But I. Don't. Care."

He closed his eyes as if her words hurt.

"I asked you who you were. Now I know. You're just a great guy who's trying to do his best for Jesus. A guy I love.

Who cares about Greek, anyway?" Had she really spoken those words?

Now came the tricky part. She added a breeze to her voice. "Hey, if you really want to learn it, I happen to know a great tutor."

He frowned.

She nodded. "Free."

"I don't know, Abs. I . . . Maybe I'm not cut out for ministry."

"Are you kidding?" Now this she hadn't expected. "You're a natural. Didn't you listen to the fishing expert? Just use your gifts. I'll help you with Greek. And you build relationships, find the empty spots, and fill them with truth." She took his other hand. "You have a way of getting under a person's skin and making them rethink their life."

"And do crazy things like enter a fishing contest?"

She shook her head. "Like win a fishing contest."

He laughed, and the sound of it released the knot in her chest. "Babe, you not only landed the muskie of the year, but—" his voice lowered as he reached up and wove his fingers into her hair—"you reeled in my heart. Hook, line, and sinker. I love you so much, home-run gal. And if you're really serious, I'll take that tutoring offer." He touched his forehead to hers. "On one condition."

He was so close she could smell his cologne—Polo? The guy hadn't changed much in a year. Or, wait. Yes, he had. He'd grown from campus hotshot to campus hero. To the hero of her heart.

"What condition?"

"If I pass, you'll marry me."

She smiled as her sister walked down the aisle to her groom. "Make me a promise?"

"Anything." He held her face in his incredible hands, shooting warmth through her entire body.

"I don't want to go fishing on our honeymoon."

He laughed. And then he kissed her. Strong and full of honesty, and she knew.

This one was a keeper.

TROPICAL SALSA

Great with grilled fish (or chicken, pork, chips)!

Ingredients:

- 1½ cups diced fresh pineapple
- 1 cup diced fresh mango
- ¼ cup diced red pepper
- ¼ cup diced cucumber
- ¼ cup chopped red onion
- ⅓ cup chopped cilantro
- 3 T. mild Anaheim pepper, finely chopped (may use hotter variety of pepper, or omit green pepper altogether for a sweeter salsa)
- 1 clove garlic, minced
- Juice of 1 large lime
- Salt to taste

In medium bowl, combine all ingredients; stir well. Season with salt as desired. Serve at room temp or chilled.

Makes about 3½ cups.

ABOUT THE AUTHOR

SUSAN MAY WARREN is the bestselling, Christy and RITA Award–winning author of more than forty novels whose compelling plots and unforgettable characters have won acclaim with readers and reviewers alike. She served with her husband and four children as a missionary in Russia for eight years before she and her family returned home to the States. She now writes full-time as her husband runs a resort on Lake Superior in northern Minnesota, where many of her books are set.

Susan holds a BA in mass communications from the University of Minnesota. Several of her critically acclaimed novels have been ECPA and CBA bestsellers, were chosen as Top Picks by *Romantic Times*, and have won the RWA's Inspirational Reader's Choice contest and the American Christian Fiction Writers' prestigious Carol Award. Her novels *You Don't Know Me* and *Take a Chance on Me* were Christy Award winners, and five of her other books have also been finalists. In addition to her writing, Susan loves to teach and speak at women's events about God's amazing grace in our lives.

For exciting updates on her new releases, previous books, and more, visit her website at www.susanmaywarren.com.

ALSO BY SUSAN MAY WARREN

Deep Haven novels

Happily Ever After
Tying the Knot
The Perfect Match
My Foolish Heart
The Shadow of Your Smile
You Don't Know Me

Christiansen Family series

Take a Chance on Me
It Had to Be You
When I Fall in Love
Always on My Mind
The Wonder of You (coming July 2015)
Evergreen: A Christiansen Winter Novella

PJ Sugar series

Nothing but Trouble
Double Trouble
Licensed for Trouble

Noble Legacy series

Reclaiming Nick
Taming Rafe
Finding Stefanie

Team Hope series

Flee the Night
Escape to Morning
Expect the Sunrise
Waiting for Dawn: An E-book Novella

The Great Christmas Bowl: A Novella